The Rostov Ascension

MATTHEW ALLEN

by Matthew Allen
mattallen.ma@gmail.com

ISBN-13: 978-1481856461
ISBN-10: 1481856464

" I will gather the remnant of My flock out of all countries where I have driven them, and bring them back to their folds; and they shall be fruitful and multiply. I will set up shepherds over them who will feed them; and they shall fear no more, nor be dismayed, nor shall they be lacking," says the LORD.

Jeremiah 23:3-4

Dedicated to the "good shepherds," who live
and die—and when necessary, kill—
in service of a higher calling.

The Rostov Ascension

Prologue

Sakakah, Saudi Arabia
Two Years Ago

THE OIL PROCESSING FACILITY WAS DEATHLY STILL just before the earthquake rumbled through the region at 1:07 a.m., measuring 6.4 on the Richter Scale. It lasted for nine seconds, shaking oil pumps and derricks, rattling nerves, and waking up everyone within a hundred miles. Lights came on immediately in the dormitory where emergency personnel slept for reasons such as this. If fires broke out in any of the wells, it was imperative they be dealt with quickly.

Above ground, the impact of the quake was minimal. No fires. No injuries at the facility. Two oil platforms and an outlying security shack sustained minor structural damage, but they would be repaired easily. What no one saw was the damage beneath the surface. Tectonic friction had opened a fissure deep below the facility, extending to the east as far as Kuwait, and to the west beyond Jordan and into Israel. Over the next few days, technicians at the facility reported a slow but noticeable drop in subterranean oil pressures. It was puzzling for a while, but the levels soon stabilized. After a week, life went back to normal. After a month, everyone had forgotten about the event that would alter the region forever.

Odessa, Ukraine
One Year Ago

ALONE IN THE DARKENED HOTEL SUITE, the assassin stared at the dying man knowing that both of their lives would be soon changed forever. It wasn't supposed to end like this. The politician wasn't supposed to die. And while the assassin, ironically, didn't actually kill Sergei Bukharin, he knew that is how it would appear, and he had allowed for it. Now both men could move on.

Jacob Rostov, dressed head-to-toe in black, knelt down and checked for a pulse. Bukharin's glassy eyes stared strangely up at him but Rostov knew they were beyond sight. Beyond help. The poison had done its job. As the once-invincible powerbroker breathed his last, Rostov silently wished him good luck.

Rostov stood. It was time to disappear. When he resurfaced his identity would be complete. It would take time, he knew, but not as long as one might think. The connection had already been made. Now he simply needed to let everything take its course. When it was safe, he would surface. And then, finally, he would pursue his real enemy.

Chapter 1

New York City
Present Day

Not yet noon and already the heat was stifling. Tendrils of heat vapor from broiling asphalt and metal were clearly visible rising from the street, shimmering in the air like ghost trails. Surrounded and held captive by huge concrete and steel buildings that blocked the wind, the sidewalk and street were like an oven, slowly baking everything into virtual oblivion. To Jacob Rostov, strolling along the sidewalk dressed in a black clerical robe, the heat brought memories of more sinister places and how this was nothing like what he had experienced in Saudi Arabia, or Iraq, or the Negev. There, you could *feel* the moisture being sucked from your body by the arid winds and unforgiving desert sun. The heat here, by comparison, was merely unpleasant.

As he walked, a thin bead of sweat trickled past his ear and down his neck. He dabbed the sweat with a handkerchief and felt a small tremor course through his hand. Though he had planned everything carefully, there was no guarantee he would come out of this alive. A random police unit could stumble across the hit, although he had taken precautions in the event of such a development. There was a remote chance he was being set up and would be taken out after the hit—a loose end severed from the source to deflect attention from the real players. Though possible, he reassured himself it was extremely unlikely. He was simply too valuable to them.

Still, the excitement and uncertainty of the moment had their effect. To counter the surge of adrenaline flooding his bloodstream, he breathed deeply through his nose and slowly exhaled through thin lips, using his diaphragm to control the flow of air. The tremor quickly went away, and Rostov carefully surveyed the street. Nothing seemed wrong or out-of-place. Thin pockets of determined pedestrians filtered along beside him. Some were moving quickly with their heads down, lost in their own worlds. Others moved slower, their heads up, as if absorbing the sights, sounds, and smells of the city. The stench of car exhaust was irritating, especially as it mingled with the smell of roasted garlic and onions, beef falafel, pepperoni pizza, and hotdogs. Added to the faint but pungent odor of sweat, dirt, and urine that never ceased to permeate the air, it was the smell of the big city. Somehow everyone got used to it.

As Rostov neared the hotel entrance, a taxi waiting across the street alerted him by honking three times. Rostov caught the driver's eye and the driver nodded. The target was coming. Rostov slipped on a pair of thin gloves, reached inside the front of his robe and gripped the handle of a Tokarev automatic. A Westernized version of the 7.62-millimeter sidearm used by the Russian Army, the 9mm pistol was an inexpensive throwaway, but it was reliable and accurate enough, and untraceable. Screwed to the extended barrel was a six-inch long, cylindrical suppressor. Every surface of the gun and suppressor had been wiped thoroughly clean. Even the bullet casings were free of the latent fingerprints that a New York Police Department forensics team would eventually dust for.

A uniformed doorman stepped outside and held the door for two men exiting the hotel. "Good morning, Senator Richardson," he said.

"Morning, Frank," replied the silver-haired senator as he stepped through the doorway.

Rostov tipped his head and smiled pleasantly at the passing senator, but Charles Richardson didn't even register Rostov's presence. It was nothing personal—the senator tended to ignore anything that didn't immediately concern him. The doorman, having completed his task, retreated to his post inside, leaving only Rostov outside with the senator and his bodyguard. A cell phone began trilling "Hail to the

Chief," and Rostov almost smiled. Richardson raised the phone to his ear as he continued distractedly towards the street.

Sloppy, Rostov reflected, unimpressed. The senator must have believed he was untouchable; otherwise his security would have been better. He would have had at least one more man in front and one behind, and they would have been scrutinizing the solitary priest as a potential threat. Rostov again made eye contact with the cab driver and received the final nod. *All clear.*

As Richardson reached the black Lincoln Town Car, the driver opened the door. Across the street, the taxi honked one last time and the driver yelled, "*You crazy son of a three-legged camel! Where did you learn to drive?!*"

With his targets distracted, Rostov raised the pistol. The most immediate threat, the bodyguard, took the first bullet in the back of the head. The "wet" suppressor functioned perfectly as thick fluid inside the canister absorbed the sound of the explosion and reduced the subsonic discharge to a muted *clack*. The hollowpoint round also performed as designed, quickly expanding inside and terminating all brain activity. Before the body hit the ground, Rostov pivoted and fired again. *Clack*. The senator, struck just behind his left ear, crumpled to the sidewalk. Rostov fired a third time and struck the driver in the left temple. The man's body sagged against the open car door and slid to the curb.

Rostov surveyed the scene. All three were down. All head shots. Mission accomplished. "*Allahu Akbar!*" he intoned clearly, not because he was a Believer, but solely for the effect the phrase would have on anyone within earshot. Any witnesses would remember not what they may have actually seen, but what the easily recognizable Arabic phrase had conditioned them to believe: the senator had been killed by an *Islamic terrorist.*

Rostov lowered the pistol into his robe and calmly walked away. At the first intersection, he slowed. A man dressed in a dark tailored suit, watching the scene behind him, quietly said, "All clear."

Rostov resisted the urge to look back. His cover unit had told him all he needed to know. He turned right and continued calmly, turning right again at the next intersection. With his hands still underneath his robe, he unscrewed the suppressor and slipped it into his pants pocket. From the same pocket he withdrew a rat-tailed file and slid it up and down the inside of the Tokarev's barrel. Without breaking stride, he disassembled the pistol and casually tossed the parts down a storm drain.

Two blocks later he ducked into an alley, removed the black wig, fake mustache, gloves and cleric robe, and stuffed them in a dumpster. Wearing faded blue jeans and a New York Yankees jersey, he continued down the alley and turned right. After a quick scan of the street he approached a dark blue Ford Expedition parked at the curb. A rear door opened, he pulled himself inside and the large SUV disappeared into traffic.

Munich, Germany

SIX TIME ZONES AWAY, IN THE darkening sky above downtown Munich, a storm was brewing. Sporadic sprinkles of rain fell harmlessly to the ground from dark storm clouds floating ominously in from the north. Off in the distance, occasional flashes of lightning, followed by deep explosions of rumbling thunder, announced the impending deluge. In minutes, the city would be drenched.

Erich Neumann studied the clouds overhead briefly. Standing on the sidewalk dressed in a brown leather trenchcoat and hat, he looked like a 1940's-era Gestapo agent. He was a detective lieutenant in the State Security Division of the *Bundeskriminalamt*, the German national police. Neumann looked to his left and saw headlights approaching. He eased into an alcove in the apartment building behind him. Seconds later, an Audi A4 slowed and turned into the parking structure across the street.

Russell was home.

Neumann returned to the leading edge of the alcove and studied the street. Traffic had thinned out. There were a few pedestrians, but they all seemed preoccupied. Across the street, Russell carried a pizza box to the front of his apartment complex. Neumann slipped a Marlboro between his lips, cupped his hands and lit it. Just then, the door behind him opened. He turned and saw a young boy in a rain suit.

"*Kommen Sie hier, Junge*," Neumann said. *Come here, lad*.

"*Ja?*"

"*Polizei*. I'll give you five euro to deliver this letter across the street."

"*Warum?*" *Why?*

"*Fünf Euro*," he repeated.

The boy hesitated. Then he thrust his hand out.

Neumann gave him the envelope and the money. "Apartment 13," he said. "Be careful crossing the street."

The boy stamped his heels together, saluted, and quipped sharply, "*Jawohl!*," then crossed the street laughing to himself.

CIA CONSULAR OFFICER MIKE RUSSELL entered his flat, locked the deadbolt and set the pizza down in the small kitchen. He shrugged out of his damp raincoat and placed it on a peg by the front door. He turned the TV on, watched for a few seconds, then returned to the kitchen. As he opened the pizza box, he heard three raps on the front door.

Russell went to the door and looked through the peephole. No one was there. He unlocked the deadbolt, opened the door and peered out. There was a boy walking toward the stairwell.

"Hey!" Russell yelled.

The boy looked over his shoulder, waved, and said, "*Ein Briefumschlag für Ihnen, mein Herr!*" *An envelope for you, sir!*

Russell glanced down at the envelope on the doormat. There was no return address. He yelled to the boy, in German, "Who's it from?!"

The boy shrugged and said, "*Ein Mann draussen.*" *A man outside*.

Russell considered going to investigate, but whoever had sent it obviously didn't want him to know who he was. Curious, Russell finally took the letter inside and closed the door. He opened the envelope with a pocketknife and withdrew three folded sheets of plain white paper. The bottom and top sheets were blank. The inner sheet was a list of names. As he read through the names, his attention was drawn to the television.

"—*bringing you breaking news on the assassination just minutes ago of a popular American senator. We have confirmed through the NYPD that Charles Richardson, the widely esteemed and sometimes controversial senator from New York, was shot and killed by as yet unidentified gunmen outside of his New York penthouse. Considering the anniversary of the Trade Center terrorist disaster tomorrow, some experts have already declared that al-Qaeda is indeed alive and kicking despite years of relative inactivity*—"

Russell looked at the sheet of paper in his hand and saw *Charles Richardson* at the bottom of the list. "My God," he muttered. "What is this?"

His phone rang.

"*Mein Gott*," the caller said. "I didn't know it would happen this soon." He spoke passable English, with a slight German accent.

"Who is this?" Russell demanded.

"I can't give you my name, but I am a friend."

"You're not behind this?"

"Absolutely not! I was trying to prevent this."

"Tell me who you are."

"I can't. Not right now."

"Why not?"

"It's not safe."

"So, what am I supposed to do with this?"

"There's no time now. Take it to your agency. They must know immediately. More deaths will follow this one, I am certain."

Russell was speechless.

"Sorry," the caller continued. "We're all in danger. That was a warning. Be careful."

"Is this al-Qaeda?"

Silence.

"Hello?" Russell said. "*Hello?*"

Nothing. The caller was gone.

Tel Aviv, Israel

GENERAL GIDEON BIRAN'S LIVING ROOM was alive with activity, but the mood was somber. Men whispered to each other when they needed to speak. Those that didn't need to speak kept their mouths shut as the security team from Tel Nof Air Force Base electronically swept the house.

Colonel Hayarkon, the officer in charge of security at the base, watched a technician reassemble a telephone receiver. "Did you find something?" he asked. The technician placed a metallic object in the colonel's hand. Hayarkon studied it briefly, then showed it to General Biran. It was a tiny disc, similar in shape to a small watch battery. "You were right to be concerned, general."

"A phone tap?"

"*Ken.*" *Yes.* "It's one of ours."

"*Aman?*" Biran asked warily, referring to Military Intelligence.

"What I mean is, the technology was developed here in Israel. It's a passive microtransmitter. Mossad once used this type, but that was years ago."

Biran exhaled softly, and said, "Am I under investigation?"

"If you are, I haven't heard about it. But of course, it's possible."

With the coalition government growing more and more politically unstable, painfully divided over no-win territory disputes, constant skirmishes with insurgent militias, and the larger, daunting quest to secure a peaceful infrastructure, Biran knew nearly anything was possible.

"Look into it," he said simply.

"Of course, *adoni.* Immediately."

"Is this model commercially available?"

The colonel shrugged noncommittally. "You know how it is."

"*B'seder,*" Biran replied. *Okay.* "Where do we go from here?"

"I'll handle this quietly and keep you informed. You know I can't guarantee a timetable."

"I understand."

The general stepped into the kitchen and handed the microchip to a handsome, desert-tanned young man in his early thirties—his son, Avi.

"A passive microtransmitter," Avi Biran observed. "It looks like one of our designs. You were right, *abba*. It's not a good sign."

"No, it's not," General Biran agreed. "I can't believe this is internal, though. It's too deep for Hezbollah or Hamas. Maybe Syria. Obviously, we'll have to put my staff on alert. But, Avi—" He paused as he considered the ramifications of what was happening. "I'm worried about Elen. She's extremely vulnerable."

"Then we should warn her."

"I don't know what to tell her. It may be nothing."

"Even so, you can't let this go. Maybe just send her an e-mail?"

General Biran nodded distantly and said, "I suppose that will have to do. But what if she really *is* in danger?"

Avi pursed his lips. "I'll see what I can do when I get back to Paris, *abba*." He looked at his watch. "For now, just tell her to be careful."

"Right."

Chapter 2

Long Beach, California
Next Day

DEEP IN THE HEART OF SOUTHERN CALIFORNIA, the city of Long Beach was basking in the warm glow of the final weeks of summer. Twenty miles south of Los Angeles and barely a block from the long, white sandy beach from which the city was named, the Long Beach World Trade Center was both a lighthouse and a beacon to the new economic world still struggling to be born in the new Millennium. State and federal flags atop her communications array were at half-mast, in honor of her sister buildings in New York that were destroyed—and the thousands of people whose lives were snuffed out—by the most infamous act of terrorism in history. The city, country, and the world were already on the mend, though, and life, as much as was possible, had returned to normal.

Only two blocks from the WTC, the Main Public Library boasts a modern, concrete and glass, two-story structure filled with thousands of books, magazines, videos, microfiche files, music CDs, paintings, works of art, and much more. Inside, Kevin Edwards was trying to enjoy a welcome day off from life, work, and everything else that sucked. The volatile and unpredictable economy had hurt his graphic design studio. His girlfriend of six months had decided, only a month ago, that she wanted to move back home to Virginia. Homesick, she'd said. He couldn't really blame her. Their relationship was having serious ups and downs anyway. Serious enough that he didn't want to move across the country to see if things would work out.

Not with his business, friends, and family here. Well, what remained of his business.

He was only marginally depressed. Not clinically, he was sure. He knew all he really needed was to get lost in a good book for a couple of days. That meant fiction, although he had decided on classical instead of modern. Something epic. Sad. And well-written. He was in the D section, lightly fingering book spines as he methodically progressed from left to right.

His finger stopped at a large hardback.

Alexandre Dumas.

He slid the book out and skimmed the first few pages, remembering the first time he'd read it and how much he'd enjoyed it. Back in middle school. A wave of nostalgia swept over him as he flipped through several more pages. "You really *are* depressed," he muttered.

He shook his head absently. Then, satisfied with his selection, he turned and promptly collided with another patron, knocking her books to the ground. "I'm so sorry!" he said, stooping down. "Here, let me get those for you." He scooped her books up and handed them back with an amused expression.

"Thank you," she said. "What's so funny?"

"Oh, nothing." He couldn't think of anything else to say. *Absolutely stunning*, is what he was thinking. She had long dark hair, beautiful skin, dark eyes. She was exquisite.

"*The Count of Monte Cristo*," she said, reading the book title in his hand. "That's a bit of a read, isn't it?"

"Oh, yeah," he said, clearing his throat. "I haven't read it in years." *Hi, my name's Kevin.* He looked down at the book while he thought of what to say. In doing so, he failed to notice the concealed look of concern that suddenly crossed her face as she looked off in the distance behind him.

An odd-looking man in a dark suit was trying not to stand out. He had been staring at her. She was used to the looks she got from men everywhere, but the way this man looked at her—it just didn't seem right.

"It's one of my favorites," Kevin finally said.

"Hmm," she muttered.

"Yeah, it's a classic. Suspense, political infighting, jealousy, injustice, romance, revenge. Just what I need—" His voice drifted off. "Anyway, I'm sorry I knocked your books down. I should watch where I'm going."

"Oh, don't worry about it."

She returned her attention to the bookshelf and Kevin moved on. Something felt odd about the encounter and he wondered why her appearance struck him as unsettling. Absently, he recalled the story in his hand. Then it hit him. But the coincidence was—

As if on autopilot, he turned and walked back to the shelf. She seemed distracted. He cleared his throat and said, "Excuse me. I'm sorry if I'm bothering you."

She was focused on the man in the suit. He was looking away from her, though, trying to appear nonchalant. As she scanned the area her gaze fell on a second man in a dark suit. She turned to face Kevin with a questioning look.

"I, uhh," Kevin continued haltingly, "Can I just tell you that, umm, well, there's a character towards the end of *The Count of Monte Cristo* that I—" He couldn't go on. This was stupid. He turned to leave.

She made a quick decision. He didn't seem wrong. Not like the suits. *They* were wrong. She might need someone to create a diversion—and she needed time to think. "Don't worry," she finally said. "I don't bite."

Kevin grinned sheepishly. "I'm sorry."

"Not at all. What about this character?"

"Well, her name is Haidee. She's from an exotic, faraway country, and I've always imagined her as the most beautiful woman in the world. Fell in love with her when I was ten." He chuckled softly. "Well, you look so much like how I pictured her." He paused. "Oh, God, I'm sorry. You must feel—"

To her credit, she smiled at him and managed to laugh. "Forget about it. I'm flattered." She leaned closer and kissed him on the cheek. "You're sweet. That one's from Haidee." *Let those guys ponder that*, she thought.

Stunned, Kevin smiled at her, but she had already turned away.

ELEN BIRAN AVOIDED LOOKING DIRECTLY at the two suits as she made her way to the exit. She dropped off her books at the checkout counter and left empty-handed, carrying only her purse. Inwardly, she admitted she was flattered by the attention she always got. But it was horrible timing today. And it was ridiculous. Men were such physical creatures. *What do they know? Like moths drawn to a flame*, she thought. It wasn't a flattering analogy. *They see something pretty and they want it. Why?*

She stopped in the concrete courtyard in front of the library, distractedly soaking in the fading warmth of the setting sun. Her attention was drawn to the long row of halfmasted flags whipping gently in the wind. She surreptitiously checked her reflection in the window and scanned the area behind her for more suits. Nothing stood out. A cool ocean breeze picked up suddenly, and she placed her hands inside her jacket pockets, hugging the coat closer as she walked away from the library.

Yesterday afternoon, she had gotten the e-mail from her father. It was still vivid in her memory:

> *Elen, it's difficult to explain why, but I'm concerned you may be in danger. Something strange is going on here. Take every precaution to ensure your safety, hamoodah. See you soon. Love, Abba.*

In another time and place she might have dismissed the warning as a joke, but her father was never flippant about situations like this. In Israel she had learned to avoid crowds whenever possible, as well as the obvious hotter areas of terrorist activity. Security was simply too important to be taken lightly. It was the inherent yet unpredictable instability of the region that had necessitated her move to the United States three years ago. She was tired of the violence, the blind hatred that unjustly killed and maimed innocent lives. Not that the United

States was immune from violence.

America was beginning to understand the terror that Israel had been dealing with for over fifty years. *Terrorists!* Evil men who targeted women and children. Noncombatants. They were like a cancerous infection that destroyed a little piece at a time, seeping inexorably deeper into the country's nervous system. She frequently wondered if the infection would ever be stopped. More importantly, she wondered *who* would stop it. Maybe the U.S. president could finally team with the Israeli prime minister. Together, maybe they could—

She had stopped walking and was now standing next to a hotdog vendor in the courtyard. From the corner of her eye, she saw Kevin approaching. Suddenly, she grew wistful. How long had it really been since she'd been fond of someone? Someone special?

He was dressed well. He seemed nice. Intelligent. Cute. She scanned the exit of the library again. No suits.

Were you just imagining things?

As he walked by, he winked and gave her a lazy salute. She smiled and shook her head, amused. He stopped and did an about-face. "Did you learn that in the army?" she asked, wondering *why* she had asked even as she did.

"No, ma'am. High school marching band."

She laughed.

"Umm, look," he said, stepping closer. "I'm not a weirdo, okay? I've got a good job. Well, actually, my business isn't doing so well. Because of the economy and all. To tell you the truth, this last month has been pretty rotten."

Elen scanned the exit again. No suits.

"But," he continued. "Instead of doing drugs or blowing everything in Vegas, I just decided to come to the library to find a good book. And maybe, just *maybe* pickup the girl I've been looking for ever since I was ten." Kevin grinned innocently.

She couldn't stop the smile that came to her mouth.

"So," he continued. "There's a coffee shop across the street. Let me buy you a drink. Maybe a cappuccino or a mocha? Whipped cream on top? What do you say?"

She hesitated—still no suits at the exit—then said, "Yeah. Why not?"

"Great! I promise you won't regret this. By the way, my name's Kevin. Kevin Edwards. What's yours?"

"Elen."

"That's a nice name. Pleez'd ta meetcha, Elen."

"WHAT THE HELL WAS THAT all about?" the man dressed in the dark business suit asked softly.

"Beats me," his partner replied.

The first man lowered his binoculars and keyed a small radio mic. "This is One," he reported. "Does anybody know who the guy is?"

Silence.

"*Negative, One,*" a disembodied voice finally responded in his hidden earpiece. "*Subject unknown.*"

"Recommendations?"

"*Wait one.*"

The two men watched the couple enter a trendy coffee shop across the boulevard. Thirty seconds later the response came: "*One, observe and determine if the new subject is a threat. Nothing else changes.*"

One keyed his radio and quietly replied, "Copy."

"THIS IS HAPPENING SO FAST," Elen said as they found an outside patio table, drinks in hand.

"Yeah," Kevin agreed. "I have to admit, I've never done anything like this before."

Her look said she didn't believe him.

"Honest!" he said, grinning. "So, what do you do?"

"I'm a student."

"At Long Beach State?"

"No, at UCLA."

"What are you doing this far south?"

"Meeting a friend for dinner. At her uncle's house." She looked at her watch and frowned. "I'm actually supposed meet her pretty soon."

"Do you need to take off?"

"I've got a few minutes."

Kevin nodded, then said, "I'd hate for you to be late on account of me."

"Really? That's sweet of you."

"Can I walk you to your car? We could talk on the way."

"Sure."

ONE LOWERED HIS FIELD GLASSES and pondered the situation. He keyed his lip mic and said, "Six, this is One."

"*Go ahead.*"

"They're heading back to the parking structure. I'm a little confused by the guy. Recommendations?"

"I've got a funny feeling about it," Six admitted. "His timing is rotten."

"I suppose he could just be some shmoe trying to get lucky. Do you suppose he's trying to warn her?"

"Hell if I know. Two, keep an eye on him; designate Tango-2. When they split up, One, follow Tango-1 to her car. Three, you're One's six."

"Roger, Six. What if he's a player?"

"Be careful."

"HISTORY AND PSYCH, HUH?" Kevin said as they walked toward the parking garage. The book from the library was tucked under his left arm. "That's cool. My dad did that, too. Degrees in History and Psych."

"What does he do?"

"Retired. Used to work for the sheriff's department. Now, when he's not out tormenting himself on the golf course, he's just an all around good guy."

Elen nodded distractedly.

"What does your dad do?" he asked.

Her eyes flared for the briefest moment. "Why are you so interested?"

"Just curious."

With growing circumspection, Elen looked around. She saw the man in the suit again, across from the parking garage. *Not even trying to hide now,* she thought.

"There's that look again," Kevin said.

"What look?"

"I don't know how to describe it."

She raised her eyebrows expectantly.

"I'm really just a teddy bear, Elen. I know you can't tell simply from appearances, but I'm probably one of the nicest guys you'll ever meet. Honestly."

"You're quite sure of yourself, aren't you?"

"It's the truth."

"I'll admit, you don't strike me as the serial type."

He smiled. "What's bothering you?"

"It's hard to explain."

"Life that rough, huh?"

"Right now, yeah." She looked back. The man was gone.

"You know," Kevin said. "Most guys are notoriously inept at picking up signs, and I'll be the first to admit I've ignored my share along the way. But, am I missing something here?"

Elen shook her head.

"A boyfriend, maybe?"

She looked away and muttered, "I can't believe I'm doing this."

"Doing what?"

Elen stopped. "Are you always this—" She paused, unable to think of the word she wanted.

"Funny?"

"I was thinking more on the line of neurotic."

Kevin smiled, and said, "Hey, I'm not psycho."

Elen made a halfhearted attempt to smile. "I appreciate your attempts at levity," she said, walking again. "You seem like a nice guy. But—"

"Wait. Before you blow me off, let me say something. And I'll be totally serious. Elen, you're the most beautiful woman I've ever seen. God's honest truth. You probably think I'm just trying to get you into bed, but I'm not. I can honestly tell you that's not me. I—"

"Wait," Elen said, cutting him off.

"What?"

The man in the suit was back. With his partner. As they entered the parking garage, Elen looked around and picked up her pace. *Don't panic.*

"What is it?" Kevin asked, suddenly wary.

"Are you serious?"

"Yeah."

"You're not interested in getting me in the sack?" The disbelief in her voice was palpable. She looked behind and saw that the two men had matched her speed.

Kevin still hadn't caught on. "Hey, slow down! So I'm not your average Joe. What can I say to convince you?"

"I don't know," she replied. "What can you?" It was a harsh response and she regretted how it came out. But she had other things on her mind.

Kevin matched her pace and said, "I guess I don't know, really. But, will you give me a chance to prove it?"

"Sorry. No time now. Are you with them?"

"With who?"

Elen's face softened as she studied him. "You seem like a decent guy, Kevin. I mean that. You're cute. Intelligent. Under different circumstances, I think we could even be friends."

Kevin's eyes narrowed at the implied rejection.

"But," she continued. "This just isn't a good time for me."

"I don't understand."

"I can't explain."

"Please," he said. They were next to his Honda Pilot. He took the keys out of his pocket. "This is me. Can we stop for a second?"

Elen did. "Kevin, thank you for your interest." She saw the suits closing in. There was no doubt this was going to get ugly. Fortunately, she had come prepared. "You have no idea who I am. I'm flattered, but this can't work. I'm sorry."

She hurried away, dropping her coffee on the pavement.

† † †

"DAMN," TWO SWORE INTO his mic.

"*Where's Tango-2?*"

"They've separated."

"*If he's one of them, we have to act now.*"

"Affirm. Take him out, then back us up. We can't let her get away. One, Three, take her now! Move, move!"

ONLY TEN PACES FROM HER CAR, it seemed to Elen that time had stopped. She noticed a new man on the other side of the parking structure. She looked behind her and saw the other two closing in. She looked around for help. Except for a parking attendant booth at the exit there was no one around, and there didn't appear to even be an attendant inside the booth. She was alone. Suddenly, to her right a large car screeched to a stop, pinning her car in. The moment of truth had arrived. She reached inside her purse as the driver stepped out of the vehicle.

TWO GUNSHOTS SUDDENLY THUNDERED inside the structure, and Kevin whirled to see what had happened. He heard another boom and suddenly wondered what in the world had struck him in the abdomen. Filled with excruciating pain, he dropped to his knees. Another gunshot boomed and the glass above his head shattered. He ducked out of the way as two more shots slammed into the car door beside him.

"*ONE'S DOWN! SHE'S GOT a gun! Two, get over here!*"

ELEN WHIRLED AND DOVE BETWEEN two cars as a flurry of gunshots sprayed out, tearing into metal and punching holes in the glass beside her. From a crouch, she twisted her body and raised her pistol with both hands. Moments before, she had gotten the drop on One. Surprise. He was lying prone on the concrete, blood pooling around his skull. Another suit appeared in her sight picture and she squeezed off two rounds, barely missing his head as he ducked away.

† † †

"I'M TAKING FIRE!" Three reported. "But she's pinned down. Be careful, Two."

"Yeah, right," Two muttered as he crouch-walked toward Elen's position, his gun raised and ready. This was getting out of control, and he was going to put a decisive end to it. Fast. He moved quickly to where she was pinned between cars. That's where she had fired at Three from—

She wasn't there!

Spinning to his left, he suddenly realized his mistake and immediately dropped to the ground.

Too late. Elen had already stepped to the side of a concrete pillar and fired at him from a distance of less than twenty feet. He took a bullet in the chest and one in the throat. The vest stopped the first one. Not so lucky on the second. Elen saw blood coming from the neck wound and she immediately fell back under cover.

"TWO'S DOWN!" Three reported.

"Get out of there," Six ordered. "Fall back."

"*Copy.*"

ELEN EJECTED HER MAGAZINE and counted the remaining rounds. Of an original ten, she had four left, including one in the chamber. And, stupidly, she reflected, there was no spare magazine in her purse. Before leaving this morning she had thought that taking the gun was a silly precaution. Not to mention illegal. But acting on her father's warning had saved her life.

She reinserted the magazine and peeked around the corner in time to see the third assailant running away.

KEVIN SAW THE GUNMAN GO DOWN clutching his throat. *Who fired? Elen?* He stood and walked numbly toward the scene, trying to process it. His vision began to blur around the edges.

"Kevin!" Elen yelled. "Are you all right?"

"Took one in the side," he grunted. "Oh, man, I feel like garbage—lightheaded—bleeding."

That much was obvious. The lower half of his shirt was drenched. He needed to get to a hospital quickly.

"My car's pinned," she said. "Give me your keys. We'll take yours."

Kevin didn't hear the last part. He'd already fainted.

Chapter 3

KEVIN AWOKE GRADUALLY AS HIS MIND LINGERED between illusory realms of consciousness. He discerned a faint buzzing sound and his eyes fluttered open. Darkness turned into a light blur. As his focus slowly improved, he was able to identify the top of the inside of his Honda. Turning his head, a rush of pain stopped him from wanting to go any farther. Instead, he took a deep breath, closed his eyes and tried to block the pain out.

When the pain receded, he opened his eyes again. From his poor vantage point, all he could see was a dark window. Occasionally, a point of light would seem to carom off of the otherwise featureless surface, so he was at least able to determine that the truck was moving and that it was nighttime. He tilted his head to get a better view, but the throbbing intensified and he was unable to stay awake—

HIS FOREHEAD FELT COOL and damp. He was in bed. Someone softly stroked his forehead. He managed to open his eyes. "Elen?" he whispered.

"Shhh," she said, pressing her fingers gently across his lips. "Don't talk."

"Whe—?"

"Shhh," she insisted. "You have to rest. You've lost a lot of blood."

His eyes fluttered shut. "Water," he croaked.

With an effort, his eyes opened and he saw Elen dip a washcloth into a bowl. She placed the dripping cloth on his lips and squeezed gently, sending a small cascade of cool water into his parched mouth. As it trickled down his throat, he coughed.

"Just take your time, Kevin," she said, dipping the cloth into the bowl again. He swallowed easier the second time, and felt himself nodding off to sleep. Before he lost consciousness, he felt her lips press against his forehead.

SLEEP WAS DEEP, DREAMLESS and painless. He awoke briefly and heard someone moving, but it faded.

THE NEXT TIME HE AWOKE it was nighttime. He felt disoriented and frustrated by his inability to track the passage of time. In one sense, it seemed he'd been out for only a few hours, but in another it felt like days. When he found the strength to look up, he couldn't find anything to reveal how long he'd been asleep. He was briefly annoyed before blacking out again.

RETURNING TO THE LAND OF THE LIVING once more, he knew he must be getting better. It was daytime and he could feel some strength return. With a clearer mind, he was also able to recall fragmented images of the shootout.

Elen. The gunmen. The dead gunmen. Getting shot.

"Elen?" he said weakly.

Nothing happened. He closed his eyes for a moment, breathed deeply, then tried again: "*Elen?*"

A door creaked softly. The pleasant scent of vanilla wafted into the room, and he smiled. Elen walked softly to his bedside and said, "How do you feel?"

"That's a good question," he replied, stretching his back stiffly. "I guess I feel better. But did anyone get the license plate on that herd of elephants?" He eased himself into a sitting position on the side of the bed, inhaled deeply, and felt oddly pleased that he didn't vomit.

"Poor thing," Elen said. "Maybe if you close your eyes, Helga the old forest witch will kiss your forehead and magically return your lost powers."

"That would be nice." He smiled with a narcotic-induced, fatigued happiness, then closed his eyes. It was quiet once again.

Peaceful.

He felt the air change around him and sensed Elen was moving closer. Her lips pressed gently against his forehead. He wasn't sure if he was being stupid, but, for some reason, at that moment it all seemed worth it.

She stroked his hair and said, "Thank you, Kevin."

He looked at her. "I should be saying that."

"No," she insisted. "Thank you. For saving my life."

"I only remember getting my ass kicked. How did I save your life?"

"Well, you got in the way. That bought me just enough time."

Kevin looked confused. "Elen?"

"Yes?"

"What the Hell happened?"

"I don't know."

"Who were those men? Why did they attack you? Why did they shoot me? What the Hell is going on?"

"Those are all good questions, Kevin. Unfortunately, I don't know."

Kevin's gaze narrowed, as if something had just occurred to him. "Is that why you were so distracted? You knew they were following you, or something?"

"I suspected something."

"Really?"

"Yeah."

"Inside the library?"

Elen nodded slowly as she looked away.

Kevin whistled softly. "I was just getting in your way. And their way. I had no idea." He paused reflectively.

"Anyway," Elen said. "You must be hungry."

"Yeah. I think I could eat a horse."

"Then let's get you some breakfast."

She helped him to his feet. Carefully touching his side, he pressed his hand on the large bandage that covered the left half of his abdomen. It was clean and tight. He guessed whoever had worked on him had done a good job. Elen handed him a clean shirt. He gingerly put it on, then followed her out the door.

They entered a modestly furnished dining room and Kevin's stomach growled. He eased himself into a highbacked wooden chair and said, "I can't believe how hungry I am."

Just then, Elen's roommate, a very attractive blonde wearing baby blue UCLA sweats, walked in, carrying two large plates. Each plate had fluffy, scrambled eggs with small chunks of tomato and cheese, toast and hash browns. "I was going to make them omelettes," she said. "But I lost my patience."

Kevin grinned, picked up a fork, then looked at Elen questioningly.

"Anna," she said. "Meet Kevin. Kevin, this is Anna—my longtime friend and lesbian lover."

Kevin nearly choked.

"Elen, you're going to Hell," Anna said. "Give the guy a break."

Anna Cohen, blessed with beautiful light-colored hair, bright green eyes, a very pretty face and a keen sense of humor, smiled at Kevin. "It's a pleasure to meet you, Kevin. And don't listen to her. She's full of crap, which is something you'll find out the more time you spend with her." She paused, inviting a comeback from Elen, then winked at Kevin and said, "Let the truth prevail."

Kevin's eyebrows went up.

"Thanks for the introduction," Elen said. "Anna's my roommate. And my best friend, as you can tell. We served in the army together."

"You were in the army?"

Elen nodded and replied, "In Israel, serving in *Tzahal* is a requirement."

"Za-what?"

"Tzahal. The Israel Defense Forces."

"You're from Israel?"

"Yep."

"I bet you have some interesting stories."

Anna and Elen exchanged knowing smiles. Not exactly happy smiles, though.

Kevin dug into his scrambled eggs. "Anna," he said. "You're the best. I think I've died and gone to heaven."

"Flattery will get you nowhere, partner," Elen cautioned with a wry smile.

"Oh, I don't know, Elen," Anna countered. "A little flattery never hurt anyone. Especially coming from him."

"You leave him alone," Elen warned with a playful frown. "He's mine, now."

Kevin squirmed at the repartée, and they laughed at him. After a sobering look from Elen, the two became serious and the conversation lapsed into silence. While Kevin continued to eat, Anna went into the kitchen and started cleaning up.

"Anyway, Kevin," Elen said. "I'm glad to see you're feeling better. I was concerned for a while."

"Well, thanks," he replied between mouthfuls. "I certainly appreciate you not letting me bleed to death. How are you doing, by the way?"

Elen's face was serious as she took a moment to collect her thoughts. "I'm fine, Kevin, thanks. Listen—I really don't know the best way to say this." She sighed.

Kevin stopped eating, wiped his mouth with a napkin, then gently set it down. "What's wrong?"

She shook her head. "I think we've knocked over a gigantic hornets' nest."

"How?"

"Are you familiar with the ATF?"

"Who isn't? The Bureau of Alcohol, Tobacco and Firearms. Pretty hard-core federal law enforcement guys."

Elen nodded.

"Wait," Kevin said. "What's going on? What do they have to do with anything?"

"Well, I couldn't believe it at first, and to be honest I still don't believe it. Anyway, those men who chased me and got killed apparently worked for the ATF."

He cleared his throat, and said, "You're saying those guys were feds?"

Elen shrugged.

"Well," Kevin continued, "I don't understand. I never heard them say they were cops. My dad was a cop. I know what they're supposed to say to you. And some dude just shot me, too. He didn't say anything. Just pulled the trigger."

"I know. It's not right. None of it's right."

"I've heard of some pretty crazy stuff. But this is really freakin' crazy. Did you talk to the police?"

"No."

"Why not?"

Elen almost laughed. "You don't understand."

"You can't talk to the police? Why not? Are you in some kind of trouble? Maybe I can help you. I could ask my dad for—"

"No, you can't ask for anything. Please."

"Okay. Look, I trust you, Elen. I just met you, but I trust you. Okay? Just tell me what's going on."

"Okay," Elen said. "First of all, I don't think they were federal agents."

"Because?"

"Or, if they were, they were unsanctioned, or corrupt, or whatever. What I mean is, well, here, look at this." She handed him a sheet of paper. "The day before this happened, I received an e-mail from my father. He's in Israel. A general. Look here," she said, pointing. "'*I'm concerned you may be in danger. Something strange is going on. Take every precaution to ensure your safety.*'

"Kevin, it's not like him to say things like this unless something really bad is happening. Frankly, at the time, I didn't know what to make of it. But I was worried."

"What does this have to do with the ATF?"

"Well, when I talked with my brother yesterday, that's the conclusion he reached. They're either corrupt agents, or not legitimate at all. He has no idea why they would pose as ATF, except that they must have deep connections."

"But how could he know they're not legit?"

"Because, Kevin, the timing is just too coincidental."

"Coincidental with what?"

"With my father's warning."

"I don't follow."

Elen sighed tiredly and said, "My father was probed by some sort of secret intelligence unit. Someone went into his home and installed listening devices, and some items disappeared from his office at work. One of those items was a picture of my family. Someone was probing for a weakness to exploit." She paused and added, "Apparently me."

"But why?"

"I don't know."

"Okay. But where does the connection with the ATF come in?"

"The news reports."

"News reports? How long was I out?"

"Almost two days."

"Two days?"

Elen nodded. "I went to a private doctor to get you stitched up. You're really lucky, you know. The bullet went clean through and didn't hit anything vital, but you still lost a lot of blood. You've been on pain meds the last two days."

Kevin nodded grimly. "So, what do the news reports say?"

"Basically, in an ATF operation to apprehend two suspects, two agents were killed by the suspects who escaped, et cetera, et cetera."

"We're both *suspects* now?"

"Unfortunately."

"So, two federal agents—*supposed* federal agents—are dead and everyone believes we did it. Is that it? I don't suppose there would be much understanding on the part of any law enforcement type who happened to hear our explanation. Right?"

Elen shrugged.

"But don't you think we could contact someone who—"

"I don't trust anyone right now," Elen replied matter-of-factly.

"Not even me?"

"Don't be so melodramatic. Of course I trust you. And Anna. And my brother and my father."

"Who fixed me up? You trust him, too? Don't doctors have to report gunshot wounds to the police?"

"He's a private doctor. A *sayan*."

"A say-what?"

"A *sayan*," she replied. "A helper. Someone who does what he can to support Israeli interests, including being discreet."

"How does that work?"

"Long story. He's a doctor who won't report anything."

"Okay," Kevin said, letting the subject drop. "So, where do we stand? Where are we?"

"Near UCLA."

"How come the police haven't knocked down the door yet?"

"Because this place can't be traced to me. Or to Anna, for that matter."

"Okay. But how is it the police even figure we're suspects and not victims caught in the crossfire?"

"Well, my car was left at the scene with bullet holes in it. I'm sure the police found the registration inside the car. With me nowhere to be found and a couple of dead bodies at the scene, I'm sure they came to their own conclusion."

"And one guy got away," Kevin said.

"I counted four bad guys. *Two* got away."

Kevin nodded as it all became clear. "So, as you drove us away, they saw the license plate, gave it to the cops, and then ID'd me through the registration. It was their word against mine and I was on the run. Still, Elen, they *have* to be feds, don't they? This wouldn't have gone as far as it has if they weren't."

Elen nodded dully. "I'm still not sure, but I tend to agree."

"Assuming they are, then—Elen, why do dirty feds want *you* so badly?"

"Kevin," she replied with an exhausted smile. "You've hit the nail on the head. I honestly don't know why. Except it revolves around my father somehow. I've never been in trouble with the law."

Kevin picked up his fork, resumed eating, and said, "How do you know so much about this sort of business, anyway?"

"I grew up in Israel."

"Yeah?"

"Israel is very different from America, Kevin. We've all had to protect ourselves since before I was born. It's just a way of life."

Kevin appraised her with new eyes. There was much more to this beautiful woman than he had ever imagined. He looked around, then said, "How do you really know we're safe here?"

"Trust me."

"Is this a safe-house?"

Elen nodded.

"How did you get us to a safe-house?"

"Another long story, Kevin. The bad news is, we can't stay here much longer."

"Why not?"

"It's only temporary. For emergencies. My brother is finding a place for us to go."

"Where is he?"

"Honestly, I don't know at the moment."

"Then how is he going to help us?"

"He has contacts."

"As in 'intelligence' contacts?" Kevin replied. "What, does he work for the Mossad or something?"

Her eyes narrowed. "Look, Kevin. He's going to help us. Trust me. For the next couple days, we just have to lie low and wait for him to come up with a plan."

In the other room, Anna switched on the television set. The words that came from it electrified Kevin.

"*On the latest FBI manhunt—*"

The picture developed into an image of Kevin and Elen. He walked to the couch and immediately recognized the coffee shop on the screen.

"*Although the fugitives remain at large, the FBI expect to make an arrest soon.*" The picture zoomed in on the two sitting at a table. "*Seen here in a recent surveillance photo, the two suspected terrorists were meeting to finalize plans for what the FBI believe is a forthcoming terrorist action.*"

Kevin gaped at the screen, then looked at Elen in disbelief.

"*The couple should be considered armed and extremely dangerous. Under no circumstances should they be approached. If seen, please call the number on—*"

"Terrorists?" Kevin muttered in disbelief.

"We'll be fine for the next few days," Elen said as she looked up at the ceiling, hoping it was true. Quietly, she added, "Come on, Avi."

Westwood FBI Office, Los Angeles

"THERE'S BEEN NO SIGN OF THEM, sir," FBI Special Agent Bryce Maurer reported. "They've completely disappeared."

"That's not possible, Agent Maurer," Assistant Director in Charge Terence Smith said.

"Sir, over the last two days we've checked all of the hospital records in a thirty mile radius from Long Beach, including Irvine"—he counted on his fingers as he spoke—"Yorba Linda, Santa Monica, USC Medical, UCLA. I even checked Catalina Island. They haven't shown up anywhere."

"Then extend it to a hundred miles."

"That'll take a lot of time."

"That's not my problem, Agent Maurer. You're keeping tabs on his parents?"

"Of course, sir. We've put taps on their house, his office and his home."

"NSA is monitoring his cell phone," Smith added. "In the meantime, how about double-checking all of his business contacts, friends and acquaintances, cousins, aunts, uncles. I don't care. Dig something up. Just do whatever it takes, and find them."

"Yes, sir." Maurer turned smartly on his heel and promptly marched out of the assistant director's office. In the hallway, he passed a man in a dark business suit but took no notice of him. He was too concerned about how he was going to find the fugitives.

ASSISTANT DIRECTOR SMITH HAD A BOTTLE of antacid in hand when he heard a quick rap on the door. "Come," he said tersely.

The man Maurer had seen in the hall entered the ADIC's office and closed the door softly behind him. His visitor identification badge read: DAN STEVENS, BATF.

"Yes?" Smith asked wearily.

"Any developments?"

"None yet," Smith replied as he shuffled papers on his desk.

"Any sniffs?"

The Assistant Director shook his head. "Nada."

"Okay. Thanks." He turned to leave, but seemed to change his mind. "Was that Special Agent Maurer who just left?"

Smith nodded.

"The lead investigator?"

"Yes. Why?"

"I just want to coordinate some details with him."

"Fine," Smith replied carefully. "Just don't step all over his toes, okay?"

"Of course." *Dumbass.* He turned to leave.

"Agent Stevens?"

"Yes?"

"I've been wondering."

"What's that?"

"How in the world did you guys screw this up so badly?"

Stevens paled.

"And why did you try to take this down with only three other agents—without a warrant?"

"It was the call on-scene. We had reason to believe they were about to fall off the grid, so there was no time for a warrant or a team. We had to act fast. Unfortunately, we failed."

Smith snorted softly. "That's the understatement of the year."

Stevens turned away before Smith could see his eyes narrow menacingly. *Screw you,* he thought as he walked out the door.

Chapter 4

Charles De Gaulle International Airport
Paris, France

AVI BIRAN DISEMBARKED THE AIR FRANCE flight from Athens just after midnight. The airport was less crowded than usual, which was the way Biran liked it. He cleared customs using his Israeli passport and hefted his lone carry-on to his shoulder as he exited the terminal. Once outside, a taxi immediately stopped for him. He waved it off. As the cab moved on, a dark BMW flashed its lights as it pulled to the curb. He got in. The sleek, Série-5 Berline eased away from the curb and joined the light flow of airport traffic.

"So good to see you again," a man in the back seat said warmly. "Did you leave Athens intact?"

"Athens was wonderful," Biran replied, glancing briefly out the window. "I see Paris is still in one piece."

"It's a big city. I do my best."

Biran laughed as he metamorphosed into his cover identity, Canadian businessman Alan Donovan. He shook hands with his partner and best friend, David Anan. Superficially, both were junior partners in an import-export firm based in Quebec. In reality, the two were veteran intelligence officers employed by *Ha Mossad le Modi'in ule Tafkidim Meyuhadim*—the Institute for Intelligence and Special Tasks.

"How is your father?" Anan asked quietly.

"He's doing well, I suppose. But some disturbing things have happened lately."

"Oh?"

"A few weeks ago he noticed a man regularly following him on the street. The guy always wore the same leather jacket and sunglass-es, but my father was never able to get a close look. Then, some things disappeared from his office. Family pictures, personal memen-tos, his coffee cup. Small things." He shook his head. "He keeps a tight office so it's easy for him to notice when things change. The weird thing is everything reappeared the next day, exactly where they were supposed to be."

"The secretary?"

"She insists she didn't touch anything."

"Does he believe her?"

"Yeah. She's a good girl. In any case, several days ago we discov-ered a tap on his home telephone. Aman has been watching him ever since."

"A probe?" Anan wondered aloud.

"Probably. When I talked to him, I told him to send Elen an e-mail and warn her to be careful, just in case. The next day, she was attacked."

"I saw the news. Is she okay?"

"She's fine," Biran said. "They're at a safe-house waiting for me to come up with a plan to get them out of the country."

"Incredible," Anan muttered. "So, who's the guy?"

"He's a nobody as far as Elen can tell. He just happened to be in the wrong place at the wrong time. And he got shot somehow."

"That's why she took him along? Why didn't she just leave him there?"

"She couldn't," Biran said simply. "You know how she is."

Anan nodded. "What about the attackers?"

"It's not really clear. They appear to be connected with the ATF. Beyond the superficial, it just doesn't wash, though. Probably a cov-er, but none of it makes sense yet."

"Jeez, Avi. What the Hell?"

"I wish I knew," Biran agreed sullenly. "Since we know Elen's not a terrorist, and in light of the probes on my father, I think it's in her best interest not to get caught."

"Should we contact *Al*?"

Biran considered the suggestion, but quickly discarded the idea. *Al* was a supersecret cell of veteran Mossad officers operating without diplomatic cover in the United States, and both men knew they would never expose themselves for an unsanctioned operation. "I don't think so," Biran finally said. "They're on the wrong side of the country for one thing, and they've already got enough to worry about. I've got another idea, though."

They arrived at their operational flat twenty minutes later. Inside, Biran flipped through a small notebook of phone numbers, then dialed his cell phone.

The line rang three times. "Hello?" a voice answered.

"It's been a while, Mike. Take any Med cruises lately?"

Silence. "Avi?"

Biran laughed and said, "How's your family?"

"Great, my long lost desert-dwelling friend. What can I do for you?"

"Are you secure?"

"Not completely. It's an open line."

"Okay." Biran ran off a list of the things he wanted.

"No problem," Mike said. "Give me 'til, say, lunch time tomorrow."

"Thanks. There'll probably be more, so I'll bring you up to speed tomorrow."

"Okay. You take it easy."

Biran disconnected the call, leafed through the notebook and dialed again.

Westwood, California

THE RINGING PHONE STARTLED ELEN. She'd been waiting so long for it to ring that it was a shock when it finally did. She quickly scooped it up and said, "Yes?"

"No names. It's me."

"Oh, thank God. How are you?"

"I'm doing fine. You?"

"Hanging in there but getting a little nervous. What's up?"

Avi explained the arrangements. "After you get squared away, rent a car with your new ID and drive to Quebec. Stay away from airports and cross the border as close to Quebec as possible. Leave the car in the U.S. and take a bus over. Now, on the way there, take your time. Don't speed. Whatever happens, don't do anything to attract attention to yourself. Stay at places that aren't extravagant but nothing too cheap. Cover your hair and wear sunglasses. Do whatever you can to change your appearance. You know the drill. Follow?"

"Yes."

"When you get there, call this number." He told her a string of digits. "Subtract my six-digit birthday from that and you'll have the correct number. From there, you'll either get in touch with me, or a friend who can contact me. By then I should have some idea about what's going on."

"*B'seder*," Elen said. *Okay.* "Thanks."

"You're welcome. You take care, sis."

"You, too. Bye." She hung up and turned to see Kevin standing behind her.

"Everything okay?" he asked.

"Yeah, that was Avi. Have you ever been to Canada?"

By nine o'clock they had eaten dinner, watched more news, followed part of a hockey game, then discussed escape route contingencies. Elen used the time to teach him a few lessons of tradecraft and Kevin absorbed all of it. While the TV droned on, Elen slumped back in the sofa and closed her eyes. Kevin looked at her and smiled.

Her breathing had become shallow, and he wondered if she was still awake. He studied the shadows on her face, how they accentuated the soft curves of her cheeks and nose and eyes. After a few minutes, he turned away, let his mind relax, and closed his eyes.

WHEN KEVIN AWOKE HE WAS alone on the sofa. He looked around and noticed movement out of the corner of his eye. Elen was sitting against the wall, concealed in shadow. Moonlight from the window, however, reflected a twinkle in her eyes and he could tell she was staring at him.

"What time is it?" he asked.

"A little after two."

"Is everything okay?"

"Yeah. I guess." Her voice sounded distant and brooding.

"Is it finally sinking in?"

"I think so." Her head came to rest against the wall with a thump. "It hasn't felt real. I mean, look at us. I really have no idea who you are. And vice versa. Yet here we are. In a run for our lives."

"I know," Kevin said. "It feels so out-of-control."

Silence.

Kevin sensed she wanted to say more. He cocked his head in her direction and tried to discern her thoughts. With her face in shadows, it was impossible. He smiled reassuringly and felt a curious bond beginning to form between them.

"You know," she said softly. "I've never considered myself emotional. At least, not controlled by my emotions. But right now, I feel so empty. Alone."

She sniffed and Kevin realized she was on the verge of tears. It put an ache in his chest. "Elen, there's nothing wrong with feeling that way. It's part of our nature. You can't hold it in for long without it tearing you up inside."

"I know."

He walked over to her and saw her eyes were glistening. He sat down next to her and put his arm around her. A single tear trickled down her cheek and he gently wiped it away. "I'm on your side," he said softly. "I'll never do anything to hurt you, I swear. I know this is a mess, Elen. Never in my wildest imagination—" He shook his head. "I just want you to know. Over the last few days I've come to see something in you, something that—"

"Don't," she interrupted softly.

"I—"

She put her finger to his mouth and said, "I know."

Kevin shook his head.

"I know," she repeated. She smiled at him, touched his cheek gently and said, "Just hold me."

Kevin wondered if his heart was going to burst as she laid her head on his chest. "Remember what I said? About what I wanted, or didn't want, from you?"

"Yes."

"You can trust me."

Elen wrapped her arms around him.

Kevin closed his eyes briefly and felt an intoxicating peace flood through him. For a few precious minutes he forgot about their predicament and simply lost himself in her embrace. He gently stroked her hair until he sensed she had dozed off. Then he smiled, and closed his eyes.

WHEN KEVIN AWOKE AGAIN, he had a pain in his side. He looked at the clock on the wall. 5:55. Still early. Recalling their conversation brought back a flood of emotions, including a sense of unease. It had been like a surrealistic dream. Magical, almost. Kevin stroked her hair affectionately.

Elen opened her eyes and smiled. "We should get ready to go."

"Yeah."

She stood slowly, and lumbered into the kitchen. "Go ahead and shower, if you want," she said. "I'll make some coffee."

Twenty minutes later, Kevin emerged from the shower, refreshed, dressed in jeans and a polo shirt. He didn't shave. It would take a week before the beard started looking decent. After breakfast, Elen showered and got her things ready to go.

In the main room, Kevin heard someone lightly rap on the front door. It was Anna.

"Morning," he said. "How are things?"

"Settling down a little, but I still can't go back to the apartment. Too hot. I think there's an FBI van across the street from the complex."

"Where are you staying?"

"At a friend's."

Elen came into the room.

"Hey, Elen," Anna said. "You guys ready to go?"

"Let me just make a quick phone call."

As she went into the other room, Kevin turned to Anna and asked, "What are you going to do after we leave?"

"Lay low for a few days. I'll head back to the apartment when things quiet down."

"Don't you think the FBI will want to question you?"

"Maybe. But they don't have any proof of my involvement. I don't see there's anything they can do. Besides, if I have to, I can always call the consulate."

Kevin grunted softly, unconvinced.

When Elen returned, she looked at them and said, "What are you two plotting?"

"Oh, nothing," Kevin said. "I'm just wondering how safe it is for Anna to go back to your apartment. The FBI must suspect her involvement by now, don't you think?"

Elen nodded, and looked at Anna.

"Don't worry about me," Anna said. "I'll be fine."

THE DRIVE TO CULVER CITY took thirty minutes by way of the often-gridlocked 405 freeway, and traffic was heavy. Anna found the building where they were supposed to meet their contact. She pulled into a small shopping center nearby. After exchanging good-byes, Kevin and Elen exited the vehicle and Anna drove off without looking back.

Kevin was apprehensive as they approached the shadowed doorway of the old office building. A dirty-looking vagrant was leaning against the wall, uncomfortably close. As Kevin approached the door, the old man spoke in a guttural voice, "You two sure's a cute-lookin' couple."

The man's features were veiled in shadow by the hood of a decrepit jacket. Kevin couldn't see the lopsided grin on his dirty face. Kevin simply nodded noncommittally, approached the door with a wary eye, and pressed the door ringer. Nothing. He wondered if anyone inside had heard it. He waited, pressed it again, and still nothing happened. Finally, he turned away.

"Leavin' already?" the vagrant asked.

"There's no one here."

"You sure?"

Kevin turned, looked at Elen, and said, "Yeah, I'm pretty sure."

"Well, I'm here!" the vagrant said.

Kevin allowed a smile to break through. "I see that. But I'm looking for someone else."

The vagrant moved away from the wall and walked towards them. Elen stiffened and Kevin stepped toward the vagrant, stopping the man several feet short.

"Is there any way you can help a poor old guy?" the man asked.

Kevin shook his head and said, "Look. I'm sorry you're down on your luck, but I can't help you."

"Well, maybe I can help *you*, then." The vagrant withdrew a cell phone from his coat and said, "Take this. Walk down the street and wait by the Burger King. Someone will call when we're sure you're clean."

Kevin was taken aback. He looked at Elen for help.

"Take it," the man said. Kevin did. With an expansive gesture of gratitude, the man disappeared around the corner of the building.

"Come on," Elen said, taking Kevin's hand. "Let's go."

They followed the man's directions. Three blocks later, the phone rang. Kevin answered it immediately.

"At the next signal," the caller said, "go to the other side of the street and wait at the corner. A black Honda Accord will pick you up."

Kevin disconnected the call and took Elen's hand as they crossed the street. Thirty seconds later, a black Honda stopped beside them. The front passenger window rolled down and a tanned face wearing fashionable sunglasses smiled at them. With his head inclined towards the rear door, he said, "Get in."

Kevin helped Elen inside, then sat down beside her and closed the door. He looked at the driver. "Where——"

"Not yet," the man in the passenger seat said. "Just sit back for a second while we make sure we're clean."

Kevin leaned back and put his arm around Elen's shoulder. The driver navigated a quick path to the freeway. Forty-five seconds later they reached Interstate 405 and took the southbound onramp. Eight minutes later they reached Interstate 105. Heading east, clear of the San Diego Freeway's congestion, they were soon cruising at just over seventy miles an hour. The driver kept the Honda in the second lane from the left and stayed with the flow of traffic.

Finally, the man in the front passenger seat turned sideways and said, "All right. Looks like we're clear for now."

"Who are you?" Kevin asked.

"My name's Joe. I don't want to know your names. I'm here for security, and to deliver you safely where you're goin'. Tuck yourselves in. We're not stoppin' for a while."

"What? I thought that—"

"That was just the pickup. Don't worry. You got everything you need?"

Kevin looked at Elen.

"Yeah," she said softly.

"What's next?" Kevin asked.

"Just relax and enjoy the ride."

Kevin looked out the window, set his cheek against the top of Elen's head, and sighed.

TWO HOURS LATER, KEVIN SENSED a decrease in road vibration, opened his eyes, and saw a small town surrounded by desert. The car slowed as it neared the end of the exit ramp. "Where are we?" he wondered. "Barstow?"

"Barstow it is."

"What are we doing here?"

"You'll find out soon enough." The driver pulled into a parking lot. "Now," Joe continued, "we just ferried you across the river, so to speak. Keep that cell phone." He inclined his head toward the rear door and said, "Good luck."

Elen opened her door and got out. Kevin hesitated and looked at Joe with curiosity. "You're a Marine. Right?"

"What makes you say that?"

"I could just tell. Thanks for your help."

Joe nodded.

"*Semper Fi*," Kevin said as he got out of the car. He joined Elen and they watched the Honda leave the lot. As it left, the phone rang. Kevin answered it immediately.

"To your right, do you see a white Grand Cherokee?"

"Yes."

"Come on over."

Kevin led the way to the Jeep and helped Elen get in. As he shut the door, the Jeep took off.

"Welcome to the underworld, my friends," the driver said. He appeared to be in his early forties, had short hair, and was wearing wrap-around, amber-lensed shooting glasses.

"Were we just on the Styx?" Kevin asked.

"In more ways than you know."

Elen squeezed Kevin's hand. He touched her forehead where a stray lock of hair had fallen over her eyes, and gently brushed it to the side. Meanwhile, she studied the driver closely. He was wearing sand-colored military fatigues. "Are you our final contact?"

"Yes, ma'am. In the flesh."

"Where are we going?"

"My shop's only a few minutes away. Sorry about all the cloak and dagger stuff."

His voice trailed off as he turned up the volume on the radio. Five minutes later, he pulled the Jeep into a small business lot, drove to the back and parked. As they walked inside his office, a telephone rang. The driver answered it, grabbed a pen and started writing. "Not a problem. You bet. Take it easy." He hung up and said, "Sorry about that. My name's Mike. Your brother and I go back a bit, so you've got nothing to worry about. Anyway, let me show you what I've got."

He walked over to a heavy file cabinet, unlocked the lowest drawer and withdrew a large backpack. He placed the pack on the desk and withdrew two cell phones. "One for each of you," he said. "Untraceable. You can use them anywhere. I already gave your brother the numbers. Here," he said, extending two business cards.

Elen took a card. The phones were identical but she noticed a small red sticker on one and a blue sticker on the other. On the card, the numbers were written in respective colored inks.

"Next," Mike continued. "Contingency funds. Nine thousand." He placed the cash on the table, reached into the bag and produced two semiautomatic handguns. He hefted one and said, "Now I don't recommend using these, but it never hurts to be prepared." He racked the slide back into a locked position. "Walther PPK. Three-eighty. A little more pop than a twenty-two, but not as much as a nine. Pretty much self-defense only. Each holds six rounds plus one. Two spare mags each. Ready to go." He released the slide and it sprang forward with a satisfying *clack*.

"James Bond is in the building," Kevin said.

Mike chuckled. "Don't go getting any ideas."

"Never."

"You're familiar with firearms, I take it?"

"A bit. I've been around them most of my life."

"Good," Mike said. He set the Walther next to its partner. "Then you know to be real careful."

"Of course."

"Fine. Moving on. Two leather waist packs. Each has a compartment for access to your wallets, phones, and a secret pouch for the PPKs. Here's your typical cloak and dagger gear: ball caps, sunglasses, bandannas, scarves. You can buy anything else on the way." He placed everything on the desk and walked towards a small studio. "Follow me. Elen, step inside and take a seat on the stool. I'm gonna take a couple pictures."

Elen did as she was told and sat down.

"Okay," Mike said. "Look at the red light. Great. Now throw on one of those sweaters." She did. "Okay. Tilt your head a little to the right and lift your chin a little. Perfect. Okay. All done. Next."

Kevin smiled, exchanged places with Elen and went through the identical routine. Mike came around the corner, handed each a pen and paper, and said, "You need new names."

They had already discussed what they were going to do. Kevin wrote the name Kyle Johnson. Elen decided on Erika Johnson. They would be married—it made the most sense. Mike took the papers, confirmed the spellings, and disappeared around the corner. Five minutes later, he returned and said, "I just need you to sign your new names. The vaguer the better." He held up a computer drawing pad. Both scrawled indecipherable signatures. Mike retreated to his office and returned with their new identities. "Passports," he said. "Stamped with visas for authenticity. Nevada DL's. Two business credit cards."

"Wow," Elen said. "That fast?"

"They're legitimate, too. The bills will even get paid, so don't go crazy." Kevin couldn't tell if he was serious. "Now," Mike continued, "ditch anything that identifies you as who you were." He showed them a small furnace. Kevin was reluctant. Mike said, "I know. You gotta do it though. They're only a liability now."

They both knew he was right. When they finished, they got back in the Jeep and Mike dropped them off two blocks from a car rental lot. There was no need to let people make a connection. Kevin hefted the backpack to his shoulder, lowered his head back inside the car, and said, "Thanks."

"No problem. Good luck."

Eager to be moving, Kevin took Elen's hand. The two fugitives were soon strolling the dusty streets of Barstow in silence, each left to personal thoughts of the unpredictable future in store for them. When they arrived at the rental lot, Kevin opened the door for Elen and followed her inside.

A pretty, well-dressed saleswoman stepped away from the counter and said, "Can I help you?"

"Yeah," Kevin replied. "Can we get a midsize rental?"

"Certainly. For how long?"

"A couple weeks. Maybe longer."

"No problem," she said as she tapped computer keys. She stared at the screen and said, "Let's see. Is a Ford Fusion okay?" She quoted the rate.

"We'll take it," Kevin said.

"Excellent. It looks like we have a green one and a white one. Do you have a preference?"

"White," Elen said.

"Okay." The associate typed into the computer, then said, "I just need a credit card."

"Here you go," Kevin said. He withdrew his new Visa card and driver's license, and set both on the counter.

As THEY DROVE OFF, KEVIN half-expected to see a line of police cars in the rearview mirror. He kept the speed at a safe pace and tried to relax. Two unremarkable hours after leaving Barstow they exited the freeway on the outskirts of Las Vegas. They found a nondescript Holiday Inn, checked in without a problem, then detoured to the mall for some shopping. After getting clothes and accessories for the trip, they stopped for dinner at *Chili's* and found a secluded table at the back.

A waitress arrived and took their orders. As she left, Kevin leaned back in his seat, surveyed the room, then turned his attention to Elen. He was amazed at how well she was adapting to the chaos. She seemed relaxed, as if she didn't have a care in the world. He, on the other hand, was almost sick with worry. He wanted to emulate her attitude of resilience and mental toughness—they were qualities he would need as well if he was going to survive this mess.

Elen reached for his hand and said, "Just don't think about it for a while."

He smiled, then turned to survey the room again. At a table fifteen feet away, two police officers were discussing something and one was looking at him as they talked, almost as if the officer was studying a mugshot photo and memorizing unique details. Kevin's breath shortened. He smiled at the officer, then nonchalantly returned his gaze back to Elen. "I don't think this was such a good idea after all."

"What do you mean?"

"Don't look," Kevin said, "but there are two cops a few tables over. One of them is looking at me a little too closely for my taste. You think he's gay?"

Elen had just taken a drink and struggled to keep it down. Kevin grinned. Elen swallowed quickly, took a deep breath, and said, "Ahhh. Don't do that to me!"

Kevin glanced back at the officer and was relieved to see they were no longer an item of interest. Still, considering the situation, he didn't like it. "I think we should get the food to go."

"Fine," Elen replied.

Ten minutes later, they were back at the Holiday Inn. Elen opened the door to their room and burst out laughing. She set the food on the dresser, turned to face him, and threw her arms around his neck. Kevin returned her embrace, but she suddenly let go and moved away.

Kevin said, "Are you sure you weren't drinking a Long Island Iced Tea back there?"

She grinned.

"What's gotten into you?"

"The look on your face when you said—Sorry. It's just you looked so funny."

"Thanks. I live only to entertain, madame. For my next act, I—"

"Shut up," Elen said quickly. She put her hands behind his head, gently shook him, and said, "Shut up, shut up, shut up." Their faces were inches apart. She was smiling. She looked at his lips, then his eyes.

Kevin put his hand on her cheek and said softly, "What are we doing?"

"I don't know."

"What do you want to do?"

Elen hesitated, then said, "I don't know."

"What should we do?"

"I don't know."

Kevin leaned in. Elen drew back, just out of reach, but the smile was still on her face. Kevin put his arm around her and drew her close.

"Food's getting cold," Elen said.

"Yeah?"

She nodded.

"You hungry?"

"Yeah."

"All right, all right," Kevin said, letting her go. "Let's eat."

Chapter 5

Munich, Germany

A PARTLY CLOUDY SKY CAST THE CITY with an invigorating glow, generating a nearly tangible sense of harmony and peace. Mike Russell couldn't help but be inspired by the sensation as he strolled down the diminutive Burkleinstrasse. "*Pardon, madame,*" he muttered as he carefully sidestepped an elderly woman. He could have spoken German, or even English for that matter, but instead chose the Gallic tongue— for no conscious reason he could think of. All three languages are understood by most people in Munich.

At the next corner, Russell slowed to a halt and looked up at the street signs, as if unsure which way to go. In reality, he was checking the surveillance team's position behind him. He noticed the team had thinned out considerably. Russell hoped now they would finally break form and make a mistake. To him, it had become something of a game. He had a small map in his hand. He studied it as he crossed the street and headed north along St. Anna Strasse. He slowed his pace, studied the buildings along the street, and glanced back again at the intersection.

"Recovering well," he muttered to himself.

He was certain they were a decent team. But they were at a disadvantage. Russell *knew* where he was going, and they didn't have the foggiest idea. Still, he had to be careful. He didn't want to alarm them into thinking he was anything more than an oblivious attaché-slash-tourist trying to find his way through a foreign city. So far, he had managed to get good looks at four of them. That was sufficient for the time being. He really wanted to identify the leader, but doubted he would get the chance.

As he continued north, Russell noticed three young men exit from a *biergarten* ahead. They appeared drunk, talking loudly to each other in coarse German. Russell edged away from them, closer to the street, not wanting to give them any excuse to focus their drunken energy on him. He passed even with them and started to relax.

But it was too soon.

The three men swerved in his direction just as a black Mercedes sedan screeched to a halt on the street beside him. The trap was sprung perfectly. Unable to get away from the boisterous trio, Russell was pushed toward the car. A rear door opened. A pair of strong hands reached out of the back and grabbed Russell firmly, pulling him quickly into the car. One of the three "drunks" slammed the door shut, and the vehicle sped off.

Inside the Mercedes, a severe-looking German frisked Russell. "*Lehnen Sie vorwärts*," he said. *Lean forward.*

Russell calmly said, "I'm a consular official with the U.S. Embassy."

"*Vorwärts lehnen!*"

Russell shrugged his shoulders, shook his head, and said, "Look, you're going to have to speak English. *Sprechen Sie Englisch?*"

The man sighed in surrender and repeated himself in accented English. Russell complied. The man checked his back for weapons, found nothing, and said, "*Danke.*"

Russell leaned back in his seat. "What's going on here?"

"*Polizei*," the man in the front passenger seat growled. "You will know soon enough."

Russell realized he was better off saying as little as possible. *Police, huh?* Whoever these people were, they were serious. In his mind, he also knew he was the one at a considerable disadvantage now. Having no chance of immediate escape, he told himself to relax and let the scenario play out. *But what would an untrained attaché do? Be frightened, of course.* If he allowed himself to relax, that would be a sure indication of his intelligence training. So, instead, he opted to foster a slightly nervous appearance—and hope he wasn't overdoing it.

The driver slowed, turned left at Prinzregenten Strasse, and pulled the car over to the curb. The security man in the front-passenger seat got out and opened Russell's door. "*Losgehen*," he said. *Move.*

Russell stepped onto the sidewalk to see the first man surreptitiously pointing a silenced pistol at him. A coat was draped over the man's arm, concealing the weapon from passersby. Russell allowed his eyes to grow big at the sight of the weapon, hoping to further sell the idea of his innocence.

"Move," the man said tersely, indicating with his head that Russell precede him on the sidewalk. "Your games mean nothing, by the way. Don't do anything stupid."

Russell noticed this man's English was substantially better than his colleague's. In his mind, Russell decided to dub him *One*, and the colleague in the backseat, *Two*. "What's going on?" he repeated hesitantly. "Have I done something wrong?"

"Silence."

Russell allowed himself to appear sufficiently cowed, silently praying that One didn't suffer from an itchy trigger finger. This was definitely not the time to test the man's resolve. Two came around the car as One pushed Russell along the sidewalk, finally taking a distanced position of cover should their captive attempt anything foolish. *Another mark for them*, Russell noted in his mental flowchart of the situation. *They're not stupid. I could take one of them, but not both.*

"To your right," One said.

Mike obeyed and followed the concrete path into a large park called *der Englischer Garten*, resigned to the fact he was in no position to escape. With a silenced pistol, One could easily shoot him before he made it ten paces, then disappear before the *polizei* arrived to investigate. Besides, he reasoned, there weren't enough people around to create the necessary diversion if he even hoped to have a chance. The location and the time had been chosen well. Nevertheless, he found it odd that they had taken him here in the first place. If they intended to harm him, it didn't make sense to do it in such a visible environment. *But shooting me isn't their intention*, he quickly surmised. *No, they want me alive. Maybe to talk to someone?* It was as good a guess as any.

Moments later, his suspicions were confirmed. One directed him to a solitary park bench and said, "Sit."

Mike sat down and sighed as he studied the park, looking for the smallest sign of danger. Nothing caught his attention. *Just a typical day in the park*, he assessed with a lopsided grin.

"It seems odd to see a man in your position smiling, Herr Russell."

Mike turned to face the newcomer. He was a tall man who bore an obvious air of authority and spoke English with an accent that was neither British nor American. He was smoking an American cigarette.

"I beg your pardon?" Russell said.

The man sat down on the bench. "I am Detective Lieutenant Erich Neumann of the Bundeskriminalamt. I have been ordered to follow you." A knowing smile began to form on his otherwise stoic face. "My superiors think you are a spy."

The line was delivered flawlessly. A slightly raised eyebrow completed the statement and at the same time turned it into a question. Surprised by the man's directness, Russell couldn't think of anything to say.

"What?" Neumann said. "No witty comeback? How about this." He paused, continuing in a typically drawn, British manner, "Spy? I simply have no idea what you're talking about, old boy."

Russell noticed that while Neumann's mouth smiled, his eyes did not. They remained cold—firmly detached from the situation. "I'm not British," Russell said. "I don't know what you're talking about."

Neumann's eyes narrowed as he studied the young man before him. "I commend your training, Mister Russell. You handle stressful situations very well. You're an asset to your agency."

"What are you talking about?"

"I apologize for my colleagues' zeal in picking you up in such a manner. I assure you it was a miscommunication. I pray they didn't frighten you?"

"Excuse me?"

"*Bitte*—please," Neumann said with a raised hand. "You are not in danger. This is Germany. We are friends. Allies."

"What do you want?"

"Relax, Mister Russell. Markus," Neumann said quietly, speaking to the nearest security guard.

"*Ja?*"

"We're fine here. Make sure the area is secure. *Danke.*"

"Certainly," Markus replied as he turned away to investigate the park.

Once he was out of earshot, Neumann leaned closer to Russell. "Please forgive the melodramatic formalities, Herr Russell. I assure you I am not playing counterintelligence games with you. But, sometimes I have to keep up appearances. People are watching, after all. This is Oskar," he said, indicating the remaining man. "You are well trained, Mike. I like that. May I call you Mike?"

Russell shrugged.

"That's why I sent you the list," Neumann continued. "This is a very delicate situation, and I need someone in the Agency I can trust. I've been watching you for a while, and I think you are that man."

Russell looked away. "I don't know what you're talking about."

"Look. We're professionals here. Listen to what I have to say. Okay? I don't have much time."

"I'm listening."

"Good. I've studied your record with the State Department, and I know you are, in fact, a rising star in the Agency." He paused to assess the effect of his words. "Yes, I have seen your personnel file. Don't be too surprised. I have many connections. But, why am I talking to you like this, you wonder?" He shook his head. "I have to be very careful. There is a mole at the U.S. Embassy in Berlin."

"What?"

"I'm talking about a very serious problem, Mike. But it doesn't stop there. There are moles in BKA, too. My superiors can never know I'm speaking to you in these terms. Thus my ruse to get you aside." He paused to consider his words, then continued, "The list I sent you serves a dual purpose. First, it should convince you of a very serious threat to the people on the list and thus the quality of my sources. Second, it will also confirm the identity of your mole. How, you wonder?" Neumann smiled. "Well, I can tell you who your mole is."

Russell's eyes narrowed as he studied Neumann's face. He detected no guile, but that was hardly enough to prove the veracity of the lieutenant's statement. "Who is it, then? Who is he working for? The Russians?"

"Hardly. You know as well as I do the Russians are in disarray. They haven't the resources to carry on an operation like this anymore. No, this is much more serious, although right now you would not believe me if I told you."

"You can tell me the identity of the mole, but not who he's working for?"

"Correct. You have no idea who these people are, how dangerous they are. In time I think you would believe. But not now."

"Well, end the suspense. Who's the mole?"

Neumann stared him directly in the eyes, and said, "Your station chief."

Russell coughed, then started to stand, but Neumann stopped him with a raised hand.

"Please, do not leave just yet. I understand your reaction, but I assure you it is true."

"What evidence do you have, Erich?" Russell asked as he sat back down. "May I call you Erich?"

"The list," Neumann replied. "The list is more important than you can imagine at this point. Your station chief understands this, because he is one of them."

"One of whom?"

"It's complicated."

"Well, that's just too damned bad," Russell replied coldly.

"Like I said, you would not believe me if I were to tell you, Mike, only because you are not ready to believe." He paused to collect his thoughts. "But here is the proof. Check to see if your report has been forwarded up the chain of command. The list certainly warrants that much attention. I'll bet your station chief has quashed it, because he doesn't want that information to go any farther than Berlin."

Mike shook his head, unconvinced.

"Don't take my word for it," Neumann said. "He'll even demand you give him the original list and any related documents and files you may have started. How is that?"

Russell pursed his lips. If it was disinformation, he decided there was no harm in continuing. *If it's real—no*, he thought. *I'm not even going to consider that.* "Okay," he said quietly. "I'll check it out."

Neumann stood. "Do you remember the biergarten on St. Anna Strasse?"

"Of course."

"When you see I'm right, meet me there tomorrow. Seven p.m."

Russell nodded.

"*Auf Wiedersehen*," Neumann said. He walked away, flanked by his security guards. Russell looked at his feet and sighed. He had been picked up by a foreign counterintelligence agency, though technically an allied one, and warned. *The station chief. A mole?* He realized it wasn't impossible, but it seemed highly unlikely.

Russell walked away from the bench knowing he had some work to do before this was going to blow over. He opened his pack of Marlboros, put a fresh cigarette to his lips and lit it. He blew out a large cloud of gray smoke and replaced the lighter in his pocket. Intelligence work was frequently boring as Hell. His job usually entailed a lot of sitting and waiting and thinking. Not now. Slowly, he began to smile as his body tingled in anticipation. He was on the edge of something. Possibly something big.

Los Angeles, California

THE CLOCK ON THE WALL of the hotel room read half-past ten in the morning. Sitting on the bed with his back against the headboard, Rostov was studying a map of Los Angeles on his iPad. He could have used his smartphone map, but at the moment he preferred the larger picture because it helped him visualize routes and locations.

He was staying at the Radisson, a pleasantly anonymous hotel along the 405 freeway. He could have stayed at the Beverly Hilton, or anywhere else for that matter. Cost wasn't an issue. He was paid a salary of $10,000 per week, plus expenses—over half-a-million dollars annually, deposited tax-free into his Cayman Islands bank account. It was a great arrangement for both sides. His employer had money to burn for his special services, and he was only too happy to oblige.

He set the iPad down, stretched his arms, and walked to the window to assess the traffic situation. It was bad, as usual. Still, he guessed he had a window of opportunity between eleven and two to get the job done without getting mired in traffic. He muttered a curse at the unpredictable nature of traveling in Los Angeles, then closed the thick drapes covering the window.

He retrieved his wallet from the dresser, opened it and studied the official-looking ID card inside that backstopped his alias as FBI Special Agent Jacob Ross. Satisfied his credentials were ready to be displayed—although, only in an emergency—he holstered his Beretta 9mm, put the rest of his gear into a black bag and left the room. Out of habit he avoided the trapped confines of the elevator and instead took the stairs three flights to the lobby. He had already checked out online, settling the bill with a corporate American Express Card.

Five minutes later he was driving north on the freeway. He lifted a cell phone and dialed.

"Stevens," a voice answered.

"Dan. It's Jacob Ross."

"Hey! Are you in town?"

"Just got in last night."

"Jet lagged?"

"A bit. I've been doing a lot of traveling, that's for sure."

"You did a nice job in New York, by the way."

"You mean the art exhibit?" Rostov asked innocently.

"Yeah, whatever," Stevens replied. "You know what I mean."

"Wasn't there. Didn't do it. Can't prove a thing."

"Amen to that."

Rostov said, "So, what are you up to these days?"

"Jeez, man. I don't know if you heard, but I really stepped in it the other day. Then I slipped, fell down, and rolled around just for good measure."

"What happened?"

"Hold on a sec." There was a muffled conversation in the background, then Stevens came back on the line and said, "Sorry about that."

"Where are you?"

"UCLA."

"What are you doing there?"

"Interviews." His voice suddenly got softer. "Anyway, I lost control of a situation down in Long Beach, and—well, it's a long story. Hey, you're not here to whack me, are you?"

"Very funny," Rostov replied.

"Yeah, ha ha," Stevens said in a humorless voice. "Well, I've been tagging along with the FBI, but they haven't been much help."

"How did they get involved?"

"That's part of the long story."

"Can you handle it?"

"I think so. I could sure use your help, though."

"I'm already booked."

"All right. Hey, you wanna get some drinks later?"

"Possibly," Rostov replied. "I'll have to see how my schedule develops."

"Okay. I don't know how long this is going to take, so just"—

"Damn!" Rostov interrupted. "Sorry, I'm about to miss my exit. I'll call you later."

He disconnected the call, dropped the phone on the passenger seat and barely squeezed into the exit lane. The black Toyota Camry he cut off in the process braked hard, coming within inches of his bumper. Rostov saw the driver make an obscene gesture. Whoops. He waved an apology.

The Toyota followed him through the stop sign at the end of the exit ramp. Rostov checked his mirror again and saw the Toyota was lowered with tinted windows, and he could hear hip hop music coming from inside. It finally occurred to Rostov that he cut off a crew of gang members. When they followed him around another turn, he reached inside his coat and scanned the residential neighborhood. He found a secluded side street darkened by overhanging trees and pulled over. As the Toyota pulled in behind him, he screwed a suppressor to the extended barrel of his automatic.

Rostov got out and turned to face the Camry, keeping the Beretta hidden. He slowed his breathing as he prepared for the inevitable confrontation. Naturally, his heart was pounding with the surge of adrenaline, but he knew how to control it. When the doors of the Toyota opened, the music seemed to double in volume. Four young black men emerged wearing baggy pants, dark sunglasses, gang-colored bandannas, and several thousand dollars worth of gold chains. One of the gang members took a drag on a joint and handed it to his homie.

The leader approached with an automatic pistol prominently displayed in his waistband. It was a bad move. He would never be able to draw it in time.

"Hey, what are you boys up to?" Rostov asked.

"Who the Hell do you think you are?!" the leader asked incredulously.

Rostov raised his left hand in apology, and replied, "No need to get hostile, my friend. My mistake."

"I ain't your friend, punk! What's your problem, white boy?!"

"Sorry, man, I'm just a tourist."

"Well then, maybe it's time you *visit* a *hospital*."

Rostov sensed his FBI credentials would only make the situation worse. He had to deal with them quickly. He scanned the neighborhood and saw that nobody was watching. "You boys know what you're doing?" he said. He stared at the leader. "You're about ten seconds from dying, my friend." To the remaining gang members, he said, "You're eleven seconds. You're twelve. And you're thirteen."

The leader hesitated when it finally occurred to him that Rostov's right hand was hidden. Rostov thought the situation might diffuse then, but one of the gang members said, "Ice? We gonna let this white punk diss us like that? We needa bus' some caps in his *sorry* ass right *now*."

With those words, Ice's resolve strengthened and he reached for his gun. Rostov's Beretta was up in a flash. He fired once and Ice fell to the ground with a sucking wound in the center of his chest. Rostov stepped to the right and shot the second one in the throat. The third went down with a double-tap to the head. The last gang member simply stared in shock as the unbelievable scene unfolded in front of him. Showered with blood and brain tissue, he lost his grip on his gun and staggered backwards in disbelief.

Rostov approached him and saw for the first time that he was just a boy—maybe fifteen or sixteen years old.

"Please," the boy begged.

The Beretta flashed once more and the boy fell over, settling in a contorted heap. Rostov checked Ice and saw he was still alive, clutching his chest and coughing blood. Ice tried to point his gun. Rostov shot him in the head, then surveyed the area for witnesses. None. At least, none who would talk to the cops. He returned to his car, got in, and drove away.

Amateurs, he thought, suddenly angry. *Street thugs. Punk kids without a future.* Though he'd never expected them to pose a serious threat, he was still surprised at how easy it had been. He'd fired four times in less than three seconds. Six rounds total, and every round had struck home.

IT TOOK ROSTOV FIFTEEN MINUTES to get to the country club. On the way, he managed to calm down a little. Now, he had to take care of the actual business of the day. His target was an avid golfer and Rostov wanted to do a quick reconnaissance. Through a contact, he knew the target was playing golf and would most likely finish within the hour. If possible, Rostov would end the contract here. If not, he would wait.

He avoided the parking lot. Instead, he parked on the street a short distance away and walked back to the clubhouse. Wearing a dark suit, he nosed around inside the golf shop to get a sense of the environment. He examined an expensive set of clubs, then noticed an attractive young woman nearby. She had been looking at him, but glanced away when he looked in her direction. He casually approached her, and said, "Hi, how are you?"

"Fine, thanks," she replied hesitantly. "And you?"

"Not bad, actually, considering I just survived my first freeway gunfight."

Taking it as a joke, she laughed softly—freeway shootings are an occasional source of morbid humor in Los Angeles. She turned to study him, and said, "Well, I don't see any holes. I guess you're all right."

He patted himself down, sighed deeply, and said, "Yeah, thank God." He looked at the club in her hand. "If you're looking for a set of clubs, I wouldn't recommend the ones you've got there."

"Really? Why not?"

"Wrong shafts. Wrong flex. You need a ladies' set."

She looked at the club in her hand. "What makes you think it's for me?"

Rostov laughed. She was quick. "Just a hunch," he replied. "Are you looking to buy a set of clubs?"

"Why? Can you get me a good deal?"

"No," he said, stifling a chuckle.

"Then I guess not."

"And if I could?"

She grinned coyly. "I don't know. Maybe I would just lead you on for a while. Make you think I was going to purchase."

"Do you do that a lot, then?"

She smiled. "Occasionally, when I'm trying to kill some time."

"Is that what you're doing here?"

She continued to smile, but didn't reply.

He looked into her eyes. She was intelligent, beautiful, and appeared interested in the conversation. A natural flirt. Probably just waiting for someone to finish playing the day's round. He extended his hand and said, "My name's Jacob."

"Heather."

"Are you waiting for someone to finish?"

She nodded.

"Me, too." He glanced out the window. "God, what a beautiful day. Do you want to join me outside? I'll buy you a drink."

"Wow, you move pretty fast, huh?"

Rostov smiled.

"I still might buy these," she said, hefting the club in her hand.

"Ahh, come on. Anyway, I can tell the assistant pro wants you out of his hair."

"Oh? How do you know that?"

"It's in his eyes. He clearly doesn't appreciate pretty girls toying with him. You know, leading him on and such."

"And you do?"

"Occasionally. When I'm trying to kill some time."

"Did I just miss something here?"

"Not at all. Come on. There's a table in the shade. I need someone to cover me while I stake this place out."

She laughed, put the club back in the rack, and said, "Okay, why not?"

He opened the door for her and they went outside. A short distance away, Rostov saw a girl in shorts and a club shirt stocking her motorized refreshment cart with drinks. "Can I get you something?" he asked.

"A soda's fine," Heather said. "Thanks."

He went over to the cart girl and returned seconds later with two bottles. They sat down at the table and popped the tops off. "Cheers," he said.

"Cheers."

Rostov looked around, studied the layout of the course, and nodded appreciatively. The manicured fairways exuded a deep green glow and the magnificent oak trees surrounding them appeared healthy and majestic. There was even a large waterfall embedded in rock behind the eighteenth green. "It's so beautiful here," he said.

"The course looks nice, too."

"Is this your first time?"

"Yeah. Are you a member?"

"Yeah, sort of. My dad's a member and I just tag along sometimes."

"Do you golf?"

"Not very well. Actually, I'm just visiting my parents for the week."

"Oh? Are you in college?"

She laughed. "Thanks for thinking I'm that young."

"What? You don't look a day over twenty-one." She smiled at him, and he wondered what might have been, under different circumstances. She was intelligent and easy to talk to. Beautiful. Gorgeous, really. He'd just wanted someone to provide cover for him, but he sensed she was actually interested in him. His lifestyle didn't lend itself to dating. All the traveling. And killing. He'd been married before, but she left because he was away from home too much. It was inevitable, really.

"So, what do you do?" Heather asked.

"I'm a consultant," Rostov said. "I travel a lot. Some of it's interesting. Some of it's—" He wobbled his hands. "But, I have to admit it's a nice job."

"Do you live around here?"

"Just visiting. Actually, when I'm not traveling on business, I stay at my house in the Caymans."

"Wow, really?"

"Have you ever been there?"

"Last year," she replied. "It's *so* beautiful. Incredible diving."

"Do you scuba?"

"I love it. Dad's a diver, too."

Rostov smiled, lost in thought.

Heather was silent as she studied him closer. "Are you married?"

Rostov hesitated for a moment, actually surprised by the probing question. "No," he finally replied. "At least, not anymore."

"What happened?"

"Are you always this direct?"

Shrugging, Heather answered, "You seem like a direct kind of guy."

He smiled at her and looked away. "She left me," he said. "Two years ago." He looked at the ground and sighed deeply. "Cancer," he lied easily. "It wasn't diagnosed in time and she was gone inside of two months."

"I'm sorry."

"Sometimes life can be cruel."

"Yeah," Heather agreed soberly, looking away.

Rostov followed her gaze and saw a group of golfers finishing. His attention was drawn to a man putting on the eighteenth green. It looked to be a fifteen-footer—not an easy shot, but makeable. The player stroked the ball cleanly and Rostov sat up straighter to watch. The ball disappeared in the hole and a muted chorus of *well-done's* erupted from the green. As Rostov studied each of the players, his gaze stopped at the man second from the left.

Target acquired.

Rostov considered Heather for a second and felt surprisingly torn. He knew it would completely violate his own rules, but—she was really attractive. Smart. Beautiful. He slipped his cell phone out of its case and studied it for a second. "Damn," he said softly. "It looks like I have to get back to work." He stood up to leave. "It was nice to meet you, Heather."

"Yeah, you, too." She smiled warmly. "Have a safe trip."

"Thanks." He started to walk away, then stopped. "Heather, can I ask you a personal question?"

"That depends."

Rostov smiled disarmingly. "Are you seeing anyone?"

Heather bit her lip, and said, "Are you always this direct?"

"You seem like a direct kind of girl."

She smiled. "I might be."

"What? A direct kind of girl? Or seeing someone?"

"Maybe both."

Rostov smiled, and said, "Can I buy you dinner tonight?"

"You want to buy me dinner?"

"Absolutely."

"But you don't even know me."

"Yeah, I do. Your name's Heather."

She laughed. "Well, I don't know you."

"Yeah, you do. My name's Jacob."

"I don't know."

Rostov withdrew a business card. It was blank except for the name JACOB ROSS. He scribbled a phone number on the back and said, "I'm staying at the Sheraton in Santa Monica. That's my cell." He handed her the card. "Maybe you could come over this evening? We could have a couple of drinks at the bar. Then we could go out for dinner. I've got a nice Italian place in mind. Maybe sit by the pool afterward and talk? What do you think?"

"Hmmm," she stalled, trying to seem disinterested. "I'll think about it."

"Okay," he said, smiling with uncertainty. "Well, sorry, but I have to go. It was a pleasure to meet you."

"Likewise."

As he left, Heather felt a sense of loss. Replaying their conversation in her mind, she shook her head in disbelief. In such a brief amount of time, it seemed they had communicated far deeper than she would have thought possible. He was so confident. *Magical* almost. She definitely wanted to see him again, but something didn't seem right. She realized she was a little frightened by him. By his charisma. His charm. His ease with words. His personality was a force. But it was too late now—she knew she had to see him again.

ROSTOV RETURNED TO HIS RENTAL CAR. He was being careless and stupid. He knew it. The woman was a distraction he didn't need. He had to put her out of his mind for the time being. He took off his coat, replaced it with a dark windbreaker, and replaced his dress shoes with dark sneakers. A Los Angeles Dodgers baseball cap and Oakley shades completed his disguise. He debated on returning to the entrance of the club to wait for his target, but then considered it a bad idea—

Heather might see him. As much as he wanted to see her again, now was the wrong time.

From the car, the view of the club was good. He decided to wait. Ten minutes later, his target finally emerged. Rostov started the car. The target's Lexus exited the parking lot and turned away from him. Rostov pulled his car onto the street and accelerated to catch up. A quick search for surveillance vehicles came up empty. He knew from experience that time is the enemy of the bodyguard and sentry, and the ally of the stalker. Maybe his target, if he had even taken the initial threat seriously, just felt secure and was no longer worried about his safety.

When the Lexus entered the onramp to the freeway, Rostov accelerated to close the gap. The Lexus was out of sight briefly, but he wasn't concerned about losing it. He knew where his target's residence was located. Several minutes later, the Lexus signaled and changed lanes, presumably heading for the Wilshire Boulevard exit. As Rostov followed, he allowed two cars to come between them, hoping at least one would follow the Lexus and not take the eastbound fork toward the business district. It wasn't meant to be. Both cars went east and Rostov was forced to hang back in the westbound exit ramp, hoping his target didn't spot him.

He followed his quarry west on Wilshire, past the Veterans Administration facilities. When the Lexus turned north onto San Vicente, Rostov allowed another car to come between them as they drove past the trendy shops and markets lining both sides of the street. He followed the Lexus onto Bundy Street and into Brentwood. He couldn't help but be reminded of the infamous event in 1994, only a few blocks away on Rockingham. The murder trial and shocking acquittal had been the polarizing event of the decade in Los Angeles.

Rostov smiled distantly at the absurdity of life, then refocused on the task at hand when the Lexus suddenly turned right, forcing him to accelerate to catch up. When he reached the next corner the target turned right again. Rostov was immediately wary. After another right turn he broke off the tail and swore under his breath. His target had employed a cheap countertail technique, but as cheap as the trick was it was effective. If he had continued to follow he would have been burned.

Rostov pulled into an empty driveway, paused for a moment, then turned around. Under his breath, he muttered, "You can run, but you'll only die tired."

Chapter 6

University of California, Los Angeles

"THANKS FOR YOUR TIME, MA'AM. Good-bye." Bryce Maurer ended the phone call with a flourish. He pressed the END button on the cell phone in an exaggerated manner, and in the process revealed his mounting frustration.

"No luck?" Dan Stevens asked.

"Nada."

In the last two days, he had spoken to twenty-five people, mainly students, believed to be associated with Elen Biran. He had a list of twenty more names to call. Nobody seemed to really know her well, the consensus being she was friendly but distant. Half of them suggested he contact her roommate, Anna Cohen. He had already tried, several times, but it seemed she had disappeared, too. That made Maurer a little suspicious, but he really didn't know what to do about it. He looked up at the sky and stretched his arms.

"How about lunch?" Stevens suggested.

"I'm not hungry."

"You sure?"

"Yeah. You go ahead. I'm going to try Cohen again."

"Okay," Stevens said. "Call me if I can help."

"Right."

As Stevens walked toward his car, Maurer reflected on the troubling assignment. He understood why Stevens was so interested in the investigation, but he was also confused. Instinctively, he knew ATF wasn't telling the whole story. Neither Elen Biran nor Kevin

Edwards had a previous criminal history, nor did they have any links to organizations that promoted terrorism. Biran was Israeli, but being from a war-ravaged country didn't make her a terrorist. Besides, Maurer reasoned, Israel was not *in* the terror business. Edwards, on the other hand, was completely mystifying. He had no background or apparent motivation for this sort of thing. A model citizen by all appearances, the son of a retired cop, and suddenly he works for terrorists? It didn't make sense.

Despite his misgivings, Maurer simply knew he had to find the two fugitives. His best approach toward that end appeared to be through Anna Cohen. He picked up his cell phone and dialed.

Westwood, California

ANNA STUDIED THE VAN OF FEDERAL AGENTS watching the apartment. She was unrecognizable in her disguise: a colorful shawl, sunglasses, and maternity clothes that made her look seven to eight months pregnant. She had avoided returning to their apartment for the last week, but now she was anxious to get inside. There were papers she needed to study, and she wanted to check the answering machine. She secretly hoped Elen would call, but she didn't really believe her best friend would be so careless. Resisting the impulse to go to the apartment, she turned around and walked in the opposite direction.

Brentwood, California

ROSTOV WAS GETTING ANGRY. It wasn't a normal reaction for him and he was surprised. His target had suddenly gotten smart. After breaking the tail earlier, the man had called for a security team. More than anything, Rostov was angry with himself. He blew the surveillance at the club. Blew the tail. He was getting sloppy.

Focus.

He watched the team position themselves in a perimeter around the target's Brentwood estate, a beautiful three-story mansion with immaculate brickwork and shrubbery. The Lexus was parked in the half-circle driveway in the front. From the safety of his own car two blocks away, Rostov raised his binoculars and studied the house. The security wasn't the best he had seen, but they appeared competent. That changed things. He preferred getting in close, but he counted seven security guards. The men were deployed in a tight semicircle around the Lexus. Acceptable defensive positioning. Each had a good field of fire for an oncoming attacker. He could take out half of them before they realized what hit them, but it would be risky. They were primarily a visual deterrent, intended to discourage any hapless moron who wanted to kill their principal. Against a determined professional, they were hardly more than an annoyance. Still, they were dangerous, and he would have to be careful.

He reckoned several more were posted inside. Without an inner security detail he could simply sneak into the house and do the job. But if the security team knew what they were doing, they would secure the estate inside before allowing their principal access to the house. For the job in New York he had used a support team. This one was solo. If he got reckless, he could become the target, bottled-up with nowhere to go. He shook his head at the thought. Surprise might be on his side but it hardly outweighed the negatives. That left one other possibility.

He started the car, drove around the block and parked. Inside the car, he changed into an expensive jogging suit, then walked back in the direction of the estate. He started jogging. The ball cap covered his face and he kept his gaze down. He veered toward the house, crossing the street in front. The estate was centered at the heart of a T-intersection, perfect for what he had in mind. He counted his paces for about two hundred yards. Finally, he halted and looked up at the sky as if catching his breath. Slowly, he turned to see if he was being watched. The road curved slightly and the estate was just barely within view. None of the guards seemed interested in him. He studied the rooftop of the house across the street and mentally calculated his sight line and distance.

It should work.

Rostov completed a circle of the block and finally reached his car. Once inside, he picked up his phone and dialed.

"Hello?" a wary voice answered.

"Is this Norm's Auto Wrecking?"

"No."

"This isn't Norm Basirian?"

"Get lost, pal."

"Sorry. Wrong number." Rostov disconnected the call and waited. Twenty seconds later, the phone chirped, Rostov answered and said, "I need a three-oh-eight, the garment bag and a couple of sandbags." He was silent as he listened to the response. "Good. I'll be there in twenty."

After twenty-two minutes of navigating through heavy traffic, Rostov pulled into a nondescript office park. Shortly, a short man dressed in jeans and a hoodie approached the car, carrying a black garment bag over his shoulder. Rostov pressed a button to unlock the doors. The man placed the bag inside and shut the door. Rostov handed him an envelope, then quickly drove off.

Paris, France

"MERCI BIEN," BIRAN SAID with disappointment in his voice. "Good night." He replaced the telephone in its cradle and rubbed his eyes. It was late, and the last twenty-four hours had been frustratingly unproductive. He was convinced the man who had followed his father was directly connected with the men who had stalked his sister. The problem was he couldn't prove it.

David Anan entered the room and noticed his friend's gloomy expression. "No luck?"

Biran shook his head, exhaled loudly through his nose, and muttered, "What the Hell's going on?"

"Keep digging," Anan replied. "Something has to turn up soon."

Santa Monica, California

ROSTOV PULLED HIS CAR INTO another business park just as his phone rang. He flipped it open and answered, "Yeah."

"Take the last one," the caller said. "Keys are under the visor. There's a jumpsuit in back."

"Thanks."

Rostov drove to the back and saw a row of three unattended cable company vans. He parked, got out and took the garment bag with him over to the last van. The sliding side door was unlocked. He stepped inside and slid the door shut behind him. As promised, the keys were under the visor.

Fifteen minutes later, he drove the van into an alley near the target's house, slowed down, and looked for the dumpster that marked his spot. Finding it, he eased the van next to it and parked. He emerged from the van wearing a tan jumpsuit with the cable company logo embroidered on the back, a toolbelt around his waist, and a tan ball cap on his head. He grabbed the garment bag from the rear of the van, closed up the van, and walked over to the house he'd selected.

A wooden gate barred entrance to the back yard. It was a simple latch, though, and it was unlocked. Rostov slid open the latch and entered the yard. He closed the gate behind him and stood still, listening. No sound from the house. No dogs. He walked around the side and checked the windows.

No one home.

He looked back at the gate and saw a tool shed in the corner of the yard. A ladder was propped against it. Rostov shook his head. This was too easy. He set the garment bag on the ground next to the house and walked over to the shed. He nosed around inside but there was nothing that interested him.

Rostov came out and hefted the ladder to his shoulder, carried it to the house and propped it against the edge of the roof. The garment bag was bulky, but he managed to carry it up the ladder easily. On the rooftop, he placed the bag at the edge closest to the target's house, unzipped it and opened it. The sides of the bag folded flat so the inside became a padded shooting mat for him to lie on.

The sniper rifle was disassembled in a hard case. Rostov opened the case and put the rifle together: barrel, receiver, buttstock, scope, silencer. He inserted a full magazine of .308-caliber match-grade ammo, then racked the bolt back and forward, chambering a round. Ready to go, Rostov lay on the mat, cradling the rifle in the crook of his elbows. He lifted the binoculars to his eyes and studied the estate in the distance. The Lexus was still in the driveway. The number of security personnel outside had dropped from seven to five. The other two would be inside. Perhaps there was a good surveillance team out hunting for him. Not likely, but possible. He completed a sweep of the neighborhood through the binoculars.

Nothing.

He set the binoculars down and pulled a piece of paper from his pocket. He found the target's phone number and punched it into his cell phone. It was answered after four rings.

"*Hello?*"

"Judge Henning?" Rostov asked.

"Who's calling?"

"This is Special Agent O'Neill with the FBI. I wanted to let you know we've apprehended a suspect in the area. We believe he may have been following you. We can hold him for a while but then we have to release him. If you can come over and give us a statement we can continue to hold him and hopefully even charge him."

"Thank you," Henning replied. "When's a good time?"

"I'll be in the office for the next hour."

"I'll be right over. Thanks, Agent—" He paused.

"O'Neill, sir," Rostov replied.

"Thanks, Agent O'Neill. I appreciate your hard work."

"It's our pleasure, sir."

Rostov set the phone down, rested the rifle on a sandbag and settled into a comfortable position. He pressed the Kevlar-fiberglass buttstock firmly into his shoulder and peered through the scope. Moments later, the door opened. The first man through was security. He signaled to the men outside as Rostov eased his cheek against the stock. He found a perfect weld with the crosshairs situated directly on the center of the doorway. 210 meters. Rostov was utterly confident he could put the shot within centimeters of his aiming point. Finally, he saw movement in the doorway. Two more guards exited the front door, then Gordon Henning finally emerged.

Rostov centered the crosshairs on Henning's head, exhaled half the air from his lungs, took the slack in from the trigger, then gently squeezed. A match-grade .308-caliber bullet travels in the neighbor-hood of 2,500 feet per second. While a silencer can take the edge off the explosive discharge, it can't completely "silence" a high-velocity rifle shot. Even so, the report is usually so muffled as to be virtually unrecognizable, and detecting a shooter's location after one shot is nearly impossible. Rostov's bullet, traveling faster than sound, en-tered Henning's left ocular cavity and blew the back of his skull out a split-second later. The lifeless body dropped like a marionette clipped of its strings and settled to the ground in a disheveled heap.

For a moment, everything seemed unnaturally still, as if Nature itself was shocked into silence. Then the security team recovered and dove for cover. Rostov ejected the spent casing onto the mat, cham-bered another round and quickly acquired another target. A guard took cover behind the Lexus but his head was exposed as he searched for the hidden sniper. Rostov squeezed the trigger. The rear window of the Lexus shattered, deflecting the bullet just enough so it only grazed the man's forehead.

"Stay down," Rostov growled as the man ducked out of sight.

Rostov ejected the empty shell and placed both shells into a pock-et of the shooting mat. He quickly disassembled the rifle, secured it inside the mat and zipped up the bag. Gear in hand, he navigated his way down the ladder, returned the ladder to the shed, then slipped into the alley.

Eastern Utah

ELEN WAS FIRST TO SEE THE SIGNPOST for Grand Junction, Colorado. She looked at the clock display on the radio. 5:15. It had been a long day. Earlier, they'd decided to stop in Grand Junction and take the rest of the night off.

"Wishing we could have flown instead?" Kevin asked.

"Yeah, we could be in Quebec by now. Heck, we could probably be in Paris by now."

"Do you think we'll be going to Paris?"

"I don't know."

"Avi didn't say?"

"He didn't get that far."

"Well, I guess we'll be flying out of Quebec to somewhere. It actually makes sense. With the exception of Tijuana, Vancouver is the quickest route out of the country from L.A., but it's probably one of the first places the FBI would check. I suppose we could shave a day or two off of the trip by heading for Toronto or Montreal. I'm sure Avi has a good reason for Quebec—maybe because nobody in their right mind would drive from Los Angeles to Quebec to get out of the country."

Elen smiled distractedly and looked out the window.

"What are you thinking?" Kevin asked.

"Oh, I'm just worried about Anna. I've got a really bad feeling, like we never should have left her." She sighed. "I wish we'd had more time to think it through."

"Maybe we should call Mike. See if he can help."

"I want to, Kevin. I really do."

"Then let's call him."

Santa Monica, California

ROSTOV RETURNED THE VAN and parked it beside the other two. In the back of the van, he took off the jumpsuit and placed it next to the garment bag. He opened the bag and the hard case inside, then wiped down the rifle. He put the empty shells in his pocket, returned the keys to the visor, then wiped down everything else he had touched. Satisfied, he left the van unlocked and returned to his rental car.

Fifteen minutes later, he arrived at the Sheraton, checked in, and took a shower. When he finished, he got dressed and turned on the television. News. The four dead gangbangers were leading the day so far. Quite a story: *Was there a gang war in L.A.? Who would be next?*

What an eventful day. Five people were dead as a result of his handiwork. Though he did find a certain satisfaction in doing his job well, he didn't take pleasure in killing. In the course of his business he'd encountered a few psychopaths, men who took special pleasure in torturing and killing. He kept them at a safe distance, never getting close. That wasn't why he killed. As distasteful as it was, he had a clear goal in mind. A mission. An assignment. He'd tried to diffuse the fight with the gangbangers. Tried to give them an out. But it wasn't meant to be. When there was no other option, he just did what he had to do to survive. Nothing more.

His cell phone rang. He looked at the caller ID, didn't recognize the number, but suspected it was who he hoped would call. "This is Jacob," he said.

"Hi, Jacob."

"Heather?"

"Yeah. How was your afternoon?"

"It was good, thanks. And yours?"

"It was good, too. You working?"

"No, I'm done for the day."

"You hungry?"

"Starving."

"So, where do you want to take me to eat?"

Rostov smiled. "Is Italian okay?"

"Sure."

"I know the perfect place. Do you want to meet me or should I pick you up?"

"I'll meet you."

Smart. "Okay," he said. He gave her directions, turned out the lights and left the room.

Grand Junction, Colorado

ELEN PLACED THE PHONE ON THE DRESSER and said, "He'll do what he can. He's not sure what that will be since we have no idea where she is and her cell phone isn't safe. I gave him the apartment address in case she ends up going there. I suppose it's the best we can do."

"I wish we could do more," Kevin said.

"Me too."

"I'm sure she'll be fine, Elen. Both of you are forces to be reckoned with."

Elen smiled.

"Are you hungry?" he asked.

"I guess so."

"What do you say we go out for dinner?"

"Are you sure that's a good idea?"

"Probably not. But what the heck? I'm starving."

Beverly Hills, California

THE INTERIOR OF THE RESTAURANT was impeccably detailed and illuminated. The ambiance was perfect. Rostov was waiting for her in the lobby as she came in the door. "Thanks for coming," he said as he gave her a single white rose. "You look beautiful."

"Thank you," Heather replied, smiling serenely as she took the rose and placed it under her nose. "It smells wonderful, Jacob. You sure know how to sweep a girl off her feet."

Rostov grinned, kissed her gallantly on the back of the hand, then let her take his arm as he led her to their table. She was immediately disarmed by his innate and casual charm, and the peacefulness of being near him. It was almost like stepping out of black-and-white into vibrant color. When the waitress came to take their orders, Rostov deferred. Heather selected chicken parmesan and a glass of merlot. Rostov ordered the same and asked for the bottle.

They settled into an easy dialogue as they talked about small things and sipped wine. Rostov was pleased she spoke with intelligence and thoughtfulness. Physically, she was breathtaking. She was slim in a healthy way, obviously athletic but with curves in all the right places. She had pleasant features, a beautiful smile and warm eyes. Her neck was slender and elegant. He allowed himself a glance below her neckline to the low-cut white silk blouse that accentuated her feminine grace, and reflected on how nice it was to take his mind off work.

"I saw that same look on your face at the club," she said. "It's like your mind never stops churning."

"Sorry," he said.

"What are you thinking about?"

He laughed softly and immediately answered, "How beautiful you look. And how nice it is to be here with you."

She smiled. "Thank you, Jacob." She looked around for a moment, then added, "This place is amazing."

"I agree. So, anyhow, tell me about yourself. What makes you tick?"

"What do you want to know?"

"Well, where did you go to college?"

"U.C. San Diego. I graduated with a Child Psych degree. I also took sign language classes so I could teach deaf children at a special school in La Jolla."

"Wow. Then you're obviously not afraid of a challenge."

"True. But, really, helping deaf children communicate and have a fulfilling life is amazing. I can't imagine doing anything else."

"How long have you been teaching?"

"The last four years. After my niece got an ear infection she ended up losing her hearing. That's what got me started."

"I'm sorry," he replied.

"It's been tough for her," Heather said. "But, she's a trooper. A real sweetheart."

"I can imagine."

Grand Junction, Colorado

"KEVIN, KEVIN, KEVIN," Elen chided, shaking her head. "Always thinking about the big picture."

"That's me. Now, eat your food quickly before I see a policeman and run off somewhere."

She laughed.

He took a bite of cheeseburger and melodramatically said, "Mmmm, that's good."

Elen couldn't help but enjoy his company. He always seemed to know the right thing to say. He was so easy to get along with and in just a few short days it seemed they'd been lifelong friends. There was definitely a physical attraction between them, but it didn't seem to preoccupy him too much. He was different, in a curiously attractive way.

"What are you thinking?" Kevin asked.

"Oh, nothing," she replied, not wanting to share *that* thought just yet.

"Do you like beer?"

"Sometimes."

"I could go for a pint of Guinness. What about you?"

"I'm fine with water, thanks."

Kevin caught the waitress' attention and ordered. When she returned with the beer, Kevin pushed the glass toward Elen and said, "Try it."

"God, that looks like it could come out of my car."

"Ahh, it's not that bad."

Reluctantly, she took a sip and cringed. "No thanks." She pushed it back to him.

Kevin chuckled. "Maybe it's an acquired taste."

"Maybe it's a guy thing."

Beverly Hills, California

"WHAT ABOUT YOU?" Heather asked.

Rostov smiled. There was no way he was going to tell her what he did for a living. Depending on how things developed, he might tell her a little more at another time, but for now he would use a cover-story based largely in the truth. "I'm a security consultant," he said. "Mainly corporate work."

"What does a security consultant do?"

"Train security personnel, mainly. Sometimes I handle sensitive security issues."

"Do you ever work for the government?"

"Occasionally, but private sector gigs pay better."

"You were in the army, I bet. You have a military kind of air."

"Yeah?"

"You're very confident and in control of yourself. It's like you're not afraid of anything."

Rostov laughed softly.

"Seriously," she said. "You look pretty successful, too."

"You could say that."

"Well. Can I ask you a serious question?"

"Sure."

"What does this dinner mean to you?"

He smiled, caught a little off-guard. "Are you always this direct?"

She laughed softly. "You seem like a direct kind of guy."

"Well, I think you're very attractive, of course. And also very intelligent. Unique. You intrigue me."

"Do you always say the right things?"

Rostov smiled reflectively, then replied, "Maybe I try to. Am I doing well so far?"

"Maybe."

He laughed again. "I just want to get to know you, that's all."

"But you don't live here, right?"

"That's true."

"So what do you—" She hesitated.

"What do I want?" he asked. "I just want you to have a wonderful dinner at an amazing restaurant. Enjoy yourself. It's such a nice change of pace for me. I just want to spend the evening with you and enjoy your company."

"Well, thanks. To be honest, I *am* having a wonderful time and I enjoy your company. But, can I ask you another serious question?"

"Please."

"Do you sleep with a lot of women?"

"Wow," Rostov replied quickly, coughing on his drink. "You *are* direct."

"Saves time," she said.

"True." He paused reflectively.

"Ahh," she said quickly. "Don't answer that."

"Well, what do you think?"

"I think," she replied slowly, looking into his eyes, "that you're a good man."

Rostov smiled halfway, caught off-guard again. He could tell she meant it. If she only knew.

She saw the look on his face and intuitively knew it was a warning. "I'm going to get hurt, aren't I?"

He shook his head as he gazed intently into her eyes, then quietly but emphatically replied, "No, you're not."

She smiled, not sure she believed him. She sipped her wine and said, "What an improbable encounter."

Rostov lifted his glass. "To improbable encounters."

Grand Junction, Colorado

KEVIN LOOKED AT HIS WATCH. 8:55. He was standing up to his chest in the shallow end of the hotel's pool, the white bandage on his side a reminder of how close he had come to facing his own mortality. The wound was healing fast and he hoped a dip in the pool wouldn't create a problem. The pool was heated, and he lowered his body under the surface. Holding his breath, he began counting. When he had first started doing it, years ago, he found it difficult to go past forty. He'd learned not to give in to the burning sensation in his lungs, and soon he was staying under water for over a minute. Having convinced his mind it was possible, each subsequent time became easier. As he reached *eighty-three* in his mind, he could no longer fight it. He surfaced and inhaled deeply.

He was facing the other direction when he heard footsteps near the edge of the pool. Kevin turned around as Elen eased herself into the pool. She was stunning. She didn't let him stare, though. She slipped in until the water came up to her neck.

"That's a gorgeous suit," he said. "I had no idea you would wear it so well."

"You don't look so bad yourself." She swam closer. "So, Kevin. What's your story?"

"What do you mean?"

"Well, you asked me out. But, you haven't come on to me. What's the deal?"

He smiled. "Oh, I don't know."

"I don't buy that for a second. What's holding you back?"

"Respect, I suppose."

"Respect for what?"

"For the situation, I guess. And for you. Your family. My family.

God, even."

"Really? What do you know about God?"

"Just that he's there."

"Yeah? How do you know that?"

Kevin smiled, and said, "I'm looking at one reason."

"Ohhh. Nice answer."

"Thanks."

"Seriously, though," she said. "How do you know he's there?"

"I don't know. I just sense it. Don't you think so?"

"Honestly, I don't know. I think a lot of Jews sort of see God as a—a force, I guess. Not so personal, maybe, as Christians see him. A friend of mine from school used to invite me to her Christian church every week. *Every* week. I was surprised she would keep doing that, so after a while I finally ended up going. It was different than I expected."

"What do mean?"

"That's the funny thing. I don't know what I expected. They talked about Jesus and Abraham and Moses, and God creating the world, the commandments and stuff. They were really passionate about Israel being God's *chosen* people. When they found out I was Jewish, *and* from Israel, they were so—excited, I guess, that it was weird. I always thought Christians were sort of antagonistic to Jews. Or maybe they just thought they *knew* better or something." She laughed as she reflected. "I was a sudden celebrity. Everyone wanted to touch me, like somehow I was closer to God because I'm Israeli."

"No," Kevin said with a grin. "They just wanted to touch you because you're a hottie."

Elen punched his shoulder. "Smart ass."

Kevin turned away in mock surrender and said, "Hey, easy there, Rocky. Or, should I say, Elen the Destroyer."

"Very funny."

"I bet that freaked you out a bit."

"What?"

"The way they treated you."

"Yeah," Elen said. "It *was* pretty unnerving. But they were really nice people. Didn't try to convert me or anything. They just wanted to know more about me and what's going on in Israel. Like I said, it was different than I expected." She splashed water on him, and added, "*You're* different than I expected."

"Yeah? How so?"

"Well, you're a smart guy. You're hot. You're shy, but confident, too. It's like you grew up in a different time. Honor. Integrity. Loyalty. That kind of stuff."

"Well, I just try to do the right thing, that's all."

"And how do you know what the right thing is?"

"I guess I just know."

She raised an eyebrow questioningly and raised herself out of the water just enough for her chest to break the surface. Kevin smiled. He knew what she was doing. Elen grinned as she moved closer.

"God, you look amazing," he said.

"Thank you." Elen put her hands behind his neck, leaned in close, and—

"Hey you two!" someone yelled, laughing. "Go get a room. Ha ha."

Kevin suddenly felt angry as he looked at the idiot standing on the balcony.

"Don't—" Elen started to say.

"Why don't you go play with your X-Box, you punk!"

The guy just kept laughing as he walked away, like no one had ever heard that line before.

"Better yet," Kevin added under his breath, "go find a landmine to play with."

Elen scolded him with a look.

"Sorry," he said.

"So you are human," she replied.

"I don't know. Maybe." Kevin touched her cheek and said, "You're amazing, Elen. I don't want to do anything to hurt you."

Elen furrowed her brow and blinked in surprise. For some inexplicable reason her eyes quickly welled up until a single tear trickled down her cheek.

"Whoa there, partner," Kevin soothed as he held her cheek in his palm. "I'm sorry if I touched a raw nerve."

"No need to apologize," she replied, suddenly withdrawn.

"Hey, Elen," Kevin added as he studied her face carefully. "I mean it."

"I know you do, and that's what I—I—"

"What's wrong," he prodded gently.

Elen touched his cheek and absently traced her finger along his forehead. "What I like about you," she said finally.

Santa Monica, California

THE SWIMMING POOL AT THE SHERATON was invitingly large. Including Rostov and Heather, there were a dozen people lounging in the pool area. They had already taken a dip. Now they were seated on deck chairs. She was wearing a tee shirt over a bikini. He was wearing marine shorts, with nothing else to cover his lean, muscular physique.

They talked about everything—the types of music they enjoyed and what kinds of foods they liked. Personal experiences. Memories from when they were younger. When asked, he was as truthful as possible without revealing anything she shouldn't know. As an hour with her turned into two, then three, her presence became intoxicating, and he found it increasingly difficult to draw the line between fact and fiction.

"So," she said. "Jacob. What do I know about you?"

He smiled. It was a rhetorical question.

"You're from Ireland originally, though your mother is Israeli. You speak like five or six languages, you've lived all over the world at one time or another, you travel all the time and you live in the Caymans. What a life! So, how old are you?"

"Well, let's see. You know, I guess I'm old enough I can't quite remember."

Heather narrowed her eyes and said, "Jacob, are you playing games with me?"

"*Moi?*" he replied innocently. "How old are you?"

"I asked you first."

"Fine," he conceded. "Thirty-four."

"Really? You look younger."

"Hah," he said. "What about you?"

"Guess."

"Twenty-nine."

"That's uncanny. What are you, a mind reader?"

"Among other things. You should see me at the roulette table."

The lights suddenly went out. Heather stifled a startled gasp. The lights came right back on, flickering at first, then slowly regaining intensity.

"That was weird," Rostov said. He reached for her hand. "Maybe it's time to go." She took his hand and he helped her to her feet. "Would you like to come up for a drink?" he asked.

Heather pondered the question. Studying his face, she gazed into his soft blue eyes and knew that once in his room she wouldn't be able to resist. It was inevitable, really. She'd been delaying the moment of decision for as long as possible.

Finally, she made up her mind and said, "I'd love to."

Rostov held her face gently, leaned close, and kissed her softly on the lips. His touch was electric and she was genuinely amazed at how it felt. He took her hand and guided her up the stairs to his room. The lights were already on, preset to a gentle glow. She sat on the sofa and smiled with a pleasant, dreamlike glow of peacefulness. It occurred to her that she was agreeably intoxicated. She was glad—it helped her forget how nervous she was.

"I've been thinking," Rostov said reflectively as he walked to the center of the room. "You're on vacation, right?"

She nodded.

"Well, I know it's a little soon, but I have a few days off, and—" He paused to consider the sheer audacity of his plan. Softly, he continued, "I want you to come to the Caribbean with me."

Heather was surprised. "I, uh, don't know what to say."

"Live on the edge," Rostov encouraged playfully. "Just say yes."

"But I hardly know you."

"My name's Jacob. Your name's Heather. I think we know

enough. We'll go diving, see some shows, hang out on the beach. It'll be perfect."

"I don't know."

"You'll love it," Rostov insisted. "And I promise not to bite."

She laughed. "Jacob, you're such a sweet talker. I'll probably regret it. But—okay. Why not?!"

"Great!" he said. "How about a drink to celebrate?"

Heather walked to his side and slipped her hand into his. Then she rested her head on his shoulder and replied, "I don't want anything."

"Really?"

Gazing into his eyes, she reached for the light switch and turned it off.

Chapter 7

Munich, Germany

ANOTHER STORM WAS BREWING. A sudden, booming thunderclap rever-
berated through the street, startling Mike Russell as the first tentative
drops of rain found their way to the pavement. Glancing skyward,
Russell saw a flash of lightning momentarily illuminate the dark sky.
A biting wind sent a chill down his back, making him shiver as he
looked for an opening in traffic. He saw his chance. He hurried to the
other side of St. Anna Strasse just as another sonic boom erupted
overhead.

Safely across the street, Russell checked for surveillance behind
him. None that he could see. As he approached the *biergarten*, Oskar
was standing watch outside. Russell entered the tavern and scanned
the smoke-laden interior. Neumann was in a corner booth, flanked
by guards. Russell made his way over and sat down.

Neumann pushed a pint toward him. Russell took it, nodded his
thanks and said, "How did you know?"

"You see it's true, then?"

"Something smells rotten."

"Your chief?"

Russell lifted the pint, took a drink, and said, "What exactly are
you doing, Erich?"

"I need a favor. And I need someone I can trust."

"How did you know my report would be quashed?"

"It's complicated."

"It's a long day."

Neumann sipped his beer, then said, "For me, it started about two weeks ago." He withdrew a pack of cigarettes, tapped the pack and offered one to Russell. Mike took it and lit it with his silver Zippo. As acrid smoke curled between them, Neumann leaned closer and said, "I can't tell you where it comes from. But I can tell you the source is solid."

"I play with the big boys, too, you know."

Neumann shook his head slowly. "Not these big boys. Believe me. You're safer. And my source is safer."

"I need more than that."

"Look, Mike," Neumann said. "I can't tell you. I don't want you to get killed digging into this. Or my source. What I need you to do is simply forward this to the Israelis. But not through channels."

"They probably have it already."

"Not possible."

"Why them? I didn't see any Israelis on the list."

"That's because the list I gave you wasn't complete," Neumann said. He withdrew a folded sheet of paper from his coat and gave it to Russell.

Russell studied it briefly, then said, "You can't be serious?"

"Never more so."

"Assuming I do contact them. What makes you think they'll believe me?"

"I have no control over that. Except for the other names, that is. I think they'll take it very seriously as the others drop. Just send them the list and let them deal with it as they see fit."

"But you don't need me for this. Why don't you just send it yourself?"

"I need a cutout. An untraceable one."

"Why me?"

"Because you're as far from me as I can get, and still trust. My source is afraid. BKA is penetrated. CIA is penetrated. *Sheisse*, who hasn't been penetrated? You've already seen what these people can do." He stood up to leave. "Please. Send it to them."

"Okay. But tell me one more thing."

"Yes?"

"Why are you doing this? Why would you risk your life?"

Neumann shook his head and sighed. "My country has a history. Just call it one man's desire to do the right thing."

"Really?"

Neumann nodded soberly. "Call the phone number at the bottom of the page. He can put you in contact with the Israelis."

"What about the chief? Who is he really working for?"

"All I can tell you is to be careful. You can draw your own conclusions."

With that, Neumann and his men left the tavern. Meanwhile, Russell stewed in silence. He waited ten minutes, finished his beer, then exited through the back.

Paris, France

BIRAN PICKED UP THE PHONE after the second ring and said, "*Allo?*"

"*Alain? Ici Bernard.*"

"*Bernard. Très bon*," Biran said quietly. "*Ça-va?*"

"*Ça-va*," the voice responded. "I just spoke with an American attaché in Germany. He said he needed to backchannel some sensitive information."

Biran went to his desk.

"His name's Mike Russell," Bernard continued. "He's in Munich. Here's the number—"

Biran wrote it down, thanked him, and disconnected the call. He punched in the phone number.

After two rings, a voice said, "Russell."

"Bernard said you were expecting my call."

"Yeah."

"Do you have a secure line?"

"Yes."

"What can I do for you?"

Five minutes later, Biran disconnected the call, set the phone down, and shook his head. He was relieved his father wasn't on the list, but he had never really expected him to be. He picked up the phone and dialed a private number firmly etched in his memory.

Tel Aviv, Israel

SEATED AT HIS DESK, SEMI-RETIRED SPYMASTER Moshe Yadin placed his cigarette on the rim of an ashtray, lifted the phone from its cradle, and answered, "*Shalom.*"

"*Shalom, adoni.* It's Avi Biran."

"Avi!" Yadin exclaimed warmly. "How are you?"

"I could be better."

Yadin heard the tension in Biran's voice. "Is your father well?"

"He's part of the reason I'm calling, actually. I need advice."

"How can I help you?"

"A couple things. I just got a backchannel from Germany. I think it might involve my father and my sister."

"Is Elen okay?"

"Right now, yes." Biran explained about the surveillance on his father and the attack on his sister.

"How come you didn't bring this to me sooner, Avi?"

"I needed to investigate first. I haven't been able to produce anything on who followed my father, but I think this backchannel might be related."

"How so?"

"Ben-Yakov, Zvi Hofi, and Levi Zahavy. They're all on a list that also contains the names Charles Richardson and Gordon Henning, among others."

"An assassination list?" Yadin asked. He inhaled deeply and said, "How long have you known this?"

"About two minutes."

"You did the right thing, son."

"Sir? With all due respect, I am more than a little nervous about this."

"That's understandable, Avi."

"What I mean, sir"—his voice was now barely audible—"is that I am concerned about a penetration."

Yadin's eyes narrowed. "What do you mean?"

"No proof. Just a gut sense. I don't even know if these incidents are connected. But if they are, this crosses international borders. I've heard rumors of a secret agency out of the U.N. doing black ops. Until now I've just dismissed them, but I don't know anymore. Whoever this is, they seem to have incredible resources."

"Yes, they do," Yadin agreed. He pursed his lips in concentration, then said, "Tell me again about the man who followed your father."

"Guy in a leather jacket and sunglasses. Medium build. Maybe European. Maybe Israeli. That's all I know. He disappeared."

"So, he managed to breach base security, steal items directly from your father's office, and plant listening devices at your father's home. All without being caught. He's either very talented or he has inside connections. Maybe both."

"Maybe both," Biran agreed. "This is the thing. The guy who gave me the list said his source was very worried about a penetration of German Intelligence and the CIA station in Berlin. What if somehow the Americans have been penetrated and they're pursuing this illegal manhunt for Elen? What if the same people are staging an intelligence operation against my father? What if the FBI manhunt for Elen is just a ruse to kidnap her? God, what if we've been penetrated?"

Yadin whistled softly and shook his head. "Could be a stretch, but I can't argue with you, Avi. For now, we should prepare for the worst. I'll contact Ben-Yakov."

"Okay," Biran said. "In the meantime, I want to find out who this source is."

"Well, the guy who gave you the list should have an idea."

"He's just a cutout."

"Okay, then. Simplify everything and start at the beginning."

Biran retold the entire story. The man who had followed his father was gone. Could be anyone. Biran recounted Elen's gunfight.

Yadin said, "Who's this Edwards guy?"

"It looks like wrong place, wrong time. He has no background for this sort of thing. Anyway, he was wounded. Elen got him to a safehouse where she and her roommate helped him recover. They were—"

"Wait," Yadin interrupted. "Her roommate?"

"Yeah?"

"Tell me about her."

"Her name's Anna Cohen. She and Elen served in the Army to-gether. They both went to the United States—"

"That's it!" Yadin exclaimed.

"What is?"

"Cohen. She's the connection we need."

"How?"

"Think about it for a second. You've managed to make Elen effec-tively disappear. But whoever they are, they still want her. They're going to have to find some way—a link—to locate her. Anna is that link."

"Maybe," Biran said. "And since she's their link to Elen—"

"She's our link to them," Yadin finished.

"But they've split up. I'll have to find her."

"Now you've got the direction you need, that should resolve fair-ly easily."

"I need to get to the United States," Biran said. "Can you get me out of my current assignment?"

"I'll see what I can do," Yadin replied. "For the time being, use your resources in the States to find her."

"Right. I know just the man."

Near Twenty-Nine Palms, California

IT WAS PAST MIDNIGHT IN THE Mojave Desert. The temperature had dipped into the forties and was slowly threatening to drop even more. The Mojave is unusual for a desert, as it is more dirt than sand. Tumbleweeds and scrub brush grow unchecked, giving the impres-sion of an area not unlike what old cowboy movies portray. In fact, a number of movies had been filmed in the unpopulated, arid badlands southeast of Las Vegas.

The United States Marine Corps uses the area for desert training. Master Sergeant Joe Kenton was dressed in a sniper's full-body ghillie suit, making his outline appear anything but human. The full-body camouflage suit was specially comprised of hundreds of footlong strips of infrared fabric, a concept stemming from Operation Desert Storm in the early 1990's. The IR-defeating material itself, in the light of day, would hardly be considered camouflage. But at night, the thin, crisscrossing gray stripes made a soldier effectively disappear to infrared sensors.

For this exercise, it was Kenton's job to infiltrate the area surrounding an improvised top-secret desert installation and neutralize the security detail guarding the complex. The security detail would be comprised of several warm steel targets in the shapes of soldiers. Kenton carried an old Robar SR90 .308-caliber, suppressed sniper rifle with an infrared/starlight scope. His spotter, Staff Sergeant Daniel Rodriguez, was dressed identically but carried a suppressed M16A4. Over the last two hours, Kenton and Rodriguez had stalked their way to the objective. Kenton chose an especially rough and difficult terrain to cross, from a direction he believed the recon teams wouldn't expect. From the cruel beach landing at Normandy to the deadly invasion of Iwo Jima, Marines have been trained to approach objectives from the least expected directions. And they historically fight with such ferocity and precision that in World War I the Germans called them *teufelhunden*. Devil dogs. Kenton liked that description.

The full moon was close to the horizon, in a position that created distortedly long shadows out of the myriad rocky outcroppings that dotted the landscape. It was so quiet, Kenton got the sense they might as well be on the moon. Away from the illuminated trappings of the city, a seemingly innumerable multitude of stars were visible to the naked eye. Their presence, combined with the absolute stillness of the night, served to emphasize the degree of isolation Kenton and Rodriguez felt.

From the invisible safety of an unremarkable outcropping, Kenton caught a glimpse of the objective. Both men slowly rose to their knees and studied the terrain ahead of them. While Kenton used infrared field glasses to scan the area for threats, Rodriguez used a laser range-finder to get their distance-to-target. Using hand signals, he told Kenton they were six-hundred yards away. Kenton nodded. Using his own hand signals, he told Rodriguez to continue toward the objective.

THE RECON MARINE ON POINT dropped to a crouch, raised his arm and made a fist, the silent signal to stop. The Marine behind him lowered himself to a crouch, repeated the gesture, and the entire team froze. The pointman, wearing night-vision goggles, slowly turned his head and pointed two fingers at his eyes. Then he pointed his thumb down, the signal for *enemy suspected*.

The second Marine nodded, relayed the information back to the rest of the team, and cautiously moved forward. "What do you see, Barnes?" he whispered.

"Possible movement. Ten o'clock. Sixty-meters."

The staff sergeant tilted his night-vision goggles away from his face and brought a pair of infrared field glasses to his eyes. He studied the area Corporal Barnes had indicated, and finally shook his head. "There's nothing there."

"Damn," Barnes whispered. "Where *are* they?"

THIRTY MINUTES LATER, KENTON and Rodriguez stopped again to take a range sighting. The objective was considerably larger now, and Kenton could easily distinguish the steel targets in the compound. Rodriguez lowered the range-finder and silently indicated they were two-hundred and eighty yards away. Kenton handed the IR field glasses to Rodriguez. The younger man backed into the protective shadows of a nearby outcropping and lowered himself into a crouch.

Kenton crawled away from the outcropping toward a nondescript, moderately vegetated area. It was neither bare nor thickly grown. The reason for his choice was simple. Any surveillance would be searching the shadows and the areas containing a heavier concentration of scrub brush. The area Kenton had chosen was ideal. By his estimation, it offered adequate visual protection without drawing attention by being too obvious a place to hide. And at less than three hundred yards, it was a high percentage shot, but not so close that it would negatively impact their ability to exfiltrate.

Kenton lowered himself to his belly and looked back at the outcropping where Rodriguez was hidden. All he could see were shadows—Rodriguez had disappeared. He uncovered the Robar and flipped down the attached bipod. Placing the rifle between bushes—careful not to let the large suppressor stick out and highlight his position—he took aim on the installation. The targets had been positioned so as to be visible from any direction, effectively making the two recon teams' job virtually impossible. Twenty men searching nearly four square kilometers for two *invisible* men were hardly adequate for the job. The members of the recon teams, though, had all learned to stifle complaints long ago. Every Marine knows guard duty sucks.

Kenton, now confident he was in the clear, settled his body into a comfortable firing position and took aim at the first target. He had the rifle zeroed at four-hundred yards, so from one-hundred and twenty yards closer he knew the strike of the bullet would be higher than the crosshairs indicated. He dialed-in an adjustment to the scope to compensate for the new range, then studied the bushes near the targets for wind.

Everything was completely still.

Kenton smiled as he slipped the safety into the off position and tightened his grip on the rifle. The Robar, now an extension of his being, moved imperceptibly as he made a final adjustment and placed the tip of his finger on the trigger.

MARINE COLONEL MICHAEL AMBROSE, known to Kevin and Elen as Mike, was taking a sip of coffee from a Styrofoam cup when he heard the faint metallic ping in the distance. In the desolate solitude of the calm desert night, sound travels extremely well. He was outside the communications tent, having waited for over an hour for this moment. It meant the mission was soon to be concluded.

"Go get 'em, Joe," he muttered to himself.

What Ambrose had hoped would be a quick conclusion turned into a drawn-out, ninety-minute exfiltration. Both recon teams were pissed they hadn't stopped the two snipers, and they weren't about to make life easier on them by just giving up. Especially since it was late at night, several of the Marines really wanted to inflict some pain.

But it was all for naught. Sergeant Kenton emerged unscathed in his ghillie suit by the side of the communications tent. Rodriguez was right behind him.

"Ah, Joe," Ambrose said. "Taking your time, I see."

"Yes, sir. Those recon guys wanted their pound of flesh."

Ambrose chuckled, glanced at his watch, and said, "Well, Sergeant, I'd love to chat but I've got a warm bed waiting. I've got a new assignment for you."

"Sir?"

"Follow me."

Ambrose and Kenton walked in silence to the colonel's waiting humvee. Ambrose spoke softly. "This shooting affair is turning out to be pretty serious. We have a new lead that the FBI's been penetrated."

"Penetrated, sir?"

"Afraid so," Ambrose said. "We need you to capture one of them."

Kenton smiled and said, "That should be fun."

Chapter 8

Grand Junction, Colorado

THE ALARM CLOCK ROUSED KEVIN from a deep sleep at 7:15. With a groan, he pressed the snooze button and slumped back into bed. Seconds later, or so it seemed, the alarm went off again. With a fatigued sigh, he shut off the alarm and reluctantly sat up.

"What time is it?" Elen asked.

"Seven twenty-five."

Elen sat up and ran her fingers through her thick mane of dark hair. "Morning," she said with a yawn.

"Morning. You want some coffee?"

"Not here. Let's stop on the way."

"Sounds good." Kevin stood up, yawned, and turned on the television. It was a commercial. He stood for a while in a daze, just staring at the screen. Elen got out of bed and started digging through her overnight bag. "Hey, Earth to Kevin," she said.

"Huh?"

"Wake up."

"Oh, sorry."

"How's your side?" Elen asked.

He peeled the bandage off. "Not bad."

"When you get out of the shower, I'll put a new dressing on for you."

He smiled. "Thanks."

"Kevin?"

"Yeah?"

Elen stood up, fresh clothes in hand, ready to go into the bathroom. "I just want to thank you for being a perfect gentleman last night. If you had wanted to, there was a chance you could've—" She paused.

He smiled. "I suppose now is too late?"

"Funny man," Elen said. "You're the strangest, most unique man I've ever met, Kevin Edwards. A conundrum."

"A what?"

"A puzzle."

"Does that mean I fascinate you?"

She laughed.

"Big pieces or small ones?" he said.

"Small ones."

"That hurts."

"Okay, big ones."

"That's better."

While Elen showered, Kevin watched the news. A possible gang war brewing in Los Angeles. A corruption scandal in the House of Representatives. A deadly heat wave in Chicago. A major airline in bankruptcy. Autoworkers on strike in Detroit. Kevin switched it to sports. Cardinals in a pennant race again. Yankees looked solid. Cubs not so solid. Ohio State had a close game. Florida State was back on track. Texas struggled to a fourth quarter victory. USC won easily.

Elen came out of the shower with her hair wrapped in a towel. "Anything new?"

"Trojans look good," Kevin said.

"Sports," Elen muttered.

"Gang war in L.A."

"Great."

"You finished in the bathroom?"

"Yep."

Kevin grabbed some clean clothes and went to take a shower. As the water came on, Elen sighed deeply and muttered, "Kevin, you're unreal." She started straightening out the room. At the dresser, Elen drew a pistol out of her pack. Though popularized by the James Bond films, she recalled somewhere that the Walther PPK had originally been designed for use by the German *Polizei Kriminal*, a division of undercover policeman who needed an easily concealable and reliable firearm. Probably the History Channel.

Elen gripped the Walther, ejected the magazine, and locked the slide back. She tilted the pistol to the side, peered down the barrel and studied the rifled grooves. It was clean. It was a gun. Okay. She let the slide release. It sprang forward with a resonant *clack*. Raising the pistol with both hands, she picked up a sight picture against the wall and pulled the trigger. *Click*. She lowered the pistol, reinserted the magazine, made sure the safety was on, then slipped the pistol back into the pack.

Just then the phone rang. By the third ring, she figured out which cell phone it was and picked it up. "Hello?" she said.

"Good morning, sis."

"Oh, thank God it's you. Good morning. Or, is it good evening where you are?"

"*C'est bon soir, ici.*"

"*Vous êtes en France?*"

"*Oui*. How are you doing?" Biran asked, switching to English. "Remember, this is an open line."

"Okay. Yeah, we're doing good. How are you?"

"Better than yesterday."

"Great. So, what's up?"

"I spoke with Mike to arrange——"

"The one who helped us?" Elen asked.

"Yeah."

"Who is he, anyway?"

"He works for the Defense Intelligence Agency."

"And that's safe?" Elen asked.

"I know him. I trust him."

"How much?"

"He and I go back to my days in the *sayeret*. He was a Marine liaison officer. We did some mission planning together. He's a good guy. Anyway, he mentioned you were concerned about Anna. We worked out a plan. No details over the phone. She'll be safe, though. Don't worry."

"That's great," she said.

"You and Kevin just lay low and keep moving."

"Okay."

Santa Monica, California

ROSTOV WAS STANDING IN FRONT of the mirror in the bedroom when Heather woke up. With only a bath towel around his waist, he was doing stretching exercises.

Heather smiled. Even now, with the surrealistic enchantment gone, she marveled at the sight of the beautiful man. His physique was muscular. Tight. Her smile transformed into a mischievous grin. Last night she had been absolutely breathless.

Noticing her expression in the mirror, Rostov said, "What are you grinning about?"

"Come over here," she replied coyly, "and I'll tell you."

Twenty minutes later, Rostov grabbed his phone, scrolled through the phone list, selected a number, then waited for the call to go through. "Hello," he said. "Jacob Ross. Number VX55591. Two first-class tickets, Los Angeles to Grand Cayman. Today." He listened and waited. "Yes. That's perfect. Thank you."

He disconnected the call, leaned over to Heather, and kissed her gently on the lips. "We're checked in, but we have to hurry. The flight leaves in two hours."

She smiled, slipped out of bed and headed for the bathroom. Once the door shut, Rostov dialed again.

"*Stevens*," the voice said.

"Hi, Dan, it's Jacob. I'm heading out of town for several days. Any developments?"

"None. They've disappeared."

"Completely gone?"

"*Jacob?*" It was Heather.

"Hold on a sec," Rostov said into the phone. "What is it, sweetheart?"

"Are you going to join me?"

"Yes, babe. Just a second." Heather left the door open. Rostov raised the phone back to his lips and said, "Sorry, Dan. Duty calls."

Stevens laughed. "Duty calls? Sure. This is nothing I can't handle right now, Romeo. Catch you later."

"Bye."

Westwood FBI Office, Los Angeles

SPECIAL AGENT BRYCE MAURER was frustrated. He rubbed his eyes and looked back at his computer monitor, racking his brain for inspiration. "You haven't used your credit cards," he muttered. "You haven't been to the airport. There are no hospital records for you, Mr. Edwards. No hotel records. Who the Hell are you, and where did you learn to disappear?" He pursed his lips, lost in thought. A buzzing cell phone interrupted his reverie. He picked it off the desk and said, "Maurer."

"Morning. Agent Collins here. LAPD just found Edwards' truck."

Maurer leaped from his chair, grabbed a pen, and wrote down the Westwood address. "Thanks," he said. "Has anyone canvassed the area yet?"

"Nope. We just got here."

"Hang loose then. I'll be there in five."

Four minutes later, he pulled his government-issue Ford behind a Los Angeles Police Department cruiser. "Morning, Agent Collins," he said. "What've you got so far?"

Collins pointed out the vehicle across the street. "Honda Pilot registered to a Kevin Patrick Edwards out of Long Beach. The RP called to report an unknown vehicle that had been parked in front of her house for the last several days. LAPD ran the plate and they called us. It appears the vehicle hasn't moved."

"Damn," Maurer muttered. "They ditched it." He considered the situation, and then shook his head. "We're too late, Agent Collins. They're long gone."

Collins looked at the ground and shook his head. He was first on the call and had hoped to be on the leading edge of a break.

"Still," Maurer said, "we should talk to the neighbors and see if anyone remembers something. You take care of that. Probably a dead end, but we still have to do it."

"No problem."

"There's another angle I'm looking at," Maurer said as he returned to his vehicle. "Call me if you find anything else."

"Okay."

FBI Office, Denver

SPECIAL AGENT SHANE MATHEWS stopped at the bulletin board displaying the FBI's national fugitive list. He made it a habit to check the board regularly, his ambitious way of staying ahead. He stopped at the photo of Elen Biran. Beside her was a photo of Kevin Edwards. The photos were courtesy of the California Department of Motor Vehicles.

Mathews shook his head and muttered, "God, she's beautiful." He read the brief description of the pair and whistled softly. "Wanted for the murder of federal agents," he recited softly. "Who would have guessed by looking at her?"

He continued browsing the board for several minutes before finally continuing on his way, whistling the opening to Bach's *Toccata and Fugue in D minor*. His girlfriend, only a couple of years out of the University of Colorado where she had minored in music, wanted to see a special performance that night by the Denver Symphony Brass. Among other things, the large brass ensemble was scheduled to perform the *Toccata and Fugue*. He smiled as he thought about her.

Denver, Colorado

KEVIN AND ELEN ARRIVED IN DENVER shortly past noon, less than three hours after leaving Grand Junction. Looking for a decent place to stop for lunch, Kevin exited Interstate 70 at Colorado Boulevard and proceeded south. Two minutes later, they passed the Denver Zoo and Elen pointed it out.

Kevin said, "D'you wanna see da munkeez?"

She laughed and slapped him gently on the shoulder. "You behave. Yeah. Let's go see the monkeys. Take a few hours off. What do you say?"

"Fine. I could use a break."

He drove around the block until he found the Zoo entrance. Within minutes they had purchased two tickets and were inside, strolling toward the lion exhibit. Elen studied the incredible environment surrounding them, and smiled at Kevin. "This is perfect," she said.

"Yeah. It's nice."

"You know what I especially like about it?"

"What's that?"

"It feels so normal. Like a casual date, or something."

"I guess we skipped that phase, didn't we?"

Elen smiled wistfully, then rested her cheek on his shoulder as they walked. Kevin kissed her affectionately on the top of her head.

"You know," she said. "Under normal circumstances, we would never be here."

"Yeah, I suppose that's true."

Elen squeezed his hand and said, "Well, thank God for abnormal circumstances."

"Amen," Kevin said. "Hey, you want an ice cream?"

"You trying to fatten me up for some reason?"

"Who, me?"

"No. That monkey sitting over there."

"Where?"

Elen kicked him gently in the shin.

"Ouch."

"Were you born with your sense of humor?"

Kevin rubbed his shin against the calf of his other leg. "I don't know. I think it actually sneaked up on me when I wasn't paying attention. Kind of like that kick to my shin, Pelé."

Elen laughed. "God, Kevin—" She shook her head as she realized her slip. "Kyle," she corrected. "How in the world did I ever come so close to missing you?"

"My shin disagrees with that statement, lady."

Elen squeezed his hand and said, "You know what I mean. I tried to tell you to get lost in Long Beach."

"You were pretty harsh," Kevin said.

"*Please*," Elen said.

"But I don't fault you in the least, knowing how many kooks are out there. How would you know I'm really such a wonderful guy?"

"Oh, he's cocky, now?"

"Yeah, that's me. Such an ego."

Elen leaned closer. "Well, Mister Attitude, are you going to keep me starving forever? Or are you eventually going to buy me lunch?"

"Hey, I was about to buy you an ice cream!"

"So romantic."

"Not really, huh? So, where do you want to eat?"

"Let's see what's up ahead."

After a short walk they found a sandwich shack. They ordered, got their food, and found a table in back. Elen took a bite of her sandwich and said, "Look at that." She pointed to a flyer on a pegboard.

"Yeah?"

"There's a concert tonight. Do you want to go?"

"I don't know. Do you?"

"Why not? I'm so tired of driving."

"You want to take the rest of the day off?"

"God, *yes*."

"Really?"

"You're so romantic."

Kevin laughed. "Fine. Let's go to the concert."

Miami International Airport

THE FLIGHT FROM LOS ANGELES took just over five hours, touching down shortly after 6:00 p.m. Rostov looked at his watch as he escorted Heather through the exit tunnel. "We've got an hour before we catch our next plane. Are you hungry?"

"Yeah."

"Let's grab something to eat. We won't make it to Grand Cayman until around nine."

"You live on Cayman Brac, right?"

"Yeah. It's a bit further, though. We'll spend the night in George-town, then head over to Brac in the morning."

"I can hardly wait to see your place," Heather said.

"Oh, it's nothing special."

"I'll bet it's magnificent."

Chapter 9

Denver, Colorado

THE REFINED MUSICAL ARTISTRY OF the Denver Symphony Brass filled Boettcher Hall's round stage with clear, brilliant sound. It wasn't the opposite of a rock concert, but it was close. Most men in the audience were dressed in suits, while most ladies were attired in dresses. The depth of musical expression was distinctly evident in each player as they finished the final piece before intermission, a transcription of Mussourgsky's *The Great Gate of Kiev*. As the piece reached its climax and the volume increased, the audience seemed to lean back in response to the decibel level. Even without electronic amplification, the sound was massive. The final chords rang out in the hall, the piece ended, and the audience applauded enthusiastically.

After clapping for a few seconds, Kevin stood and pointed to the left side of the ensemble. "See the trombone section? The funny looking instruments with the slides."

"Oh, yeah. I like those."

"I played one in marching band."

"That's cool."

"It was fun. I wish I'd played football, though." He laughed.

Elen smiled as they headed for the lobby. As they exited the auditorium she slipped her hand into his. The foyer outside filled quickly and Kevin guided Elen through the pockets of conversation to the main doors.

Outside, the cool air was invigorating.

† † †

SHANE MATHEWS HELD THE DOOR OPEN for his girlfriend as they came outside. The exit was tight. As Mathews tried to get past, he accidentally bumped into Kevin. "Sorry about that," Mathews said.

"No problem."

Mathews and his girlfriend walked a few steps away. "Your teacher sounds great, Shannon," he said.

"So you like the concert?" she asked.

"Yeah. It's great. Hey, do you mind if I check my messages?"

"Go for it."

Mathews pressed the voicemail button on his phone and raised it to his ear. He turned to the side and his gaze fell on Elen. As he listened to his phone, he leaned over to Shannon and said, "Hey, do you know her? She looks familiar."

Shannon looked at Elen, then shook her head. "I don't think so. Maybe she's one of your old girlfriends?"

"Very funny."

"Well, she's beautiful."

"IT'S TOO BAD MORE PEOPLE don't give this music a chance," Kevin said.

"Yeah, but there aren't any drums or guitars," Elen pointed out. "There goes most of your audience."

"True."

"I HAVE TO CALL THE OFFICE," Mathews said.

"This late?" Shannon asked.

"Sorry." He had the phone to his ear while he waited for the call to connect. "This is Agent Mathews," he said. "Is Agent Dunnigan still in?"

ELEN AND KEVIN LOOKED AT EACH OTHER and froze. They were close enough to hear Mathews' phone conversation.

"OKAY," MATHEWS SAID into the phone. "No problem. I'll be there. Bye." He disconnected the call and put the phone in his pocket.

"What was that all about?"

"There's a meeting scheduled tomorrow morning with Home-Sec. It was moved up an hour and they wanted to be sure I was there."

KEVIN TOOK ELEN'S ARM AND HEADED for the parking structure. He expected to hear a shout for them to stop. The command never came, though, and they reached the parking structure safely. "Damn," he muttered as they exited. "That was close."

"Did you see how he looked at me?"

"Yeah. It was like the wheels were spinning but he couldn't make the connection."

"What should we do?"

"Let's get our stuff and hit the road."

Thirty minutes later, they were cleared out of the hotel and back on Interstate 70, heading east. Kevin glanced at the dashboard clock and said, "It's just past nine-thirty. We should assume that agent recognized us. If we're lucky, he'll be unsure. Maybe he won't draw the connection until tomorrow. That gives us, say, twelve hours to make as much headway as possible. What do you think?"

"Well, what are we, about two and half hours from Kansas?" Elen studied the map. "Another six to Kansas City. That's nine hours, with a couple of stops on the way. From Kansas City, it's another four to Saint Louis. Thirteen hours."

"That's a long way to go."

"Yeah," Elen agreed. She studied the map some more, and said, "They'll probably set up a net in Kansas City."

Kevin took his eyes off the road to study her face. She smiled halfheartedly, and he returned his focus to driving. "I think we'll be safe if we can make it past Saint Louis by the time they start searching."

Elen was silent as she reflected on their predicament. It was tiring driving so much. Mentally and physically. They had gotten careless. If they had just stayed under the radar—

"Hey," Kevin said. "Water under the bridge."

"Stupid," she said to herself.

"We needed a break."

"I know better."

"So we made a mistake, Elen. Whoops. Let's just move on."

She breathed deeply, then said, "Okay. You're right. Let's just move on. How do you want to split up driving?"

"Whatever you're comfortable with."

"Maybe just drive until you feel tired and then we'll switch."

"All right. Try to rest if you can."

Elen reclined her seat and closed her eyes. "Kevin?"

"Yeah?"

"If you start feeling drowsy—"

"I'll pull over."

"Okay."

Westwood, California

ANNA COHEN WAS WAITING at a traffic light down the street from her apartment, studying the scene from the safety of her seven-year-old Toyota Camry. The FBI surveillance van was still directly across the street from her second-floor apartment. Even though it bore the logo of a florist, it had been parked there for the last several days. The light turned green. She went through the intersection, turned onto a side street and parked. She got out of the car, grabbed her bag and risked a glance across the street. No movement from the van. She hefted the bag and hurried into the complex.

Inside her apartment, she locked the door and breathed a sigh of relief. Nothing looked out of place. There was a flashing light on the answering machine. Twenty messages. They could wait. She went to the refrigerator, grabbed a soda and took a long drink.

There was a quiet rap on the front door.

She reacted with a start and closed her eyes. "Get a hold of yourself," she muttered. "You're not a schoolgirl." She breathed deeply several times, turned to face the door, and said, "Who is it?"

"Federal agents, ma'am."

"Just a moment."

She walked to the door and secured the chain before opening it.

"May I see your identification please," she asked through the four-inch opening.

"Certainly," Dan Stevens replied, extending his ID wallet. His partner did likewise.

She studied both carefully. "How can I help you?"

"May we come inside?"

Anna nodded, unfastened the chain, and allowed the agents to enter.

"Thanks, ma'am. We apologize for the late intrusion. I'm Special Agent Stevens. This is Special Agent Harkins."

"Would you like to sit down?" she asked.

"Thank you," Stevens said, taking a seat.

Harkins moved to the wall behind the sofa and remained standing.

Anna sat down opposite Stevens and said, "How can I help you?"

"Well, Ms. Cohen," Stevens said, "I'll get straight to the point. Your roommate, Elen Biran, is the subject of our investigation."

"God," Anna whispered. "I haven't seen her in a while. When I saw the news, I just couldn't believe it. What happened?"

Stevens leaned forward and stared directly into her eyes. "Have you had any contact with her during the past week?"

She shook her head. "I've been on vacation."

"Where?"

"San Diego."

Stevens nodded his head and leaned back into the sofa. "Can you verify that?"

"Sure. I was there."

"Can anyone else verify that, ma'am?"

"I was alone."

"Alone?"

"Yeah. Look, do you have any idea where she is?"

Stevens smiled. "I think you *have* seen her."

"Yeah, on TV. I saw the news reports like everyone else."

Stevens was impressed with how well she was handling the situation. Most people tended to wilt under serious questioning. But, he strongly suspected she was hiding something. Her answers were just too convenient.

There was a knock at the door. Stevens rose to his feet and looked at Anna. She went to the door and opened it. It was Sergeant Kenton, dressed in civilian clothes. "Oh, sweetheart," he said, stepping inside and embracing her. "God, I missed you so much. I was so stupid. Can you ever forgive me?" He turned her around so his back was to the agents, and whispered into her ear, "I'm your boyfriend, Joe. You're in danger, and I'm here to help you. Just play along." He turned her back around, released her, and said, "Honey, who are these guys?"

Anna fought with her emotions as she decided what to do. It was just crazy enough for him to be telling the truth. Finally, she said, "They're asking questions about Elen."

Kenton continued to hold her hand as he studied the two feds. "What does Anna have to do with this?"

"Sir, this doesn't concern you. We're—"

"I think it does concern me. Why are you here now? Couldn't your questions have waited until tomorrow and a more reasonable time?"

Stevens' eyes exuded barely-restrained hostility. He stepped aggressively closer and said, "Is it your intention, sir, to interfere with a federal investigation?"

Kenton closed the gap, a response Stevens hadn't anticipated. "I want to see your badges, please. Before this goes any further."

The two agents exchanged glances. Stevens nodded, and both men showed their identification to Kenton. Joe studied them and said, "Those could be fakes for all I know."

"They're real," Harkins said.

"But I don't know that. I want to speak to your supervisor."

Stevens shook his head. "Why are you being so hostile, sir? Do you have something to hide?"

"Not at all. It's just that there are rapists out there posing as officers. Late at night. It's been on the news."

"We can question anybody whenever we want to," Stevens said.

"What's your name?"

"I'm gonna ask you guys to leave," Joe said. "Unless you have a warrant, I want you to leave immediately. Anna will make herself available tomorrow at a decent time—with her attorney present."

Stevens knew, lawfully, he had to back down. He considered his options. He could leave and take up the questioning tomorrow, or he could apprehend *both* of them now and take them for private interrogation. Outside of FBI jurisdiction they could just disappear. Fewer complications in the end. The only serious impediment was Anna's boyfriend. He was an unknown and he'd already proven he wasn't a pushover. The last unknown he'd encountered had almost gotten him killed. Because of Long Beach, he had something to prove. He had to take the risk. "This can go easily for you," Stevens said. "Or it can go rough. I'm detaining you both for questioning and you *are* going to come with me."

"You have a warrant?" Joe asked. "You can't enter this house to make an arrest without a warrant. That would make this an illegal arrest."

"I don't need a warrant."

"Then on what charge?"

"Suspicion of violating the Patriot Act."

Kenton smiled and said, "Wrong answer, man. You're not a real agent."

"I most certainly am," Stevens countered. "And now you're under arrest for obstruction." He drew his pistol and motioned for Harkins to search Kenton.

Joe raised his right index finger and wagged it slowly side to side. Harkins stopped, puzzled by the gesture. Kenton pointed to the open doorway. An MP5 submachine gun slowly materialized as the man wielding it stepped into the light. Stevens put his gun down and raised his hands in surrender. He had no chance. He knew an MP5 was not available to the public. That meant whoever was behind it was serious.

"You screwed up," Joe said. "Agent Stevens, or whoever the Hell you are. Hands on your heads, turn around and get on your knees.

Now."

Harkins' jaw clamped tight as he looked at Stevens.

"Don't even think about it," Kenton said. "I know you're not federal agents, and I won't hesitate to waste you right here." Joe reached into his back pocket and withdrew a lead-filled sap. "Get any ideas and you're dog meat."

Stevens nodded, placed his hands on his head and turned his back to Kenton.

"Get on your knees. I'm not gonna tell you again."

Stevens complied. Harkins reluctantly followed suit. Kenton stepped closer to Harkins and motioned for Sergeant Rodriguez to come forward. Keeping his weapon leveled on Stevens, Rodriguez handed Kenton two pairs of plastic cuffs.

"Damn," Stevens said. "Not those things."

"I know they hurt," Kenton said, smiling. "You be good boys and I won't fasten 'em too tight."

Joe grabbed Harkins wrist. Harkins started to spin away. Joe brought the sap down hard behind his ear and Harkins fell to the floor. Kenton turned to Stevens, and said, "What is he, a moron?"

Stevens shook his head.

Kenton grabbed Harkins' left ear, pulled to the side, and growled, "You pull another stunt like that, you pathetic excuse for a hot turd, and I guarantee you'll spend every waking hour learning how to breathe out of your ass."

Anna stifled a laugh. Kenton glanced back at her and winked as he fastened the plastic cuffs on Harkins. Finished, he looked at Stevens and said, "You feeling punchy, too?"

"No. I'd like to think I'm not a complete idiot."

"A wise choice," Kenton said. "Anna? Would you please close the door?"

"Sure."

When she returned, Stevens was handcuffed and Kenton was speaking into his cell. "It's me, sir," he said softly. "Yeah. We've got two turds in the pot and our fair maiden is safe." He ended the call and said, "Toss me the headgear, Dan."

Rodriguez eased the backpack off his shoulders and set it on a chair. He pulled out two black hoods and tossed them to Kenton. Joe put them on the prisoners, then said to Anna, "You should come with us. Why don't you pack some clothes?"

Chapter 10

Georgetown, Grand Cayman

HEATHER AWOKE TO AN EMPTY BED and looked at the clock. 7:19. She was tired. Jetlagged. In L.A. it was four in the morning. A nightstand on the side of the bed held a single red rose and a slip of paper. She picked them up and caressed her cheeks with the soft petals as she read the note:

> *I'm out making arrangements for the next few days. Help yourself to breakfast downstairs in the restaurant. They'll charge it to the room. See you later this morning.*

She set the note on Jacob's pillow, then slumped back and stretched beneath the covers. She closed her eyes and was asleep moments later.

† † †

IT FELT LIKE SHE WAS FLOATING. Looking around, she was unable to discern any shapes or colors. It was cold, she realized with a shiver. Wispy puffs of vapor intermittently caressed her face until she finally rose through a thick cloud layer and saw the ocean below. There were three islands in the distance—two smaller ones in the east and a large one farther to the west. She recognized them immediately as the Cayman Islands. The view was breathtaking. The ocean was light blue, and iridescent flashes of light sparkled hypnotically off the crystalline surface.

Her attention was drawn toward the north and an immense shadow that extended as far as she could see. As the shadow progressed southward, seemingly devouring everything in its path, an icy stab of pain coalesced in the pit of her stomach. Nearing the Islands, the shadow suddenly stopped. A small extension separated itself and continued onward, finally coming to rest over the easternmost island. As she pondered the shadow's presence, she was surprised to see the large shadow pull away and disappear over the horizon, yet the small shadow remained. Before she could make sense of the strange image, she started falling—

Heather snapped awake, shrouded in a sticky film of cold sweat. Sleep was normally something she enjoyed, but not today. Not after that dream. She closed her eyes and shook her head to dispel the sinking sensation in the pit of her stomach. After several deep breaths she finally sat up. Jacob was still gone. The rose and the note were lying undisturbed on his pillow.

She eased herself out of bed, showered quickly, and dressed in khaki shorts, a white blouse and tan Birkenstock sandals. As she left the room, she noticed a young woman across the hallway shutting her door at the same time. They exchanged polite smiles. Heather continued toward the elevator. The woman came alongside just as the doors opened.

"What a lovely hotel," the woman said, pushing the button for the lobby.

"Yes it is," Heather agreed distractedly.

"Are you vacationing?"

"Yeah. Just got in last night from L.A. You?"

"Business. Hopefully with a little pleasure on the side."

Heather laughed. "Somehow I don't think you'll have a problem there."

The other woman smiled. "You know, there are some gorgeous men out there. We could go have some fun together, if you know what I mean."

"Sorry. I'm spoken for."

"That's too bad. But, I guess you won't know what you're missing." The elevator slowed its descent. "My name's Terri. I'm from Miami."

"Heather. Nice to meet you."

Just then the elevator stopped and the doors opened. Heather headed for the main lobby entrance while Terri went right, towards the dining room. Once Heather exited the hotel, Terri reappeared in the lobby, withdrew her cell phone and said, "She's clean."

HEATHER REMOVED HER SANDALS and carried them in one hand as she stepped onto the beach. It was a pleasant sensation—buttery soft white sand spilling between her toes as she made her way toward the magically clear, crystal blue Caribbean. She smiled as the sun's rays tickled her cheeks. *Paradise*, she reflected. *Simply paradise.* Her thoughts drifted to Jacob as she strolled along the water's edge. He had an incredible presence, a certain special quality to his character she couldn't quite grasp. He was handsome. He had an amazing body. *It's something inside*, she reflected. *He knows who he is, and he's comfortable with himself.* She looked down at her feet as she walked, pondering the whirlwind relationship. A short distance away, three men wearing white pants and Guayabera shirts edged closer.

Heather stopped and gazed at the water. Half-a-dozen luxury yachts floated lazily off shore. Three gigantic cruise ships were anchored farther out. A young man and his girlfriend raced by, laughing. He made it to the water first and the girl waded out to join him. He splashed water on her and she screamed. He laughed, she jumped on him, and both went under. Seconds later, he came up with her over his shoulder in a classic fireman's carry. She screamed again as he dove back into the water.

"—Excuse me, ma'am?"

Heather turned around and saw the trio of men had arrived. "Yes?"

"May I speak with you for a moment?" one of the men said.

"I'm here with someone."

"That's not what I meant," he said, stepping closer. "Actually,

Miss Reardon, we're here to protect you."

"Protect me? From what? How do you know my name?"

"My name is McGrath. Royal Islands Police."

"Is there a problem?"

"Do you mind if I ask you a few questions?"

"Not at all. What's going on?"

"How well do you know Jacob Ross?"

"I don't see how that's any of your business."

"Has he told you what he does for a living?"

Heather's eyes narrowed as she looked for help. Except for the two men behind McGrath, there was nobody within earshot.

"Miss Reardon, I don't want to frighten you, but your life could depend on what I have to tell you. We've been monitoring him for some time. What I'm about to tell you may be disturbing, but it is the truth. For your sake, you should be aware of it." He paused, then said, "The man you know as Jacob Ross is actually Jacob Rostov. He was born in Israel, in Tel Aviv. He spent seven years as an elite naval commando before being recruited into Israeli Intelligence. He's been living in the shadows ever since. We don't know much, but we do know that for a while he hopped around the globe as a member of an elite *kidon* unit. Basically, an assassination squad. Then there was a falling out. Last year, a Russian politician, Sergei Bukharin, was murdered in the Ukraine. You may remember the news reports when it happened. Rostov was linked to the crime when he disappeared following the murder and he hasn't returned to Israel since.

"Miss Reardon," McGrath continued, "Let me be clear. Jacob was banished from his own country because they couldn't control him. He's received the best training in the world and he's a very talented, *very* dangerous individual. A man like him can be a valuable resource to many political interests."

Heather looked away and McGrath realized he was losing her. "Ma'am," he said softly, trying to get his point across. "Jacob recently surfaced on our radar after being contracted by an international group of—"

Heather raised her hand and said, "I have no idea what you're talking about, but you're wrong. Jacob isn't like that. You must have the wrong person."

"Miss Reardon," McGrath countered quietly. "Jacob Rostov is an international assassin."

Heather turned to leave and quietly said, "Please leave me alone."

McGrath frowned, disappointed. "Okay. I understand your concern." He reached into his pocket, withdrew a white business card, and handed it to Heather. "This is a toll-free number where you can reach me. We can protect you."

"I don't want it."

"Please, Miss Reardon," he said softly. "Take it. It may save your life."

Heather took the card. It bore the logo of the International Red Cross. "The Red Cross?" she asked.

"That's for your protection, in case he sees it. It doesn't raise questions the way a blank card with unidentified numbers would. Or Royal Cayman Islands Police."

Heather nodded reluctantly and placed the card in her pocket.

"*Sir?*"

McGrath turned around. A member of his security team was approaching. "Yes?"

"Rostov has returned to the hotel. He's in the restaurant now."

"Thank you." McGrath turned to Heather, and said, "I'm sorry if I've upset you, Miss Reardon. I just hope, for your sake, that you take my warning seriously." He turned away and joined the two men behind him.

For her part, Heather frowned and shook her head, feeling dazed. For a while, she just stared blankly at a cruise ship on the horizon. Then she closed her eyes, wanting to erase the encounter from her mind.

McGRATH AND HIS SECURITY TEAM walked away in silence. As they reached the edge of the beach, one of the security men looked over his shoulder and said, "I think you really spooked her."

"Yeah. It wasn't the best approach," McGrath agreed. "But if I wasn't in such a hurry to get out of here maybe I could have taken my time and eased her into it. Still, the seed's been planted."

"Why don't we just eliminate him?"

McGrath shook his head. "It's not the right time yet."

"When *will* it be?"

"I don't know. Not now. Anyway, I need to get back to California. Keep an eye on her."

"Yes, sir."

BY THE TIME HEATHER RETURNED to the hotel it was nearly ten o'clock. She met Rostov in the lobby. It was all she could do to return his embrace without giving off any bad vibes. Still, he sensed something out of kilter and drew back slightly.

"Is everything okay, babe? You seem a little distant."

"I'm fine," she said hesitantly. "I had a disturbing dream, that's all. I felt like taking a walk."

"Have you eaten yet?"

"No. But I'm hungry."

They found a table in the back. Heather filled her plate with a croissant, scrambled eggs, an assortment of pineapple chunks, kiwi slices, several large strawberries, and pancakes sprinkled with powdered sugar and fruit syrup. On the table were carafés of orange and apple juice, and a steaming pot of fresh Colombian coffee.

Rostov poured coffee for both and said, "We leave for Brac at noon. I made arrangements for us to go diving. There's an old shipwreck off the coast we can explore. You're certified, right?"

"Yeah."

"Good. I just bought a couple rebreathers. It'll be a perfect opportunity to break them in."

"What's a rebreather?"

"It's a military diving rig. It doesn't put bubbles into the water like a normal scuba rig does. Great visibility."

"Did you do a lot of diving in the military?"

"Not much. I did get a chance to train with some SEALs once."

"Were you in the special forces or something?"

"Or something," he replied cagily. "That was years ago."

Heather felt torn inside. Though she had treated McGrath brusquely, he frightened her. He was a police officer and she had no reason to distrust him. But it was too much to take all at once. A small inner voice cautioned that she really could be in danger.

"Hey," Rostov suddenly prodded, interrupting her brief reverie. "Earth to Heather," he added softly.

"Sorry," she said quickly. "I just spaced-out for a second there."

"Do you want to tell me about your dream?"

"It's silly. I'll get over it."

"Fine."

She smiled and said, "By the way, thanks for the rose."

"My pleasure."

FBI Office, Denver

SHANE MATHEWS, IN KEEPING with his customary habit, went straight for the bulletin board, having second-guessed himself all night. He found both pictures quickly. *Edwards looks a little different*, he noticed. *Perhaps it's the beard.* He studied Elen's picture briefly, shook his head, and muttered, "I'll be damned."

Out of the corner of his eye he saw his boss, John Ford, the Special Agent in Charge of the Denver Field Office. As the highest-ranking agent in Denver, Ford was also one of the few African-Americans in charge of a Bureau field office.

Mathews caught his attention and walked over. "Can I talk to you, sir? In your office?"

Ford nodded his head and led the way. Once inside, Mathews shut the door. "What is it, Agent Mathews?"

"I'm ninety-nine percent sure I ran into fugitives Elen Biran and Kevin Edwards last night."

Ford pursed his lips, taking a few seconds to jog his memory. Finally, he nodded and said, "Los Angeles? About a week ago?"

"Right, sir. Anyway, I've been in the habit of keeping tabs on the fugitive board. Something definitely rang a bell last night."

"Where did you see them?"

"At the Performing Arts Center last night. My girlfriend wanted to see the concert. We ran into them at intermission."

"You're positive?"

"Definitely, sir."

"Have a seat." Ford browsed an internal field office directory, found the listing and dialed.

Westwood FBI Office, Los Angeles

ASSISTANT DIRECTOR SMITH ANSWERED the phone with a gruff, "Hello?"

"This is John Ford, SAC Denver. How are you?"

"Not too bad," Smith replied. "You?"

"No complaints. Anyhow, an agent of mine has just informed me that he ran into a couple of your fugitives last night."

"Really? Who?"

"Elen Biran and Kevin Edwards."

"No kidding?"

"My agent is positive."

"Do you have a location on them?"

"Not a precise one. It was a brief encounter. Shane Mathews is the agent who saw them. I'll put you on speaker—"

"This is Agent Mathews, sir."

"This is Assistant Director Smith. What can you tell me?" He took notes as Mathews recalled the encounter. After he finished, he set the pen down and said, "Thank you, Agent Mathews. John?"

"Yeah?"

"I'm sending Special Agent Bryce Maurer and a team out there. They should arrive in a few hours. Until then, if you would alert local law enforcement it would be appreciated."

"You bet," Ford replied.

"Thanks." Smith disconnected the call, then dialed the intercom.

"Yes, sir?" his secretary answered in the next room.

"Please find Agent Maurer and tell him to contact me ASAP."

"Certainly, sir."

† † †

Near Saint Louis, Missouri

"FINALLY," ELEN SAID AS SHE PULLED the Fusion into a Phillips station.

"Not bad," Kevin muttered. "Quicker than I thought." He was groggy, having just awakened from a nap. He'd managed to drive for six hours before handing over the driving duties to Elen. She'd been at it for the last six, and she looked sleepy. Between the two of them, they'd driven over eight-hundred miles in the last twelve hours, stopping only twice for gas.

Elen found an open gas pump and parked next to it.

"I'll get it," Kevin said as he opened his door.

"I need to stretch anyway," Elen replied. "Do you want anything?"

"Sure. Whatever looks good."

As Elen made her way inside the station's food-mart, Kevin inserted a credit card into the quick-pay gas pump. The gas pump beeped at him, approving the transaction and telling him to select a grade of gasoline. He pushed the 87-octane button and inserted the nozzle into the tank. After locking the pump handle, he stepped away.

Is there any way our cards could have been discovered by the FBI? he wondered. *What do they know? That guy—if he even made the connection—didn't hear our names, did he?*

He pursed his lips and considered the looming possibilities. It seemed very unlikely. Actually, it bordered on impossible. *Cash is safer*, the careful side of him said. *Just relax, man. Save the cash for when you really need it.* Kevin stared at the digital readout and his eyes started to glaze over. As soon as he realized what was happening, he shook his head to clear his mind.

Elen returned a few minutes later with a bag of snacks. The gas pump clicked off. Kevin replaced the nozzle and tightened the gas cap.

"What's on your mind?" she asked as they got in the car.

"I just had a thought, but—nah, it's just paranoia." He turned the key in the ignition.

"A little paranoia can be a plus in this game. What is it?"

"I was just wondering if the run-in with that agent gave them enough information to track us through our credit cards. They don't have our names, though, so I don't see how they could. Do you?"

"I don't see how. What about cash? We've got plenty of it."

"I was thinking the same thing just a minute ago. I'd prefer to save it for emergencies."

"You've got a point. I think we'll be okay."

Kevin opened the map and traced his finger along their route. "Anyway, it looks like we are about two and a half hours from Terre Haute. If you've got the strength to make it there, I think we'll be safe to get some rest."

Elen nodded. "You seem like a natural at this, Kevin."

"It just seems the harder we push ourselves, the harder we make it for them to catch us. If we don't just collapse from exhaustion."

"Yeah," Elen agreed. "I'm pretty close."

"Do you want to call it a day then?"

"No. We need to keep moving."

"All right. Let's get out of here."

Westwood, California

BRYCE MAURER FROWNED AS HE LOOKED at the agent responsible for sur-veillance of the Cohen apartment. "Agent Stevens relieved you last night, but he wasn't here when you returned?"

"Correct, sir."

"Did you check her apartment?"

"It was locked."

"I've tried Stevens on his cell, but there's no answer. I've got to go to Denver. If you can reach Stevens, bring him up to speed. Until then, keep watching the place. Miss Cohen is bound to turn up even-tually."

† † †

THE ROOM WAS BARE EXCEPT FOR a thin mattress, one pillow and two blankets. There were no windows. Dan Stevens was dressed in thin hospital scrubs and slippers. His ankles were chained together by eighteen-inch long leg cuffs. There was no toilet in the room. Stevens had to be taken out of the room in order to do nature's business.

The toilet was just down the hall. Stevens had learned nothing promising on his two trips to the head. The walls of the hallway were undecorated and solid. Concrete, he had discovered after touching them. That meant he was not in an ordinary house, but perhaps a large, fortified building. He had tried shouting several times only to be told he was wasting his breath. The walls were completely sound-proofed. Only a person in the nearby control room could see and hear what went on inside the small holding cell. Both his cell and Harkins' contained hidden microphones and ultra-miniature surveillance cameras. They were embedded in the ceiling, virtually undetectable to the naked eye. Stevens had guessed about their existence but saw no benefit in trying to find them.

He believed in the concept of reluctant cooperation, with the emphasis on cooperation. Since his captors held all the cards, nothing was accomplished by antagonizing them. They might just come in and beat him if he gave them the slightest reason to. Not that he was afraid of pain. There simply was no point in enduring it if he didn't have to. Every interrogator has a unique style. Some come in immediately and beat you until you start talking. Others try to out-psyche you in a head-on confrontation. And still others leave you alone to stew. He didn't really care. He knew how to deal with all of them. For one thing, it was much wiser to be cooperative before they threatened physical abuse. This wasn't a test of machismo, and there was nothing to be gained by being turned into pulp. That just made it impossible to escape.

The only thing he was really afraid of were drugs, and he was quite familiar with a variety of tongue-loosening chemicals. Yet another reason to cooperate. As long as he appeared genuine, drugs would be left on the shelf—or so he hoped. They tended to have unpredictable side effects. Still, he knew there were no guarantees. It would depend largely on who had captured him. And on that score he was left entirely in the dark.

† † †

"HOW LONG ARE WE GOING to hold them?" Kenton asked. He and Ambrose were alone in the control booth, studying video monitors of both prisoners.

"Avi should get here in the next day or so," Ambrose replied.

Kenton nodded and said, "What's this all about, anyway?"

"The next time you escort Mister Stevens to the head, take a good look at the back of his left wrist."

"What for?"

"Just look. It's the key to everything. Tell me what you see there, and I'll tell you what I know."

Cayman Brac

THE WATER WAS A BALMY 82°, warm, but not unusually so for the Caribbean. Heather was wearing a thin, sleeveless, fluorescent-yellow wetsuit that prevented chafing from the rebreather rig strapped to her back. As she looked around underwater, she counted over a dozen divers who had come to see the wrecked ship. She'd lost sight of Jacob—he was probably off doing his own exploration. She didn't mind, though. Diving is an intensely internal experience, solitary by nature.

Thirty feet below the surface, the crystalline waters dazzled her with sparkling beams of heavenly glory, like sunlight breaking through clouds after a storm. Transfixed, she swam through the kaleidoscope of light toward a small school of brightly-colored fish. When they veered to her right she followed them, but they were too fast. If not for the regulator in her mouth, she would have laughed with childlike pleasure.

From her left, a much larger school of tiny, silvery fish approached so close together they looked like a sheet of aluminum foil shimmering in the sunlight. Heather swam toward them, timing her advance so that half darted around her on the left and the other half on the right. She spun to watch them as they disappeared. Suddenly, she realized she couldn't see the ship. After reflection, she decided to swim back in the direction she'd come from—only, she wasn't sure which way that was. In spite of the phenomenal underwater visibility, she had no real landmarks to guide her back. Everything looked the same. She decided to surface and regain her bearings.

Before diving, Jacob had warned her about *the bends*, how nitrogen bubbles would expand in her bloodstream and cause excruciating pain if she wasn't careful. She remembered to rise slowly and breathe regularly. She leveled her ascent several feet below the surface and looked down. The bottom appeared very distant and she realized she wasn't as close to the shoreline as she'd thought. Still, the view was mesmerizing. Forgetting her concern, she swam with her head down, lost in the moment as school after school of vibrantly colored fish scurried below her. It never occurred to her swimming that close to the surface was dangerous.

ROSTOV WAS GROWING CONCERNED. He'd circled the sunken vessel three times and Heather was nowhere to be seen. As he studied the divers in the distance, his attention was drawn to one wearing a bright yellow suit. Bubbles rose from the regulator, though, and he knew it wasn't her. She must have wandered off. He reproached himself for being careless—he never should have let her out of his sight. He ascended slowly, allowing sufficient time for his body to acclimate itself to the lower oxygen-nitrogen pressure. When his head broke the surface he scanned the distant shoreline. No bright yellow suits. He turned and scanned the water surface. Nothing.

An eighty-foot yacht was cruising a hundred yards away, closer to the shoreline than Rostov was comfortable with. He ducked below the surface and swam away from the shore. He had a growing, sickening sensation in his stomach. He didn't know how well she would think under these circumstances. What was logical to a trained diver was not necessarily logical to an inexperienced one. He propelled himself forward with powerful strokes of his flippers, his thighs and calves burning with the increased effort. His arms were in tight against his sides to reduce drag.

When he crossed the shelf, the bottom seemed to just open up beneath him. It was an eerie sensation. The water was so perfectly clear he could see all the way to the bottom, and his body told him he should be *falling*. He swam to the right, initiating a search. After thirty yards, he veered back to the left and swam on a path parallel with the shore. He was only fifteen feet below the surface, scanning Up—Left—Down—Right, repeating the process in a systematic approach to locating her.

Out of the corner of his eye, he glimpsed a flash of yellow and finally saw Heather in the distance. As he swam closer, he saw she was looking down, unaware of the yacht heading straight for her. He kicked faster, hoping to gain momentum and her attention. The environment handicapped him, though. The sense of sound is extremely important and he no longer had it. Neither did she. With a wrenching pain in his gut, he knew he wouldn't reach her in time.

As HEATHER STUDIED A BRIGHTLY-COLORED school of fish, her body suddenly tingled and she remembered her dream—how she had seen the Islands from above the clouds, and the shadow that covered them. Below her, a school of fish turned black. She turned toward the surface and suddenly saw the yacht approaching. She scissor-kicked frantically, desperate to escape the collision.

ROSTOV WATCHED IN DREAD as the boat approached Heather. He reached out for her, but it was a vain gesture—he was still too far away. As the yacht churned its way unawares through the water, it didn't appear to hit her head on. Even a glancing blow could be deadly, though. If she swallowed just a little bit of water she could easily drown. He kicked fiercely and propelled himself forward, inwardly praying she was unhurt. Meanwhile, the yacht continued blissfully on, leaving a massive grave of bubbles in its wake.

Chapter 11

Rostov dove deeper, mindful of the eleven-meter safety-limit the pure-oxygen rebreather imposed on him, and equalized the pressure in his ears as he scanned for the bright flash of yellow that would reveal Heather's location. Nothing. There were just too many coral formations and undulating caves for him to check. In an odd way, he remained hopeful. If she had been hit by the yacht, he was certain he would have found her. After one final search of the area, he turned toward shore and put all of his effort into making it back as fast as possible. He extended his arms in front of him like a spear, his flippers undulating powerfully through the warm water. As he neared shore, his calves screamed in protest but Rostov didn't care.

He reached the diving pier, got out of the water and noticed a commotion a hundred yards away. A crowd had formed on the beach. He removed his fins and mask, and jogged toward the crowd still wearing the rebreather. Just then, an ambulance entered the parking lot with its lights flashing. Something serious had happened. He looked back at the crowd. Someone moved away from the circle and Rostov saw a swatch of yellow. Only twenty yards away, he slipped the tank off, dropped his gear and sprinted the rest of the way.

As he approached, the crowd opened up. Heather was lying on her back, her gear in a pile several feet away. Rostov fell to his knees beside her and scanned for injuries. Her eyes were closed. She was breathing. No obvious sign of trauma. He stroked the side of her head and said, "Heather? Are you okay?"

Her eyes fluttered open and she coughed.

"Back away," he said to the crowd. "Please. Let her get some air."

"Move away!" a new voice commanded. Rostov looked up to see a paramedic hurrying over. The crowd dispersed quickly. "You too, sir," the medic continued in a softer voice. "Please move aside."

Rostov leaned down to Heather's face, stroked her forehead, and kissed her on the lips. "The paramedics are here," he said gently. "You're going to be okay."

"Please move aside, sir. Let us do our job."

"Fine," Rostov replied, stepping back.

The paramedic turned to Heather. "How do you feel, ma'am?"

"A little dizzy."

"Are you short of breath?"

"Maybe a little."

"Do you remember what happened?"

"A boat—barely missed me. Grabbed me. Took me with it. My mask came off and I couldn't see. Then I found it. Somehow I swam back here."

"Do you have any medical conditions?"

She shook her head.

"Do you feel cramping in your joints?"

"No. I just feel dizzy."

While the emergency medical team evaluated her, the lead paramedic turned to Rostov. "I think she'll be okay, but it's possible to have complications. Dizziness could be symptomatic of dehydration, heatstroke, oxygen deprivation, or any number of things. We can take her for observation. We also have a hyperbaric chamber, just in case."

"Okay, let's go," Rostov said. "Can I ride with her?"

"Sure."

While the paramedics prepped Heather for the ride, Rostov returned the diving gear to the Range Rover and hurried back. The rear doors closed as soon as he jumped inside. Her wetsuit had already been removed and she was lying on her back, wearing only a bikini. The first medic inserted a needle into her arm and secured it in place with an adhesive strip. While he attached tubing to the IV, the other medic pressed adhesive patches above each breast and on the outsides of each thigh. He attached wires to the metal nodes in the centers of each patch, then looked at the EKG monitor. "BP one-forty over ninety," he said. "HR ninety-five and steady. Coming down a little."

Blood pressure was a little high and her pulse was a little fast, but they weren't bad, considering the situation. Rostov took her hand and said, "You're going to be fine. Just relax."

They made it to the hospital quickly. After an hour of observation—she slept while Rostov held her hand—she was discharged. Rostov handled the paperwork and called for a cab.

BACK AT THE HOUSE, ROSTOV helped Heather inside and closed the door behind them. "How are you feeling?" he said.

"A little shaky."

"You had me scared out there. What happened?"

"It all happened so fast. I was looking down, just admiring the beautiful fish all around me. It was kind of weird. I noticed a school of fish turn black, then I looked up and saw the boat approaching." She paused. "It was the boat's shadow on the fish that warned me. If not for that, I don't think I would have gotten out of the way in time. Even though it missed me, I think something snagged the tank and dragged me for a while. Maybe an outrigger or something."

"I'm sorry I wasn't there with you."

"It's not your fault."

"No, I should have been there."

Heather smiled. "Thank you, Jacob, but it's really not your fault. I was just too close to the surface. I need to sit down."

"You okay?"

She nodded her head, sat down on the living room sofa and closed her eyes. Rostov kissed her lightly on the lips. She opened her eyes and smiled dreamily at him.

"You really had me worried back there," he whispered. "Are you going to be okay?"

"Yeah. I just need to take a nap, that's all."

"All right. Do you mind if I get the Rover? I should be back in half-an-hour."

"I'll be fine, thanks." She closed her eyes.

Rostov kissed her forehead, then stepped away. By the time he reached the door, she was asleep.

THE RINGING TELEPHONE INTERRUPTED her nap. Heather opened her eyes and tried to get her bearings. Before she knew it, the phone rang three more times and the answering machine picked up. After a brief greeting, the machine beeped and a female caller said, "*Hello, Jacob. Please call the office as soon as possible. Thank you.*"

Heather sat up, took a deep breath, then stood. No dizziness. That was a good sign. She went to the bedroom, slipped out of her bikini and wrapped herself in a huge towel. On the way to the shower she passed Jacob's dresser. She paused and closed her eyes. The temptation to search it was too much to resist. She pulled on the handle of the upper right drawer. It slid out smoothly. Inside, she saw he kept his socks neatly arranged and his underwear folded. She put her hand inside the drawer and touched something heavy and metallic. She moved the socks aside and stared down at a six-inch long, steel cylinder. Next to it was a Beretta automatic.

Heather looked at the doorway of the bedroom, like a child holding a forbidden cookie. Jacob was still gone. Her heart was pounding. She picked up the pistol. Just then, she heard the front door open. She jumped in surprise and dropped the gun on the dresser, then quickly put it back in the drawer.

"Heather?" Rostov said from the other room.

She slipped into the bathroom, closed the door softly, and yelled, "I'm in here. Just going to take a quick shower." As the water heated, she slipped out of her towel and entered the stall. Her mind was racing.

Why does he have a gun?

He's a security consultant, remember?

Yeah. But what about that silencer? Aren't those illegal?

I'm sure he has a good reason for having it.

What reason would that be?

There's a perfectly good explanation.

She rolled her neck and turned around, letting the hot water hit everywhere as she struggled to resolve the conflict inside. She grabbed a bar of soap, scrubbed down, and wondered, *Why are you in such a hurry? Slow down.* With an effort, she managed to relax, and her heart finally began to ease up. She sighed deeply and closed her eyes. The hot water was soothing. After another minute, she turned the water off, stepped out of the shower and wrapped up in the towel.

Maybe McGrath is right, a small voice nagged.

She closed her eyes and shook her head. *No. That's not it.*

Are you sure?

Jacob isn't a murderer! Just shut up!

Heather wanted to scream, but knew she couldn't. Instead, she kept her eyes shut and tried to force the voice out of her mind through sheer willpower. She sat down on the edge of the bathtub and put her face in her hands. She was hyperventilating. She held her breath, then exhaled slowly. *Breathe*, she said to herself. When she opened her eyes, she let out a short, startled scream.

"Whoa," Rostov said. He had entered the bathroom while she was sitting down.

"God, you scared me," Heather said.

"I'm sorry, Heather. I just wanted to see if you're okay." He sat down and put his arm around her.

"I'm wet," she said.

"I don't mind. You're trembling."

Heather allowed herself to relax in his arms, refusing to believe the small voice inside. Then, much to her dismay, she started crying.

He put his hand on the back of her head, gently stroked her hair, and said, "I'm sorry I frightened you, babe. Relax. You'll be okay."

She shook her head, not wanting to respond—not wanting her suspicions of the truth to somehow escape of their own accord. She just held onto him until she felt comfortable looking at his face. Finally, she smiled and said, "Sorry. I don't know what got into me."

Rostov leaned closer, kissed her forehead, and said, "I never should have let you out of my sight. God, I thought you were hurt, and it scared me so much. It made me realize how much you—" He stopped.

Heather touched his face.

"I don't know how to say this," he said, looking away. "It's just that, out on the water, I realized—" He shook his head, finding it difficult to voice his feelings. Finally, he said, "I felt so empty inside. The thought of losing you." He knew it was stupid to open up like this. Unprofessional. Careless. Foolish. With conflicting emotions battling for supremacy inside, he finally said, "I have to go away on business. Only a day, I think. Maybe two. I'm sorry."

"But we just got here."

"I know." He shook his head, clearly unhappy.

"Jacob," she said softly. "Are you an—" Try as she might, she couldn't bring herself to finish the sentence.

"What?"

Heather shook her head, numbed by the reality she didn't want to see. Still looking in his face, she reached out for his hand and brought it up between them.

"What's wrong, Heather?"

She shook her head and said, "Where do you have to go?"

"New York."

"Why?"

"Business meeting," he replied distractedly.

"I was approached by a man today, on the beach."

Rostov's eyes narrowed.

"He said crazy things about you."

"Like what?"

Heather swallowed, then breathed deeply. "He said you're an assassin." *There, it's out*, she thought.

Caught off-guard, Rostov's eyes wandered around her face as he wondered how to respond. After a few seconds, he sighed deeply and made up his mind. He leaned into the shower and turned the water on. Then he reached over to the sink and turned it on. Satisfied with the ambient noise, he said, "I need you to trust me."

"What did you do that for?"

"My home is bugged."

"*Bugged?*"

"By my employers. Listen, I need you to trust me. I realize that's perhaps a lot to ask, but it's very important—for your own protection."

She studied his face, then nodded.

"Thank you," Rostov said. "I'll explain when I get back, but I have to be extremely careful. I've brought you into a dangerous situation, and for that, I apologize."

"Oh, God," she said. "I didn't want to believe him."

"Who was he?"

"Have you killed people?"

"Heather, I don't have much time. Who was he?"

"A police officer, but he wasn't wearing a uniform."

"Did he say his name?"

She shrugged.

"Heather, I don't know what he told you. Are you sure you don't remember his name?"

"Is he a threat to you?"

"I don't know."

She was silent for a moment, deciding how much she believed him. Finally, she said, "McGrath."

Rostov nodded. "I want you to trust me and stay here while I'm gone. I *want* you to stay. But, if you want to go home"—he hesitated, trying to communicate with his eyes what he felt—"if you want to go, I won't stop you. It's your decision."

"Is that all you're going to tell me?"

"For now."

Heather was quiet.

"Will you stay?"

She sighed deeply and finally nodded her head.

"Thank you," he said, taking her in his arms.

"I'm still wet," she said.

"I don't mind." He took her face in his hands, kissed her lips, and said, "Thank you."

"When do you have to leave?"

"Right now, unfortunately. I'm sorry."

"Don't be."

Rostov smiled. "Heather, I can't tell you how much you mean to me right now. I mean that."

"I just hope I'm doing the right thing."

"You are," he said. "You'll see." He went to the bedroom, grabbed a black bag and laid it on the bed. Then he went to the dresser and opened the sock drawer. Heather watched him closely, suddenly remembering that she forgot to cover the pistol. When he saw the Beretta, he turned around and raised an eyebrow questioningly.

"I was curious," Heather explained with a shrug. "I didn't expect to find anything."

"Well, now that you know, let me show you how it works." He screwed the silencer on the end of the muzzle. "Here," he said, dropping the magazine into his palm. "This lever releases the magazine. It holds fifteen bullets. Right now there's no round in the chamber. This is how you check." He pulled the slide back and showed her the empty chamber. He released the slide and inserted the magazine. "Right now, there's still no round in the chamber, even though the magazine is inside." He racked the slide. "Now, a round is chambered and the gun will fire. This is the safety. When the dot is red, the gun will fire. The white dot means it won't fire. See?"

She nodded her head.

"If someone is threatening you, make sure the red dot is showing, then aim and pull the trigger."

"Why are you showing me this?" she asked softly.

"I don't want you to be alone here without some way of protecting yourself."

"Am I in danger?"

"No," he said soothingly, hoping it was the truth. "I just don't want anything to happen to you while I'm gone. Or ever, for that matter. Now, why don't you get dressed? We can talk more on the way to the airport."

Outside, Rostov helped Heather into the Range Rover, then got behind the wheel. He looked at her and saw she was still upset. "I'm sorry, babe," he said. "Just hang in there. Everything will be fine."

"Don't take this the wrong way," she replied, looking away. "But I've never been with a"—she closed her eyes—"a man like you before."

The turmoil on her face was obvious. Rostov wondered how much he could tell her. He wanted her to know the truth, but at what cost? Anything he told her would put her in danger. What he didn't want to admit was how much danger it would actually put *him* in. He'd fought against his conscience for years, and learned to compartmentalize everything. He closed his eyes and breathed deeply.

"That look," she said softly. "It's like you're two different people. Like Jekyll and Hyde."

God, how can she be so perceptive? Rostov thought. *You saw her intelligence—well, if not quite at the very beginning, then close to it. She's beautiful. Smart. Sensitive. Caring. Vibrant. Full of life.* It struck him as a paradox. How could someone with all of these wonderful qualities be with someone like him?

Heather took his hand. It seemed like the right thing to do. And it was, yet at the same time it was the wrong thing. She had no way of knowing that the caring gesture would finally break through the façade he had so carefully constructed. As she studied him, his face transformed into one of intense, internal anguish. He abruptly looked away, opened the door and got out of the truck.

Concerned, Heather got out quickly and rushed to his side. "It's okay, Jacob," she said. "Do what you have to do. I'll be here."

He shook his head slowly and stared off in the distance.

"I mean it," she insisted. "Whatever you have to do, I believe in you."

"How can you say that?" he asked.

"I don't know. But I *am* saying it."

Rostov shook his head, looked at the ground, and muttered, "Twelve months."

"What?"

"Twelve months."

"What are you saying?"

Rostov looked into the sky. "I'm saying I've just screwed-up the last year. Preparing. Getting ready. Getting inside."

"What are you talking about?"

"I'm losing my edge."

"What?"

He sighed deeply and turned to face her. "Is killing bad?"

"Of course it is," she replied. "Well, I mean—"

He cut her off with his hand and said, "No. You're right."

"Really?"

"Of course. But it isn't that simple."

"What do you mean?"

"Is it okay to kill in self-defense?"

"Yes."

"Is it okay to kill in defense of others?"

She nodded.

"What if, in order to protect a huge number of people, you had to kill a small number of other—maybe innocent—people?"

"I don't know," she said haltingly. "I've never had to make that decision. The good of the many over the good of the few?"

"Exactly."

"Well. I can tell you I would hate to be the few."

Rostov nodded. "I suppose that's what it ultimately comes down to. But who makes the decision?"

"What do you mean?"

He studied her face briefly. "Do you know how a cancer is removed?"

"Yeah."

"There are a number of methods. Radiation and drugs, for instance. Or, surgery to cut it out. Unfortunately, with either method good tissue is destroyed in the process. It's difficult and extremely painful, but it must be done. Is the doctor wrong for destroying the good tissue?"

"Of course not. He has to in order to save the patient."

"Exactly. To save the patient."

"What's going on here, Jacob? I never liked situational ethics."

"Neither do I. But it's reality."

"Look," Heather said. "I think you're a good man. You have a charisma I've never seen before. I don't know how, but I—I think I'm falling in love with you—and I don't even know who you are."

"It's strange, isn't it? You have it, too."

"What?"

"That charisma."

"I don't think so."

"No," he insisted. "It's there. I think that's why I'm so attracted to you. Like a magnetic polarity, or something. You give me life. If I told you I'm a doctor and my job is to remove a dangerous cancer, would you understand if I had to remove some of the good tissue?"

"I think so. But what is the good tissue?"

"Unfortunately, they're people. I wish there was a better way, but this cancer is maybe the worst thing the world has ever seen."

"Really?"

Rostov nodded. "Removing it requires desperate measures. And I seem to be the most qualified for the job."

Heather shook her head numbly. "I don't know. It just seems so unreal."

"Heather, I have to convince this cancer that I'm a part of it. An important part. Because that's the only way I can kill it. For the last year, even longer, I've been establishing a mindset. I have to compartmentalize my conscience and slip into the role of a stone-cold killer, loyal unequivocally to these people. I can't act a part. I have to *become* that part. It's the only way I can gain their confidence—the only way I can identify the inner circle. Remove them, and hopefully I remove the cancer. With you in the picture, it's—" Unable to voice his real concern, he fell silent.

Heather took his hand and looked into his eyes. "Who are you, Jacob?"

Rostov looked up at the sky. Telling her would be a complete security compromise. "I want to tell you, Heather. I really do."

"But you can't?"

"I'm sorry. I may have told you too much already."

She nodded her head slowly, deliberately, weighing her options. "Be careful, Jacob," she finally said, wrapping her arms around him. "But do what needs to be done. I want you back when you finish whatever it is you're doing."

Chapter 12

Terre Haute, Indiana

"WE MADE IT," KEVIN SAID as they took Exit 7. "Finally."

Elen looked out the window and pointed to the right. "There's a Holiday Inn." After Kevin made the turn south, she suddenly blurted, "Wait. That Marriott in the back is even better. It's hidden—out of the way."

"Perfect," Kevin agreed. "Let's fill up the tank first, then get a room."

After the gas station, Kevin pulled into the driveway of the Marriott and found a parking spot near the front. Inside, the manager at the front desk greeted them with a smile and said, "Can I help you?"

"We'd like a room for the next couple days."

"Certainly."

Kevin laid his credit card on the desk, filled out the paperwork, then minutes later they flopped down on the bed, exhausted. Kevin took her hand, squeezed it gently, and said, "Have I told you today you look beautiful?"

"Ahh, that's sweet. Thank you."

Kevin kissed the back of her hand, then closed his eyes.

Elen stared at the ceiling, lost in thought. The last week was insane. The shooting. Kevin. Anna. Avi. Her father. The manhunt. Nevada. Utah. Colorado. Kansas. Indiana. Finally she closed her eyes and said, "Do you want to order room service?"

Silence.

"Kevin?"

She looked over. He was asleep.

FBI Office, Denver

"WELCOME TO DENVER," SAC Dan Ford said as he shook Bryce Maurer's hand.

"Thanks," Maurer replied. "What's the latest?"

Ford sat down behind his desk and opened a case file. Maurer sat down next to Shane Mathews. "Agent Mathews?" Ford said. "Do you want to bring him up to speed?"

"Yes, sir. We've sent photos of Edwards and Biran to all motels and hotels in the Denver area. Nothing yet. They may be using aliases. Most likely, they're no longer in Denver. We've notified as many hotels and motels along Interstate 70 as we could—up through about Kansas City—and we've sent a heads-up to local law enforcement."

"Anything else?" Maurer asked.

"Their photographs have been posted at the airports, too, but it's a safe bet they're traveling by car."

"Have you checked bus and train records?"

"Yes. No luck there. But bus records are not as thorough as the airlines."

"They're in a car," Maurer said.

"Most likely."

"These two are really good. For the most part, you can't check into a hotel without a driver's license and credit card. They could be sleeping in their car, I suppose, but I doubt that. Somehow they've managed to find lodging."

"Fake IDs?" Mathews suggested.

"That appears likely."

"They could have credit cards under aliases."

"What do you know about their backgrounds?" Ford asked.

"Nothing beyond what's in the file," Maurer replied. "ATF hasn't told us anything of any real value."

"ATF?"

"This was their baby. They lost control of it in Long Beach and tossed it in our lap. They're supposed to be terrorists, but it doesn't make sense. First off, Edwards has no criminal record. No military record. No prior watch list. He's twenty-six. Owns a graphic design studio. Father's a retired cop."

Ford looked up in surprise.

Maurer continued, "Biran is twenty-five. College student. Supposed to graduate this year. She's from Israel." He shook his head. "The Israelis haven't been forthcoming with her background. They're like that. Interviews on campus haven't produced much. We do have one lead: her roommate, Anna Cohen. But, she seems to have disappeared, too."

"Not much to go on."

All three were silent. Maurer stroked his clean-shaven chin in a decent rendition of Sherlock Holmes, and said, "There's one possibility."

"What's that?"

"I just had an idea. Maybe we can find their credit cards."

"How?"

"I'll need to go online. Can I use a computer?"

"Of course." Ford led the way across the hall, then said to Maurer, "Good luck."

Maurer sat down at an open station and started typing.

Mathews stood behind him. "What are you doing?"

The screen changed to the Web site of the leading credit reporting agency for the western United States. "Following the yellow brick road," Maurer replied softly. He navigated through two pages, then clicked on an icon that said *Authorized Entry*.

"What's that?"

"It's not very clean, but I'm going to give it a try. A hacker in L.A. showed me how to do this last year when I was on a fraud case. This'll be a little different, but maybe I can find a way in the back door."

"Is this legal?"

"It won't be admissible, but no one has to know. It could give us the break we need." On the screen, Maurer was being prompted to enter his password.

"You know how to get in?" Mathews asked.

"There are special skeleton codes. My hacker knew the code for this company, and I wrote it down." Maurer opened a small notebook, searched for the right page, and typed the code in. The screen immediately said:

ACCESS DENIED. INVALID PASSWORD.

"That's not right," Maurer muttered.

Mathews chuckled. "You had me going for a second there."

Maurer studied the notebook and tried the code again, this time slower. It showed up on the screen:

PASSWORD: **************

He pressed ENTER and waited. Five seconds went by. Then the screen changed.

Mathews said, "I don't believe it."

"I'm not sure exactly where to look," Maurer admitted. He surfed through page after page of credit card records for about fifteen minutes, copying and pasting them into a new document. "God, that's a lot of records."

"Any boundaries?"

"I've eliminated the ones who live outside of California," Maurer said.

"How about cards that are new?" Mathews suggested. "Say, maybe only a few months old?"

"Good idea, but they could have identities that go back years. I've narrowed it down to purchases made in the last two weeks."

A laser printer to Maurer's left whirred as it warmed up. Two minutes later the printout was finished. Maurer took the stack of paper, crossed his fingers and said, "Maybe we'll get lucky." After a quick perusal, none looked promising. "Well, I don't know what good that did. I'm not seeing any patterns."

"What do you mean?" Mathews asked.

"I'm looking for a string of purchases between here and Los Angeles."

"Can I help?"

"Sure." Maurer split the stack and handed half to Mathews. "Cross out the ones that obviously don't fit. Highlight any records that might. We'll eliminate the rejects, then, if we haven't found an exact match, we'll go back and tackle the possibles."

"What if they're using different names on the credit cards?"

Maurer sighed, and said, "Let's hope we get lucky, Agent Mathews."

Mathews nodded.

Warrensburg, New York

ROSTOV STARED OUT A SMALL oval window as the Gulfstream landed. The sky was overcast and it looked like rain might be in the air. When they came to a stop, he stood and put on his suit jacket, covering the gun holstered underneath his left arm. He slipped on a dark trenchcoat, grabbed his travel bag, and walked to the front.

The pilot emerged from the cockpit and opened the hatch. At the bottom of the ramp, a dark-blue Ford Expedition waited, a sizable vapor cloud broiling in the cold air behind its warm exhaust pipe. Rostov got in and the Expedition accelerated away. The private airfield was only a mile from the meeting site—the rural, corporate office skyrise of GlobalComm, International, the fourth largest telecommunications company in the world.

Two minutes later, they arrived at the rear of the massive ten-story building and pulled into the secure underground parking structure. Rostov grabbed his bag and exited the vehicle. At the elevator, he pressed his index finger on a sensor. A small button beside his hand turned green and a security camera to his right recorded his entrance. The doors closed and the elevator rose quickly. Ten seconds later, the carriage came to a stop and the doors opened.

Rostov stepped out to see a huge security guard. The guard's dark African complexion, shaved head and sharply-pressed, black military fatigues made him an intimidating figure. At six feet five-inches tall, he would have made an ideal NFL linebacker. Size didn't scare Rostov, though—not that he had any reason to be worried. He had no doubt he could dispatch the humongous security guard if it ever proved necessary.

The security giant was regarding Rostov much the same way, appraising how he might deal with the smaller man. Rostov noticed the cold look in the man's face, smiled warily, and said, "What's your name?"

"Griffin. Yours?"

"Rostov."

A smile formed on Griffin's face. "Okay," he said, nodding his head. "You're that badass mother, aren't you?"

"That's me. You look like you played some college ball. You an ex-SEAL or somethin'?"

Griffin nodded.

"How long have you been here?"

"About a month."

"Good money?"

"Bet your ass," Griffin replied. He turned to the side and said, "This way, sir."

Rostov followed him towards the security door that guarded the private communications center. Griffin stepped aside as Rostov pressed his hand against the security scanner on the wall. A button beside the scanner turned green. Rostov pressed it and the thick fire-door slid open. Rostov stepped into a brightly-lit corridor and the door hissed shut behind him. He was in a choke point. There was nothing in the hallway except another security door he had to pass through before he could enter the communications room. Rostov looked into the camera beside the door and pressed his palm against another scanner. The button beside the scanner turned green, he pressed it, and the last security door opened, admitting him into one of the most technologically advanced communications centers in the world.

"Welcome, Mr. Rostov."

The voice came from his right. He turned and saw the imposing figure of Ian Ferguson, GlobalComm's head of security. A former captain in the British Special Air Service, Ferguson was two-hundred and ten pounds of solid muscle. His employers were no slouches where security was concerned. They bought the best.

"Sir," Rostov said, nodding his head in greeting. As chief of security, Ferguson possessed the rank of colonel. Rostov, assigned to special operations within the secretive organization, was independent of the usual chain-of-command and answered directly to Ferguson. "What's going on?" he asked.

"Let's talk inside."

Rostov followed him down a corridor of rooms overflowing with technological marvels. He guessed at a price tag in excess of a hundred million, but he had no way of knowing. Most of the equipment wasn't even available commercially. "Business looks good," he said softly.

"It is," Ferguson replied. "We're constantly making improvements. How long has it been?"

"About a month," Rostov replied. "Took me a while to prepare the job in Manhattan."

"That's right," Ferguson remembered. "We've had some upgrades since then. Nice work in L.A., by the way."

"Thanks. I'd prefer being a bit more subtle, but that's what you wanted, right?"

Ferguson chuckled. "Right."

They turned down another corridor and entered a large, lavishly decorated meeting room. A heavy oak table was in the center of the room, extending from one end to the other. The walls of the room were dark. At least a dozen artistic masterpieces adorned the walls with just the right amount of backlighting. Probably originals. It struck Rostov as a paradox, yet in a way it was perfectly natural. Priceless works of art have always been the heirlooms of rulers.

Seated at the far end of the table was the President and CEO of GlobalComm, Richard Wellesley. "So good to see you again, Jacob," Sir Richard said with a warm smile. An old-money British tycoon in his early sixties, he appeared remarkably energetic and youthful.

"Good afternoon, sir," Rostov replied.

"Please, have a seat."

Rostov made his way toward the billionaire and sat down. Ferguson moved behind his boss, taking up the position of a silent observer. It made Rostov think of a king's prized mastiff, loyally situated beside his master to protect and intimidate.

Wellesley was silent for several seconds. He thought of himself as an aristocrat. Never rushed. With apparent concern, he finally said, "You have a new love interest, I'm told."

"I do," Rostov agreed.

"Of course," Wellesley said with a smile. "You know she may not see eye to eye with us."

"Yes, sir, I realize that. She knows nothing, nor does she need to."

"Ahh," Wellesley replied with a tolerant nod. "Love is wonderful. Truly wonderful."

"That it is, sir," Rostov replied. "But, with all due respect, sir, you didn't call me here to have tea and read poetry."

Wellesley laughed. "Of course not! Just a healthy warning, son, that's all. Enough said. One mustn't be boorish." He smiled benignly as he collected his thoughts. "I've been watching you closely for the last six months, Jacob. I'm very impressed with your efficiency, and quite pleased by your progress."

"Thank you, sir," Rostov replied. "I do my best."

"Of course you do," Wellesley agreed. "So, Jacob. How are you?"

"Sir?"

"How do you feel?"

"I feel fine, sir. I'm healthy. I have money in the bank. I have a rewarding job."

"Wonderful," Wellesley said. "Wonderful. Everything a man needs, eh?"

Rostov nodded and smiled uncertainly.

"Indeed," Wellesley continued as he looked away. "Do you have any complaints?"

Rostov shrugged, shook his head, and said, "No, sir."

"Suggestions? Nagging questions?"

"No, sir."

"A wise man never complains about things he cannot change, is that it?"

Rostov chuckled and replied, "A wise man never complains to his boss."

"Well spoken, Jacob. Well spoken. But seriously, I want you to be comfortable here. Be candid. Is there nothing you wish to know about us? We have many secrets, of course."

"Anything I need to know, sir, I presume you will tell me. Other than that, I know how to do my job and keep my mouth shut."

"But you're an intelligent man, Jacob. Intelligent men need to *know* things, do they not?"

Rostov nodded agreeably. "Of course. Intelligent soldiers know how to take the initiative when things don't go as planned. They can think on the spot and come up with solutions to sudden problems, and survive to teach the next generation. But a wise man doesn't ask questions so much as he listens to answers."

Wellesley smiled, pleased with the repartée. "A man who does not reveal his thoughts is a strong man, Jacob. But, he is also a dangerous man. He is a two-edged sword that can strike both ways."

"Or, he is a simpleton. Better to be thought a fool, as the saying goes."

Wellesley smiled and pointed his finger at Rostov's chest. "That you are *not*," he countered. "No. You are a dangerous man, Jacob."

Rostov simply smiled.

"I like dangerous men," Wellesley added. "Dangerous men control the world. Very dangerous men." He paused reflectively. "Who is your favorite philosopher?"

"Ahh, now we've arrived."

"Who is it?" Wellesley wondered. "Nietzche? Aristotle? Sun-Tzu? Von Clausewitz?"

Rostov chuckled. "To be honest, I've never really spent a lot of time reading philosophy. As a warrior, the obvious choice would be Sun-Tzu."

"Yes. The legendary Chinese conqueror, centuries ahead of his time, and one of the first historical proponents of developing hard tactical intelligence before heading into battle."

"Correct," Rostov said. "However—"

"Yes?"

"Anton Goethe is interesting." He pronounced it *Ger*-tuh.

"Yes, yes," Wellesley agreed, clearly liking the choice.

Genuine curiosity, Rostov mused as he studied Wellesley's face. He hoped this wasn't going to hit too close for comfort. "He once wrote that no man is so hopelessly enslaved—"

"As he who falsely believes he is free," Wellesley finished. "Remarkable, Jacob. Truly insightful. And so appropriate." He turned to Ferguson and said, "Ian? He'll do just fine, don't you think?"

Rostov glanced at Ferguson, wondering what the last exchange meant.

"Yes, sir," Ferguson replied. "Shall I continue?"

"Yes, of course."

Ferguson took a seat beside Wellesley and said to Rostov, "You've passed. Your background is impressive. Your execution flawless. We have big plans for you."

Rostov raised an eyebrow.

"You have all the innate qualities we need in a covert field commander," Ferguson continued. "You are quick on your feet. You have impeccable training. You speak half a dozen languages. You have excellent judgment. And, you have extensive experience." He opened a black folder on the table in front of him, removed a photo ID card, some loose papers, and pushed them towards Rostov. "Your new identity," he said. "You've been assigned the rank of colonel, UNOSS. Your name is Jacob Ross."

"UNOSS?"

"United Nations Office of Special Services."

"Never heard of it."

"We created it. It runs directly out of the secretary-general's office."

"You can do that?"

"Your background is contained in those papers," Ferguson continued. "You will be taking on a substantially different role now, as your new identity will enable you to travel around the world with full diplomatic immunity. That means you can carry any weapons you need, anywhere you need to. It also gives you access to any site under U.N. jurisdiction."

"I don't understand. Why the sudden change?"

"This is what we've been grooming you for from the beginning. We need an experienced, highly-trained, covert operative who can quickly and easily show up anywhere in the world. To put out fires, or, to anonymously start them, if necessary. Sound interesting?"

Rostov was silent as he considered the surprising information. He had been expecting something big, but he was completely caught off guard by this. *Colonel? United Nations?*

"Mister Rostov, do you want the job?"

"Of course. I'm honored. Thank you for the opportunity."

"Wonderful," Wellesley said. "I'll leave you two gentlemen to discuss the details. Jacob, you will be working directly for me now, through Ian. Anything you need, you'll get. Understood?"

"Thank you, sir."

"Excellent," Wellesley concluded. "Good day, gentlemen." He turned and exited the room through a flush-paneled door. When the door closed, it seemed to disappear into the wall.

"He has a flair for the dramatic, wouldn't you say?" Rostov said.

Ferguson smiled briefly, then said, "Do you have any questions?"

"What's my next assignment?"

Ferguson opened another folder, withdrew an eight-by-ten photograph and handed it to Rostov. "Her name is Elen Biran. We've been trying to secure her for over a week, but she's managed to elude us."

Biran? Rostov was thinking. *Why does that name sound familiar?*
"You want me to eliminate her?"

"No. Just bring her in."

"Who is she?"

"Her background is here," Ferguson said, sliding the file folder towards Rostov.

"Is she trained?"

"Military, yes. Intelligence, no. She's Israeli, by the way," he added, closely studying Rostov's reaction. "Is that a problem?"

Rostov nonchalantly shook his head and replied, "Should it be?"

"Good. We believe she's surfaced in Denver, along with a young man who's been helping her. The FBI are tracking them and should catch up very soon—maybe within hours. The lead agent on the case is Bryce Maurer. Your best bet is to link up with him and use your resourcefulness to take her."

"This sounds like something Dan Stevens was working on."

"What do you know about that?"

"Just that he and I spoke in L.A. a couple of days ago. He was working with the FBI."

"Stevens has gone missing," Ferguson said.

"What? When?"

"Two days ago."

"Just like that?" Rostov asked.

"Afraid so. Anyway, that's a different topic. Moving on, Colonel Ross. You'll be traveling a lot. The Gulfstream you flew in on is now at your disposal. Your U.N. salary will be added to your current contract. In the next forty-eight hours, you'll receive a cash bonus for completing your six-month probationary period."

Rostov couldn't help but smile.

"We believe in rewarding our successful operators, but don't take this for granted," Ferguson warned, suddenly turning cold. "With what we're paying you, we want your loyalty to us. Period. Do your job well, Colonel Ross, and you'll enjoy a wealthy life. Now, and in the future. I don't have to tell you what will happen if for some reason you decide to betray us. Or, what will happen to Heather Reardon," he added. There was a sinister quality in his eyes now. "I know everything," he said. "I just want you to understand that with your newfound freedom of action, we still own you." He paused to let his speech sink in. "Understood?"

Rostov nodded and said, "Of course."

"Good."

"Can I make a request?"

"Yes?"

"I could use an assistant."

Ferguson considered the idea. "Do you have someone in mind?"

"I'm not certain yet, but I would like a few words with the security guard in front. Griffin, I believe his name is."

Ferguson raised an eyebrow.

"He's perfect for the job."

Ferguson nodded his head, leaned to the side and pushed the intercom. "Griffin?"

"*Yes, sir?*" a disembodied voice replied.

"Find someone to relieve you of your post and come to the boardroom."

"*Right away, sir.*"

"Do you have his bio?" Rostov asked.

Ferguson nodded. He pressed a different intercom button. "I need Griffin's file in the boardroom, ASAP. Thanks."

While he waited, Rostov opened his new mission folder and studied the contents closely. *Elen Biran*, he said to himself. *Why does that name sound so familiar?* He shook his head, unable to recall the connection. After reading the mission brief he was still at a loss. If he'd met her before, he was sure he wouldn't have forgotten.

An aide entered the boardroom with a folder. Ferguson waved the material toward Rostov. Rostov took the folder, opened it and started reading. Thomas Deshaun Griffin was from New Jersey. Thirty-four years old. Graduated from the University of Miami. Played pro football for two years, then joined the U.S. Navy SEALs. Demolitions expert. Eventually joined DEV Group. *Impressive.* That meant he had been a member of the top special operations group in the entire United States military comprised of Navy, Army, and Marine special forces. After a brief return to SEAL Team Four, he suddenly quit the Navy two months ago.

Griffin strode into the boardroom and made eye contact with Ferguson. "You called for me, sir?" he asked.

"Yes. Have you met Colonel Ross?"

"Uh, yes, sir," Griffin replied hesitantly. "I thought he said his name was Rostov."

"Ross, Rostov—" Ferguson shrugged. "Same difference."

"Yes, sir, we've met," Griffin replied.

Rostov said, "Tell me about your career. Were you in Iraq?"

"Yeah. I also saw action in Afghanistan, Yugoslavia, Somalia, Uganda, South Africa."

"Why did you leave?"

"Ah, the Navy's gettin' too clean, sir. I got a DUI comin' back from a party and lost my security clearance. Well, I got in a fight with an officer along the way, too, so that didn't help. The officer wasn't an angel, but he had connections. They gave me a choice between a courts-martial and leaving the Navy. That's when I got recruited for security work. The money here is a helluva lot better. I miss the license to kill, though."

Rostov smiled. He knew being a SEAL required a top-secret security clearance. A ticket for driving under the influence was enough to have that clearance revoked. No clearance, no Teams. "I may have a job for you," he said finally. "If you can stop pounding on officers for a while."

"Ahh, sir, I only kick ass if they deserve it."

Rostov smiled. "I need someone I can trust to cover my six. Knock some heads around, if necessary. You look like that man. There will be a lot of traveling. Around the world, probably. You have family?"

"Divorced, sir. Two kids. They live with their mother."

"Well, you'll be away from them a lot, but I imagine you'll also get some free time along the way. You will see action. I guarantee that. You interested?"

"Hell yeah, sir."

"On a probationary basis, then," Rostov said. "You'll be working with me out of the United Nations Office of Special Services. You'll have the rank of lieutenant."

"An officer?" Griffin laughed. "That's funny."

† † †

FBI Office, Denver

Agent Maurer had been rummaging through credit card transactions for almost an hour when an interesting pattern struck him. Las Vegas, Denver. He started to get excited as he continued. St. Louis—"Terre Haute," he said, suddenly short of breath. It had been a shot in the dark. "I've got a really good candidate."

"Me too," Mathews replied. He shuffled through the printouts on the desk and said, "But the pattern doesn't start in California. It starts in Cedar City, Utah. Then Salina, Utah. Grand Junction, Colorado. Hays, Kansas. That's where it stops."

Maurer walked to a map on the wall. He studied it for several seconds, then said, "That's one Hell of a pattern. What name have you got?"

"Erika Johnson."

"This one's Kyle Johnson. Her purchases fit like a glove between his. The last transaction occurred today, at a gas station in Terre Haute, Indiana." He shook his head. "Agent Mathews, I don't believe it. I think we found our fugitives."

Los Angeles International Airport

As a perk of flying first-class, Avi Biran was the first passenger to exit the Air France flight from Paris. He had one bag, a medium-sized duffel that carried all of the essentials required for his mission. He weaved his way to the end of the jetway tunnel, only to be stalled by a crowd of Japanese tourists. The airport, as usual, was busy. A large digital clock on the wall read 3:52 p.m. He pushed his way through the crowd of tourists, grumpy and jet-lagged. The flight had left Paris shortly after one in the afternoon. Now, almost twelve hours and nine time zones later, his body believed it was the next morning. He'd napped fitfully on the plane, as always made just a little too uncomfortable by the incessant whine of the engines, the drier than usual air onboard, and the cramped traveling conditions. In spite of the first-class amenities, he hadn't rested well and he wanted to get out of the terminal as soon as possible. Customs didn't help. Airports in the United States have some of the strictest entrance standards for foreign travelers. He waited in line for nearly thirty minutes before clearing the customs desk. When he finally exited the terminal, vehicles were stacked two deep along the street as passengers were picked up and dropped off. From invisible loudspeakers he heard the recorded announcement: *The white zone is for loading and unloading of passengers only.*

To his right, he saw a man holding a sign with the name DONOVAN printed on it. He walked up to the man and said, "Do you know where I can get a good, hot apple pie?"

"No," Kenton replied, completing the code: "But, I can tell you where to find a great strudel."

Biran extended his hand and said, "Avi Biran."

"Joe Kenton. It's a pleasure to meet you."

"Likewise."

Terre Haute, Indiana

KEVIN AWOKE COVERED IN A FILM *of cold sweat. He opened his eyes and studied the room. The window was open a crack and a cool breeze filled the room. Through the parted curtains he could tell the sun was beginning to set. Elen was gone. He heard the door mechanism click. His body tingled as he reflexively reached for the pack beside him. He eased the Walther out and pointed it at the door.*

His grip tightened on the Walther as the door cracked open. He pulled the hammer back in preparation to fire. Elen entered the room and he sighed in relief. He closed his eyes, shook his head and decocked the pistol. When he opened his eyes, she was gone. Surprised, he looked around and saw her on the other side of the room, leaning against a dresser.

He smiled at her, but she didn't respond. "Elen?" he said. "Is something wrong?" Based on her reaction he wondered if she had even heard him. She seemed to be in another world. As he studied her closer, he was puzzled to see she was wearing an unfa-

miliar dark-blue windbreaker. "Where'd you get that jacket?" he asked.

No response.

"Elen?" he said, this time a little louder.

Instead of replying to his question, she simply walked towards the open window. Kevin looked down at the floor, angered that she was ignoring him. He looked at her as she gazed out the window and a tremendous sense of dread suddenly overwhelmed him. On the back of her windbreaker, in thick, yellow, block letters, was the last thing he expected to see: FBI—

Kevin's eyes flashed open and he sat up, studying the room intently. Elen was still asleep beside him and the window was closed. Shuddering inwardly, he realized it was a dream. After a few calming deep breaths, he slowly exhaled and studied the room. Everything was the same. Elen stirred next to him.

"Kevin, are you okay?"

He shook his head and forced himself to stand up. Suddenly restless, he walked to the sink, turned on the faucet and splashed cold water on his face. "It was so real," he muttered.

"What was?"

"It was so real, Elen."

"What are you talking about?"

He exhaled deeply, collecting his thoughts, then described the dream.

"Wow," she said after he finished, unsure what else to say.

"Yeah."

Elen stood and wrapped her arms around him. She could feel his tension. "It was just a dream," she said.

"I know. But I can't help thinking it means something."

"Kevin. It's a classic reaction. It's natural—your subconscious mind is working overtime and your fears are its playground."

"I wish I could let it go that easily," he replied hesitantly. "I've never had a dream so vivid. Maybe it's a warning. Maybe my subconscious knows something."

Elen studied his face. "You've got nothing to worry about, Kev. There's no way they can find us."

"I'm not so sure."

"You were pretty sure earlier."

"This is different."

"Is it?"

"I think so. We need to get out of here."

"Whoa, Kev. We just got here and we've been running at Mach-2 for the last fourteen hours. We need a break."

"This wasn't a normal dream, Elen. Somehow I just *know*."

"I don't want to discount your feelings, Kev, but I'm exhausted. I need a break."

"So do I," Kevin agreed. "So do I." He looked away.

"Kevin. I'm hungry. Let's get something to eat."

"I don't know, Elen. I think we should lay low. Lower. Let's just get away from here."

"Kevin—"

"Please," he insisted quietly.

Elen sighed, closed her eyes, and shook her head.

"I'm sorry, Elen," he said. "Just humor me, okay?"

She stepped back, and said, "So, this guy walks into a bar with a duck on his head."

Kevin grinned. "I didn't mean it that way."

"I know. I just wanted to see if you still have a sense of humor. God knows we're both going to need it."

"Thanks," Kevin replied, wrapping her in a big bear hug. "I guess I'm rubbing off on you more and more."

"Well, you be careful. I don't want any messes."

"Jeez, Elen."

"Sorry."

"You're a chameleon."

"Don't even go there, Kevin."

"Okay. Truce. Can we go now?"

"Yeah, let's go."

Chapter 13

GlobalComm Headquarters

THE PROCEDURE TOOK OVER AN HOUR. Once it was finished, a white-clad tattoo artist turned off the light illuminating the back of Rostov's left wrist. Rostov flexed his hand and looked closer. It was an intricate depiction of a Roman gladius sword in front of a stylized, flaming sun. The hilt of the sword started two and a half inches above his wrist; the tip of the blade, pointing toward his fingers, stopped at the cuff line. The entire tattoo was shaded, outlined, and highlighted in vibrant color, crafted to give a sense of dimensional depth. As the tattoo artist left the room, a tech in a white lab coat entered with a small toolbox. He took a canister from the box and sprayed anesthetic on Rostov's wrist, numbing the area. Then he pressed the tip of what looked like a very small gun against the numbed area, squeezed the trigger and injected a small metallic device under the skin. Finally, the tech applied a special ointment to protect the tattooed skin, covered the tattoo with a layer of plastic wrap, then packed up his gear and left.

Rostov looked at Ferguson and said, "What was that?"

Ian Ferguson stepped away from the wall and said, "You now possess UNOSS Level-5 clearance, Colonel Ross. A microchip was implanted and may be scanned at any of our worldwide facilities. The tattoo signifies membership within our organization, like a military unit designation."

"A microchip?"

"The future of security," Ferguson explained. "As our role continues to evolve globally, the implant is the most effective way to prevent someone from accessing or hacking our intelligence data-bases."

"You have a chip, too?"

Ferguson rolled up his sleeve. "All special operations personnel with the rank of colonel and above are given the mark."

"Why the sword and the sun?"

"It's the mark of the *Sonneschwerten*," Ferguson replied.

"Pardon?" Rostov quickly translated the name—it was obviously German—and said, "The sun swords?"

"Roughly translated," Ferguson replied. "Swords of the Sun is closer. The Roman gladius brings security to the world. The sun brings illumination. Together, they bring peace."

"The Swords of the Sun," Rostov muttered to himself.

"Welcome to the inner circle, Colonel Ross. Play your cards right and you'll have a pivotal role in the course of history."

Terre Haute, Indiana

Terre Haute International Airport was the staging ground for the FBI fugitive-recovery team. Only eight miles east of the Marriott, just off Interstate 70, Maurer was confident he was only minutes away from closing the biggest case of his career. Before leaving Denver, he'd made contact with the FBI field office in Indianapolis. Twenty agents from that office, including ten from the Special Weapons and Tactics division, made the drive to Hulman Field and rendezvoused with the twenty agents who accompanied Maurer on the two-hour flight from Denver. Maurer also had faxed pictures of Elen and Kevin to every hotel and motel in the Terre Haute area. When the manager of the Marriott received the fax, he recognized them immediately and in-formed the FBI they had just checked in.

Forty-one FBI agents loaded into ten vans and hit Interstate 70 with a police escort of four motorcycles and six squad cars. With red, blue and yellow emergency lights flashing, the entourage of federal vehicles exited the interstate at Highway 41 South and established a security perimeter around the Marriott. As the FBI vans parked outside the hotel, local police officers stretched yellow tape across the road, shutting it down.

Maurer led the way through the entrance and approached the manager. "I'm Special Agent Maurer. We believe two fugitives are staying here." He placed their photographs on the desk.

"Yeah, that's them," the manager said. "I checked them in earlier."

"Which room?"

"220. Second floor."

"Are they here now?"

"I haven't seen them leave, but I've been away from the desk."

"Okay. Can you get me a floor plan for the hotel?"

The manager withdrew a brochure from under the desk, and said, "Will this do?"

Maurer took it. "Thanks. For the next twenty minutes, nobody touches a telephone without my authorization. Is that clear?"

"Yes, sir."

"Can you get me six master keycards?"

"I'll see what I can do."

Maurer turned to an agent beside him. "I want Team One upstairs converging on our room, 220. Team Two, on the ground watching the window. Team Three, you guys make rounds of the hallways, lobby, and rec area. Team Four, you guys check out the third floor."

"Yes, sir," was the soft, chorused reply.

Ten agents formed up on Maurer and another ten formed in the lobby. "You two," Maurer said as he pointed to the hotel map. "Take this room. You guys take this one. The rest of you split up and take the rooms opposite." He paused as the manager returned with the master keycards. Maurer distributed them. "Make sure the guests stay quiet. Get them downstairs quickly and secure them in the lobby."

As the agents departed, Maurer studied the hotel map for a hole in his strategy. He turned to the lead SWAT officer, and said, "Agent Hickam, do you have a couple of guys who can cover the roof, and rappel down the side if necessary?"

Hickam grinned. "Of course."

"Okay. Get them up there. Let's go."

Hickam turned and said, "Davis and LaFontaine, on the roof with rappelling gear. Jones, Lee, Walters, follow me."

As the agents hustled over, Maurer motioned for the manager. Across the way, the elevator doors opened and six guests came out, followed by four agents. Just then the stairwell door opened and the remaining six agents came through. "All clear," one of the agents said in passing.

"Great," Maurer replied, turning to address the manager. "Look at your watch. In precisely two minutes I want you to call room 220. Let it ring twice and then hang up. Okay?"

The manager glanced at his watch and nodded. At the same time, Hickam huddled his SWAT team and said, "Ammo check." He dropped the magazine from his MP5 and checked that it was loaded with blue-tipped Glaser rounds. They were specially designed to prevent over-penetration, an inherent tendency of 9mm ammunition. Satisfied, he slipped the magazine back in and said, "Lock and load. Safeties on."

Each man chambered his firearm, leaving thumb safeties engaged; nobody wanted to trip in a stairwell and shoot a buddy in the back. Maurer followed the SWAT members up the stairwell in near total silence. They quietly assembled outside the room. Hickam crouched and placed the keycard against the card reader. Maurer stepped back and watched as the other three agents lined up on Hickam's back, MP5s pointed at the door.

Maurer signaled an agent with bolt-cutters to stand-by, standard procedure in case the chain was engaged from the inside. Maurer looked at his watch. Twenty seconds to go. Fifteen. Ten. Five. He dropped his hand and nodded at Hickam. Inside the room, the telephone rang. Using the sound to mask the click of the door mechanism, Hickam inserted the keycard and pushed. The door opened and he sprang inside, staying low to cover the entrance of the three SWAT agents storming the room to his right. They went through the motions, but it was a futile effort.

The room was empty.

†   †   †

IN THE PARKING LOT OUTSIDE the police cordon, a cameraman from a local television station was filming the unfolding scene. A few feet away, his partner spoke into a cell phone: "You've got to put this on the air! It's like Los Angeles or something. I swear there are over twenty cop cars surrounding the Marriott." He paused, listening to the other end. "Yes! We're ready to go live!"

ACROSS THE STREET AT THE Honey Creek Mall, Kevin and Elen sat at the bar inside *T.G.I. Friday's*, quietly pondering their predicament. As Kevin focused his attention on the flat-screen above the bar, he almost choked.

"What is it?" Elen asked. She followed his gaze. "Oh my God, Kevin. How did you know?"

"I didn't. It was just a dream."

"What are we going to do?"

"I'm not sure exactly, but we've got to leave now."

Kevin slid off his barstool and headed for the exit. Elen paused to leave a twenty-dollar bill on the bar, then caught up to him just outside the restaurant but still inside the mall itself. He was staring blankly out at the parking lot through the glass entryway doors.

"The Interstate is bound to be guarded," he said softly. "If they found us that quickly, they've figured out our names. We're lucky to still be here."

"If they know our names, they'll also know what we're driving. They'll know the license plate number."

Kevin nodded soberly. "We need to switch plates, but I don't know how much good that will do. If we hit a checkpoint, we don't have any other ID." He shook his head. "It's inevitable, Elen. We—"

"No," she said firmly. "It's not over. I refuse to give up. I don't think you had that dream by coincidence. To escape so closely only to be captured?" They walked in silence for several seconds. "You had a vision."

"What?"

"It's the only answer."

"Come on," Kevin muttered. "It was pure, bone-headed luck. Like you said, my subconscious was working overtime."

"I disagree."

He looked at her in disbelief, but remained silent—it wasn't worth fighting over.

"It doesn't matter," she finally said.

"No?" Kevin said. "So, what do we do now? Any tricks left in the bag?"

"Maybe," Elen replied.

"What are you thinking?"

"I don't know." She paused, then said, "We obviously need help, though."

"Yeah. Maybe from God?"

"I wouldn't turn it down if he offered."

"Well, I wouldn't either. But we still have to find a way out of here."

Elen nodded, then said, "I need a second to think." She took his hand and sat down with him on a wooden bench. She closed her eyes, sighed deeply, then opened them and stared vacantly at the floor as she searched inwardly for the elusive answer just waiting to be discovered.

While she was busy reflecting, Kevin studied the mall, lost in thought and feeling depressed. How could they possibly get out now? The police had tracked them to the hotel they'd *just* checked into. How did they do it so quickly? And what were the odds of running into an FBI agent at a *concert* in Denver? As perplexing as it was, it wasn't the only thing that felt bizarre. In the middle of a huge mall in a small college town in the middle of Indiana, he was holding hands with the most beautiful woman in the world—just prior to being caught by a squadron of FBI agents who were determined to make him spend the most productive years of his life in a federal pen. For something he didn't do. They would probably get away with it, too. Might not even get a trial. He distantly wondered what the weather was like in Guantánamo.

Kevin told himself to stop being so cynical. Oddly enough, he found Elen's presence comforting. She was such a *fighter*—full of grit and determination. She was amazing. If only God could help. *There's a thought.* What if God was the one who had brought them together in Long Beach? The timing had been so perfect. Completely unpredictable. He'd been so awed by what had happened since then that he'd never stopped to consider that maybe Someone had brought them together to prevent her from being kidnapped. Where would she be now if he'd never noticed her in the library? If he'd never plucked up the courage to talk to her? If he'd never swallowed his embarrassment long enough to pester her into having coffee with him? He knew he'd just gotten in the way of the men who wanted to kidnap her. But that distraction had been just enough to unbalance the equation in Elen's favor. She'd handled the rest, fighting back with amazing courage. What would happen to her now if he couldn't find the courage to keep fighting?

And where would I be? he mused.

He shook his head at the thought. None of that mattered anymore. Normality didn't matter. Even with the nagging possibility of a life-sentence looming, it simply didn't matter. If he hadn't been there with her, hadn't disrupted the kidnapping just by *being* there, she would now be in the hands of dangerous men—men who tried to kill him just for getting in the way. She might even be dead by now. That was a thought he wanted nothing to do with.

Kevin studied Elen. She was staring off in the distance. On impulse, he raised her hand and kissed it. She turned and smiled at him. "I suppose we had a good run," he said.

"I'm not ready to give up," Elen replied. She opened her purse and pulled out a slip of paper.

"What are you doing?" Kevin asked.

"I'm going to call the number Avi gave me."

"The one in Canada?"

"Yeah. First I need to find the codes for Quebec. There," she said, pointing to a bank of pay phones. A minute later she returned with the information. "Let's go outside. I'll make the call on my cell."

On the sidewalk in front of the mall entrance, Kevin looked toward the parking lot. "I'll be right back," he said. He jogged across the lot, then slowed to a brisk walk as he scanned license plates. He was surprised that all the cars with Indiana tags only had rear plates. He'd assumed Indiana would be like California, which requires two plates. He wanted a front plate that wouldn't be obviously missed, so Indiana was out of the question. He saw a car with a Michigan plate on the rear, but after checking the front bumper it was clear that Michigan wouldn't work, either. It finally occurred to him that this might be harder than he'd thought. The rest of the cars in the row were all Indiana plates. In the next row over, however, he saw an old Toyota Camry with an Illinois plate on the rear. He checked the front of the car, then breathed a sigh of relief. After a quick scan of the lot, he knelt down in front of the car, opened his hip pack and withdrew the Swiss Army knife he'd bought at the mall in Las Vegas. He unfolded the screwdriver head, crouched down and removed the retaining screws from the plate, then slipped it under his shirt. As he stood, the knife went into his pocket. He hoped by leaving the rear plate on the Toyota that the owner wouldn't immediately notice the front one was missing. Since it was out-of-state, Kevin guessed it was also less likely to be immediately reported missing.

He headed back to the mall entrance and saw Elen walking toward him. She was talking on her cell phone. As she got close, she winked at him. "*B'seder, toda*," she said into the phone. *Okay, thanks.* She disconnected the call.

"Was that Avi?" Kevin asked.

"No. I talked to a guy he works with, and he put me in touch with a local contact."

"Yeah? So what's the good news?"

Elen was curious about the bulge in Kevin's shirt. "What have you got there?"

"I nabbed a plate from a car that didn't really need it."

Elen smiled and appraised him with an appreciative look. "You're catching on, huh?"

"I was born for this kind of stuff, girl. So what's up?"

"I'll tell you in the car."

"All right."

When they reached the Ford, Kevin swapped plates on the rear. He had the presence of mind to remove the front plate, too, then place both in the trunk—leaving the front plate on would have been a death sentence. Kevin got in the passenger side and Elen started the car. As they left the lot, he put his head in his hands and sighed.

"What are you thinking, Kev?"

"Just praying, that's all. Looking for help."

"Praying, huh, Kev?"

"I don't know what else to do. I know we should stay off the Interstate, that's for sure. It'll be swarming with cops. What did Avi's friend say?"

"Kevin," Elen said. "Remember the safe-house in L.A.?"

"How could I forget?"

"And, remember what I told you about the doctor who stitched you up?"

"Yeah. He was a sayan, right?"

"Right. Well, there's a *shul* on the other side of town—a synagogue. We're going there to meet a man who is connected to a real estate sayan who owns a number of apartments in Terre Haute. He has an empty one—furnished, fortunately—and he's willing to let us stay there for a few days. He won't say anything and he won't ask questions."

"Another safe-house?" Kevin asked, amazed at Elen's connections.

"Exactly."

"How do you do it? In Los Angeles *and* Terre Haute, Indiana? How do you get safe-houses with just a phone call?"

"I couldn't do it without Avi. The people he works with have resources everywhere in the world."

"Unbelievable."

"Believe it."

Twenty minutes later, Elen pulled the car into a parking lot next to the small shul. "Kevin," she said. "I'm going inside to meet the contact. Both he and the sayan think I'm Mossad—it's why the sayan is helping us, but the less everyone knows the better. Do you mind staying in the car while I talk to him?"

"Is that really necessary?"

She asked him a question in Hebrew.

"Huh?"

"Is that what you're going to say when he asks you the same thing?"

"I see your point."

"Sorry," Elen said.

"No problem."

Elen parked the car and got out. She approached the entrance and nodded respectfully to an old, bearded man dressed according to Hasidic custom. He wore a black suit and a black fedora from which silvery *payot*—long, curling locks of hair from each temple—cascaded down both sides of his face. "*Shalom, rebbe*," she said. He nodded but didn't smile. To most Hasidic men, women are considered distractions. *Beautiful* women are even worse distractions—so, the old rabbi's cold reaction didn't surprise her.

As she entered the shul, the lighting inside was dim. Off to her right, two men were talking quietly. They were dressed similarly as the old man, but without fedoras. Instead, they wore yarmulkes—small circular coverings for the tops of their heads. In Hasidic custom, covering the head is a sign of respect for *HaShem*, an obliquely-religious reference to *The Name* of God. The men looked at her, briefly annoyed, then resumed their conversation.

At the far end of the shul, Elen saw the ark, an ornately-carved, floor-to-ceiling wooden cabinet which contained Torah scrolls. Beside the cabinet was a white and blue Israeli flag. Facing the ark were three older men, also dressed in black. They were *davening*—bobbing gently up and down as they recited from the prayer books. There were ten pews between the entrance and the ark, and a thick white linen curtain ran down the middle, separating the men on the left from the women who were completely out of view on the right. Elen knew it would be inappropriate for her to go any further, so she stood at the entrance and waited.

An older man sitting in the last pew turned and saw her, then got up. Another man, a younger one, also stood and put his hand on the older man's shoulder. The older man said something softly, clearly annoyed by the disruption, then sat down and resumed his deliberations. The younger man approached Elen, and said, "*Shalom*. Can I help you?"

"Yes," Elen replied in Hebrew. "I am here to meet someone. Someone who is a helper."

The man nodded, and said in Hebrew, "I am the one you are looking for. My name is Moshe. Please follow me."

Moshe was a handsome man in his early thirties, of average height, but with surprisingly red hair and a wispy red beard. He quietly led Elen down a narrow corridor and into a small office. He closed the door behind her, then opened a small cabinet. "I am a locksmith," he said, still speaking their native tongue. He took a key from the cabinet and handed it to Elen. "Forgive me for saying this, but you are too beautiful to be a spy."

"You are too handsome to be a locksmith," Elen replied.

"Alas, a locksmith I am."

"Alas," Elen said. "We live in a strange world."

Moshe smiled, but quickly sobered. It wouldn't do to get too friendly. "I will get you directions to the apartment." He went to the desk, wrote on a sheet of paper, then gave it to Elen. "How long will you need to stay?"

"Two, maybe three days at the most."

Moshe nodded and turned to leave. "I should return to my prayers," he said.

"*B'seder*," Elen replied. A thought suddenly occurred to her. "Moshe," she said. "Would you be able to help me get a rental car—no paperwork, no questions?"

"I know a man," he replied, nodding. "There is a coffee shop down the street from the apartment. I will ask him to meet you there tomorrow at noon. Perhaps he can help you."

"*Toda*," Elen said. *Thanks.*

Moshe nodded, opened the door for her, then followed her back down the corridor toward the shul's entrance. They parted without saying another word. He returned to the pew where he had been sitting, and Elen quietly exited the building.

Near Barstow, California

JOE KENTON PULLED THE CAR into an empty warehouse parking lot in the middle of the desert. The remote facility was surrounded by low foothills, nestled in a perfect location for clandestine activities. Kenton stopped the Honda next to a large warehouse door and waited for the surveillance camera to pick him up. Moments later, the large, sliding steel door opened.

Kenton pulled the car inside and parked, and the heavily reinforced door slid shut behind them. Biran retrieved his duffel from the back seat and followed Kenton toward a security door. At the door, Kenton placed his hand on a security scanner. The reinforced steel door opened and they walked through. Joe led the way down a brightly lit corridor. At the end, another security door blocked entrance to the rest of the facility. Joe placed his hand on the scanner beside it and the door immediately slid open. Colonel Ambrose was waiting on the other side.

"How are you, Avi?" Ambrose asked.

"Good, Mike. And you?"

"Pretty good. Come on, there's someone I want you to meet."

Ambrose led them down the corridor, turned left, left again, and finally right into a briefing room. An American flag was in one corner of the room. A British flag was in another. To Biran's right, in the center of the room, was a large round table surrounded by ten chairs. Near the ceiling was a sixty-inch HD television, tuned to 24-hour news, with a bank of ten smaller monitors below it. On the wall were large framed photographs of the president of the United States, the prime minister of England, and the current directors of the Central Intelligence Agency and Britain's secret intelligence service, MI6. Biran was puzzled by the appearance of two foreign intelligence agencies sharing a common facility. Because of his connection with Colonel Ambrose, he'd assumed this was an operation of the Defense Intelligence Agency.

"As you're probably wondering, Avi," Ambrose said, "this facility is a joint operation of American and British Intelligence. We go by the designation Unit Ten, but we're not officially connected with either intelligence agency."

"Okay," Biran said. "So, this is a black project?"

"You could say that. So black we're invisible."

"What do you do here?"

"We're an intelligence gathering unit. Our area of operations is primarily North America and Europe."

A new voice joined from the other side of the room: "We want to expand soon, though, to include your area of the woods, Mister Biran."

"Avi," Ambrose said, "this is Colin McGrath. Colin, Avi Biran." They shook hands. "We have a new development regarding your sister. Colin?"

"Thanks, Mike. Mister Biran, we realized yesterday your situation might dovetail precisely with our operations."

"How do you mean?"

"Well, a few days ago we began to strongly suspect the involvement of the *Sonneschwerten* in the kidnapping attempt on your sister."

"The who?" Biran asked.

"Sonneschwerten. Insiders call it the Swords of the Sun. You've never heard of it?"

Biran shook his head.

"Not many have," McGrath said. "Anyway, our suspicions were confirmed when Joe apprehended two men posing as federal agents at Anna Cohen's apartment. Colonel Ambrose noticed one of them had a tattoo on his wrist. This tattoo is an indication of his position and authority within the Sonneschwerten, which, simply put, is the clandestine paramilitary arm of a secret, powerful group some call the Council of Ten. The individual identities of this council are a closely held secret, perhaps known only by the council members themselves.

"However, we suspect they are extremely wealthy individuals ranging from bankers to government officials to prominent businessmen, primarily European and American. They have demonstrated incredible influence in all areas of European and American government. Because of this influence, Sonneschwerten agents are able to operate under various covers, including as agents of CIA, FBI, MI6, FSB, BKA, you name it. They have leverage within the governments of almost every U.N. member-nation."

"How is that possible?" Biran asked.

"Do you want the long version or the short?"

"I suspect we don't have time for either right now," Biran replied. "Taking your word for it—if this group is who you say they are—what do they want? Why are they trying to kidnap my sister?"

"Those are good questions," Ambrose said. "And while we don't yet have a clear indication of their goals, we are confident they are motivated by simple two concepts: Power and Control. On a global scale. Somehow, Elen must be vital for them to either gain power or hold on to it."

Biran studied the photographs on the wall, lost in thought. What were they dealing with? The Swords of the Sun? The United Nations using covert agents to impersonate federal officers? Even *if* that was true, it still didn't make any sense. What were they after? "Maybe they're after me," he suggested.

"Have you been approached?"

"Not yet."

"Avi," Ambrose continued. "Unit Ten is committed to exposing this Council and stopping the Sonneschwerten. We can't allow a small group of wealthy, unelected individuals to dictate the world's political and economic policies—and we don't need a secret paramilitary group enforcing those policies. If the Sonneschwerten are involved, then your goal is our goal. We want to know why they need your sister, and we want to help you stop them."

"And we want you to help us, Mister Biran," McGrath added. "Join us. In no way will your loyalty to Israel be compromised. In fact, you will be in a unique position, capable of having a critical impact on Israel's security."

Biran's brow furrowed as he considered McGrath's offer. He

would be in a unique position to serve Israel. But he was reluctant. It was dangerous to work clandestinely outside of government channels, good cause or not. "I appreciate your position," he said hesitantly, "and for bringing me into your confidence. But, I'm guessing you don't want to reveal this unit's existence to anyone. Correct?"

"For our safety, we must remain secret," McGrath agreed.

Biran nodded. "Well, as interesting as it sounds, honestly I wouldn't be able to keep an operation like this from the Office for long. I could dance around in the shadows for a while, but not the way you would need me to. I know we have a reputation for shooting from the hip, but, believe it or not, I still make contact reports whenever I network with anyone outside of Israel. Even Mike. It's standard procedure."

"Avi," Ambrose said quickly. "You—"

Biran cut him off with a raised hand. "Don't worry about this meeting. I can be creative when I need to be, and I want to help, Mike. I do. But security back home is just too tight. I'm sure you know we're constantly monitored and evaluated, and I'm not willing to risk my career over this. An ongoing shadow operation just isn't possible for me. Not without higher approval. I'm sorry."

McGrath nodded sympathetically, then said, "I appreciate your candor, Avi. I really do—" He paused as he considered how to continue. Recruiting him had been a long shot, but they hadn't lost the game yet. "Listen," he continued, "Israel and the Mossad may be safe from the Sonneschwerten for the time being, but you have to know that if *we* don't stop them, it's just a matter of time before you guys are penetrated, too. If you haven't been already."

In truth, that was something Biran feared. The Institute was an extremely small agency, by its nature an ideal environment for tight security. Since the notoriously ruthless agency fluctuated around only fifty to sixty agent-recruiting officers at any given time—a miniscule number compared to the thousands of case officers at CIA, FSB, and elsewhere—there was simply nowhere for a mole to hide inside the upper echelon of the Mossad. But Biran knew the concept was not without precedent. The KGB had managed to successfully plant informants as low-level staffers in the early nineties, although they were exposed and rooted out before they were able to cause any operational damage. Biran suspected that, ultimately, with the right motivation and resources, anything was possible.

"Look, Avi," Ambrose said. "Don't make a decision right now. What we're doing is extremely vital for American, British, and European interests. Israel is an important ally. You know that, and you could do a lot of good for Israel, Avi, by joining us. I'll just leave it at that. Whatever you decide, I trust you to keep our meeting confidential."

"Of course."

"Okay," Ambrose said. "There's something else maybe you can help us with."

"What's that?"

"Do you know an operative named Rostov?"

"Rostov," Biran repeated softly.

"Jacob Rostov," McGrath clarified.

Biran shook his head. "It doesn't ring a bell."

"Well," Ambrose continued. "We know Rostov was in the *sayeret* special forces before he joined the Mossad. Shortly thereafter, he disappeared—we think, in light of his military specialty, into a *kidon*. He was off our grid until last year, when Sergei Bukharin, the Ukrainian politician with suspected *mafiya* ties, as I'm sure you recall, was assassinated in Odessa. Everything points to Rostov. He must have screwed up, though, because he was dropped from Mossad and kicked out of Israel. Six months ago he resurfaced, doing contract jobs for the Sonneschwerten."

"So he's a contract assassin now?" Biran said. "How do you know so much about him?"

"An impeccable source," McGrath replied carefully. "Anyhow, we suspect he killed Senator Richardson in New York. In Los Angeles, just a few days ago a prominent federal judge was killed by a sniper. Again, everything points to Rostov."

Biran shook his head, suddenly sick to his stomach. "If you've been following him, why haven't you stopped him?"

"We're not ready to intervene yet," McGrath replied.

"But you're certain it's him?"

McGrath simply nodded.

"Anyway," Ambrose continued. "The point I'm getting to is he is an important figure now in their organization. Only in the last few hours we learned that he has a new role and a new identity—Jacob Ross, a colonel assigned to the U.N. Office of Special Services."

"The United Nations?" Biran said, puzzled. But just as quickly, the Rostov connection suddenly made sense. Who better to approach and kill Ben-Yakov than one of Israel's own? With cover from the United Nations, able to discreetly travel anywhere in the world and speak Hebrew fluently, Rostov could easily get inside the prime minister's inner circle. "Why do they want to kill him?" Biran wondered.

"Sorry?" Ambrose said. "Kill whom?"

Reluctantly, Biran finally admitted the true nature of his concern: "They want to kill Ben-Yakov."

"Who wants to kill him?" McGrath asked, suddenly wary.

"Rostov. Ross. The Sonneschwerten."

Ambrose replied, "How do you know they want to kill Ben-Yakov?"

"Because he's on the assassination list."

"What list?" McGrath asked.

"I discovered it in Europe," Biran replied carefully. "From a source in Germany. Some are quite prominent figures. Already Rostov has killed Richardson and Henning, if your source is correct. Prime Minister Ben-Yakov is also on the list."

"Why kill him?" McGrath asked, still puzzled as he looked at Ambrose. "Bloody Hell! Are they making a move?"

Biran stood abruptly, clenched his fist, and said, "I want to know why they're after my father, my sister, and why they want to assassinate the prime minister." He paused, looked at McGrath, and said, "Where are the men you captured?"

"Downstairs."

"Together?"

"Separate cells."

"Have you spoken to them?"

"Nothing substantial."

"Okay," Biran said. "Can you put them in a room together?"

"Of course."

McGrath looked at Kenton. Joe nodded and left the room.

Biran looked at Ambrose, and said, "Mike, this is more serious than I thought. I need answers."

Ambrose nodded his agreement.

"I'll need a pistol," Biran continued. "Preferably silenced."

McGrath walked to a steel panel in the wall and punched a security code into a keypad beside the panel. The panel slid back to reveal a shelf of six automatic pistols, silencers, and two spare magazines for each. Hanging from straps on a shelf beneath were four Heckler & Koch MP5 submachine guns. McGrath handed a Glock-17 to Biran, then closed the panel.

THE ROOM WAS A SOUNDPROOFED twelve-by-twelve holding cell with a small Plexiglas viewing port in the door. Ambrose entered first, followed by Biran. Stevens and Harkins were sitting in ordinary metal folding chairs facing the door, their hands and legs restrained with cuffs. As Biran studied the prisoners, his face was stone cold. He hated what he was about to do, but he saw no other option. Though his face was impassive, inside he was furious. The prime minister of Israel was the *leader* of his country, a symbol of stability—and Biran genuinely respected the man. At forty-six, Natan Ben-Yakov was the youngest head of state in Israel's recent troubled existence. A dominant and charismatic leader, Ben-Yakov was a voice of reason and strength in a country besieged, literally, on all sides. Biran was proud of Ben-Yakov and was incensed that these men belonged to an organization that planned to kill him. He would never forget the assassination of Prime Minister Rabin, and there was no way he was going to allow it to happen again.

Ambrose said, "This man is from Israeli Intelligence. And, he isn't happy." He stepped back, allowing Biran to take the center of the room.

Biran remained silent as he studied the prisoners. The rage was still there. But it was under control. The Glock was hidden behind his back. He turned to Ambrose and whispered, "This may be unsettling, Mike."

"Whatever you have to do."

Biran turned back and glared at Stevens. He was the man with the tattoo, and thus the answers. The trick was to convince him to give them up. To get the information quickly, he had to stun him with something totally unexpected and ruthless. It was the only way. "This isn't a game," he said coldly. "I need truthful answers, and I expect to get them."

Harkins glared at him. Stevens looked at the floor. Biran studied them in silence. In Harkins he could see defiance and the reflexive instincts of a surly dog. He was expendable. Biran raised the Glock with one hand and squeezed the trigger. Harkins' head suddenly lurched backwards, snapping forward a second later. Stevens looked behind him, saw the huge splatter of blood and brain tissue on the wall, and immediately felt sick. Off to the side, Kenton clenched his teeth and looked away.

Biran studied Stevens intently. "You strike me as an intelligent man." There was cold determination in his voice as he inclined his head toward Harkins' body. "That was for Rabin. I will not allow the same thing to happen to Ben-Yakov. Do you understand me?"

"Whoa! Hey, man," Stevens said. He attempted to smile. "Be cool. I'll tell you anything you want to know."

"I'm not going to kill you," Biran said softly, shaking his head. "But for every wrong answer, I'm going to cut off one of your fingers. Then I'm going to cut off your toes." Biran handed the pistol to Ambrose, then said to Kenton, "May I borrow your knife?"

Kenton breathed deeply, unsheathed the standard-issue K-bar and handed it to Avi. As Biran took it, Stevens saw the blade was sharpened to a razor's edge, requiring little imagination that it would cause some serious damage. "Man, that's not necessary," he objected quickly. "I already told you I'll tell you everything. I swear!"

Biran grabbed Steven's right hand tightly and put the blade between Stevens' first two fingers. Blood started dripping from the knife. Stevens clenched his teeth and looked at Biran's face, steeling himself to lose the finger.

Quietly, Biran said, "What do you know about the plan to assassinate Ben-Yakov?"

Stevens' eyes grew large. "What? What are you talking about?!"

"Don't lie to me!" Biran squeezed the hand tighter.

"Ben-Yakov?! I don't know anything, man! I don't know! I swear I don't know!"

Puzzled, Biran looked at Ambrose, who was watching him with a dumbfounded expression. Biran returned his attention to Stevens, and said, "What's your name?"

"Dan. Dan Stevens."

"Why did you try to kill Elen Biran?"

"We didn't try to *kill* her," he said quickly. "We were assigned to pick her up. That's all. Things got out of control."

"Why her?"

"I was just told to pick her up."

"You don't know why?"

Stevens shook his head adamantly and replied, "I swear."

"Who gave you the assignment?"

"My boss."

Biran pressed the knife a little deeper.

Stevens grunted through clenched teeth, then said, "Ferguson. Ian Ferguson."

"Who's he?"

"Chief of security."

"For the Sonneschwerten?" Biran asked softly.

Stevens hesitated, then nodded, still clenching his teeth.

"And you don't know why Ian Ferguson is interested in her?"

"Maybe for leverage, I guess."

"Against whom?"

"I don't know, man. I'm telling you the truth. Ferguson tells me what to do and I do it. He never tells us why."

Biran's face darkened as he reflected on Stevens' answers. He had described a thoroughly compartmentalized operation, handled at the top with professional expertise, if somewhat inept further down the line. Whatever the ultimate objective was, Stevens couldn't tell him, and chopping his fingers off—a bluff, at best—would accomplish nothing.

Sensing time running out, Stevens glanced around nervously, then said with quiet conviction, "Man, I really don't know. I swear. Just kill me quickly."

"Ready to die so soon?" Biran asked.

Stevens grunted bitterly. "No matter what happens here, I'm dead."

"Why do you say that?"

"How does this look? I lost two men in Long Beach. One more here. Whether you do it or they do it, I'm a dead man."

Biran nodded his head as he considered Stevens' predicament. He pulled the knife away and handed it to Kenton, who wiped it down quickly and replaced it on his belt. "Maybe not," Biran said as he withdrew a pack of cigarettes. "Smoke?"

"Why not," Stevens replied sullenly.

Biran placed a cigarette between Stevens' lips and lit it. Stevens puffed a couple of times and nodded his head in appreciation.

"Mister Stevens, I'll make you a deal. I can see my quarrel isn't with you. You're just trying to do your job."

Stevens nodded behind a growing cloud of gray smoke.

"If you tell us everything you know—everything—and you help me figure out what Ian Ferguson is up to, I'll let you live. And, I'll let you go. You can disappear. Anywhere you want."

Stevens glanced around the room warily, surprised yet hopeful, and said, "C'mon, man. I'll tell you everything I know. *Everything*. Hell, yeah."

Chapter 14

Terre Haute, Indiana
Next Day

OFFICER HANK WITKOWSKI OF THE Terre Haute Police Department stopped his police cruiser behind a Ford Fusion on Poplar Avenue. He noted the license plate number and checked his MDT, or Mobile Data Terminal, for proper registration. Everything checked out. He shifted into drive and pulled away. It was a tedious process, but one he realized was necessary. The Terre Haute Police Department was doing the FBI an enormous favor, he reflected, by sending him out to check for a car that probably wasn't even in town anymore. Though he had been instructed to look for a specific California tag, he decided to run local tags just to keep the boredom at bay. He continued down the street, keeping a sharp eye out for any more Fords he might need to check.

KEVIN LOOKED AT HIS WATCH and frowned. It was ten minutes past twelve. "What time was he supposed to meet us?"

"Noon," Elen said. "Maybe that means noon-*ish*. Probably just running behind."

They were sitting inside the car, engine running, waiting in the coffee shop parking lot just down the street from the safe-house.

"Kevin?"

"Yeah?"

"I need to go back to the apartment for a second."

"Why?"

"I forgot something."

"Okay," he replied. "I'll wait here in case he shows up." Kevin got out of the car and watched her drive out of the lot. He felt a sudden sense of loss. It was silly, he realized. In her presence, he felt somehow complete. When she was gone, even for a moment, he felt a gnawing discomfort in his chest. He chuckled softly at the thought, amused by the effect Elen had on him. He went over to a table, sat down, and suddenly became aware of the symphony of Nature surrounding him: the incessant, playful chattering of nearby sparrows; the non-stop, annoying mantra of a lone mockingbird; the soft, delicate cooing of doves in the trees above.

He glanced to his left and saw a police cruiser approaching. As the car pulled even with Kevin, the officer driving the vehicle looked in his direction and nodded. Though it felt awkward, Kevin nodded back and hoped he didn't appear nervous. The cruiser soon passed and progressed down the street toward—

Toward the car, Kevin suddenly realized. *And Elen.*

Kevin walked to the street to get a better view. In any other circumstance, the officer might have appeared to be making an obligatory round of the neighborhood. When the cruiser stopped behind the Ford, Kevin's heart sank.

OFFICER WITKOWSKI NOTED THE LICENSE PLATE on what he figured was his twentieth stop of the day, oddly comforted by the knowledge that a lot of his police work was dull and routine. It was an Illinois plate and not likely to be a hit. He keyed IL into the registration screen on the MDT, then the license plate number. Seconds later the response came back. It was registered properly. He scanned the rest of the screen quickly, and was about to move on when something caught his eye.

The car *was* registered—but it wasn't a 1994 Toyota Camry. He double-checked to make sure he'd entered the plate correctly. Suddenly his skin tingled with an exhilarating sense of discovery as he shifted into park and got out of the vehicle. He approached the Ford and keyed the radio mic attached to his lapel. "Control, George-

Ten," he said, giving his location. "I've found a possible match on that vehicle the feds are looking for. Possibly a stolen plate. Request cover."

"*George-Ten, copy. George-Seven?*"

"*Enroute.*"

ELEN STEPPED ONTO THE FRONT PORCH and shut the door just as her phone rang. She finished locking the deadbolt, then fumbled with her waist pack for the phone. She got it out and said, "Yes?"

"Don't leave the apartment," Kevin said quickly. "There's a police officer outside."

"Too late," Elen replied. "I just stepped out."

"Damn."

"What should I do?"

"Stay on the phone and just walk over here. He's probably checking the registration right now. Hopefully he won't notice you."

"Okay," she said. She turned around and stepped toward the sidewalk, making sure not to look in the officer's direction. As she walked away, her peripheral vision confirmed an unfortunate reality. "I think he's looking at me."

"Ma'am?"

Elen ignored the officer. "Dammit," she whispered into the phone. "What do I do now?"

"Just keep coming," Kevin replied.

"Ma'am!" the officer repeated. "May I speak with you, please?"

She knew she couldn't ignore him a second time. She feigned surprise as she glanced back at the officer. "I'm sorry, are you talking to me?"

"Yes!" Witkowski said. "Do you own this vehicle?"

"No." Elen continued down the sidewalk.

"Ma'am. Would you please come here?" It wasn't a question.

Elen stopped, stunned by the turn of events. She could run, but realized he would undoubtedly catch her. She could try to talk her way out but knew once she started cooperating they wouldn't let her go. She had a gun, but she discarded the idea as quickly as it came.

She wasn't a criminal and couldn't bring herself to shoot an innocent police officer, even if it meant her own capture.

"Should I run?" she asked quietly.

There was no response for several tense moments. "Can you talk your way out of it?" Kevin said.

"I don't think so."

"Then run, Elen. I'm coming."

"No," she insisted. "You stay away. Get out of here while you can and get in touch with Avi. That's our only hope now."

"But—"

"*Now, dammit!* Just go."

"Ma'am?"

Elen disconnected the call, turned the phone off and finally turned around. "Sorry, officer," she said. "Can I help you?"

Officer Witkowski had his right hand on the butt of his holstered Sig Sauer automatic. He was fairly certain he'd caught one of the FBI fugitives, but the unexpectedness of the encounter left him a little indecisive. Time seemed to slow as he inwardly debated on the best way to come out of this encounter alive. "What's your name, ma'am?" he asked gently. "Do you have ID?"

"Is there a problem, sir?" Elen replied, not wanting to give anything away.

Witkowski drew his weapon and pointed it at Elen. "Ma'am, keep your hands away from your sides. Show me your hands." He keyed his radio mic. "George-Ten. Possible match."

"*George-Ten, copy. George-Seven?*"

"*Almost there.*"

As he listened to the radio traffic, an uncomfortable realization hit him. "Where's your partner?" he said, looking around.

"I don't know what you're talking about. Am I under arrest?"

"Step over here. Show me your hands."

Elen was frozen in place.

"Erika Johnson?" Witkowski asked. "Elen Biran?" She flinched at the second name. "Is he inside the house?"

Elen stared blankly at him, then said, "No."

Witkowski took her reticence as a lie. He needed to secure her first, then wait for backup before approaching the house. "Ma'am, step over here."

The radio crackled: "*George-Seven, ten-ninety-seven.*"

Witkowski's partner had finally arrived. His car screeched to a halt behind Witkowski's cruiser. He got out quickly with his gun up.

KEVIN TOOK ONE LAST LOOK at Elen before heading in the opposite direction. His heart felt as if it had been ripped from his chest. Through a foggy haze of shock, disbelief, and indecision, he managed to walk away. With every step, though, the agony of separation tore his soul deeper and deeper. As he turned the corner he started to run.

ROSTOV INTERCEPTED THE RADIO TRANSMISSIONS on a scanner inside the Ford Expedition. He was buckled into the seat directly behind the driver, with Griffin beside him. The driver was part of the logistical element that preceded Rostov and Griffin to Indiana. Rostov couldn't help but be impressed with the level of professionalism and logistical precision GlobalComm wielded. The Gulfstream, another aspect of that logistical proficiency, was a beautiful aircraft. It had handled the trip from New York with ease.

They had arrived at the Terre Haute Airport earlier that morning. The Expedition met them and ferried them to a temporary headquarters. From there, it was a relatively simple operation to intercept the steady stream of communications between the FBI and the local police officers tasked with locating Biran and Edwards. After learning of the failed FBI operation at the Marriott, Rostov decided not to approach Agent Maurer directly. Instead, he opted to wait for the fugitives to surface.

"ETA?" he asked the driver.

The driver studied the Global Positioning System computerized map display on the dashboard. "Almost there, sir."

"Excellent," Rostov said, turning to face Griffin. "Let's get ready to move."

"Aye, aye," Griffin replied, withdrawing his side arm.

Rostov touched his arm and said, "Simply a deterrent."

"Understood, sir. We want her alive and unharmed."

"Correct. She's going to be on edge so I'm going to ease her inside. I want to keep her off-balance long enough to get her on the plane, and I want her walking all the way."

Fifteen seconds later, the driver executed a high speed turn, maintained complete control of the vehicle, and accelerated toward the police cruisers down the street. The Expedition came to a hard stop beside the second cruiser. Rostov got out, walked over to Officer Witkowski and studied his prisoner. Dressed in a sharply pressed business suit, Rostov was the epitome of FBI professionalism. "Agent Ross," he said, flashing his badge. "Excellent work"—he hesitated as he read the nametag—"Officer Witkowski."

"Thank you," Witkowski replied.

"Any sign of her partner?"

"No."

Rostov nodded. "We need to get her out of here immediately." He approached Elen, took her arm and said, "Come with me, ma'am."

"I can't let you take her," Witkowski said.

Rostov shook his head, clearly indicating he would brook no interference. He saw Elen's hands in cuffs behind her back. He asked Witkowski to remove them.

"I can't do—" Witkowski protested.

"Now," Rostov said. "I'm in a hurry. This is a national security emergency."

Witkowski removed the cuffs.

"Thank you, officer," Rostov said as he escorted Elen to the rear of the Expedition. Griffin opened the door for him, then made his way around to the other side, getting in just as Elen sat in the center seat. Rostov sat down beside her. The doors slammed shut and the driver pulled away.

"What's going on here?" Elen said.

Without replying, Rostov put his own cuffs on her and let her hands rest in her lap. He removed her waist pack and tossed it to

Griffin. Finally, he extended her seat belt and buckled her in.

"Who are you?"

"FBI, ma'am," Rostov explained. "I'm sorry about the cuffs, but they're standard procedure." He leaned closer and softly added, "And I have to keep up appearances, even though I know you're not a terrorist and this whole charade is crap." He paused for effect. "Don't worry. I'll get everything straightened out and you'll be free to go."

"Why the handcuffs?"

Rostov nodded his head, sighed sympathetically, and said, "I know, I know. This whole thing is confusing." He attempted a reassuring smile, and added, "The cuffs are standard procedure. We'll get to the bottom of this, ma'am. I assure you. And believe me, I'm truly sorry for the inconvenience."

BRYCE MAURER PULLED HIS CAR BEHIND the second police cruiser. He was followed by three other FBI sedans. He got out quickly and approached the scene with his gun drawn. Witkowski and his partner were kneeling behind the engine block of Witkowski's cruiser. They both had AR-15 rifles pointed at the house.

"Officer Witkowski?"

"Yes?"

"I'm Special Agent Maurer. Did you report contact with our fugitive?"

"Yes."

Maurer's eyes narrowed as he looked around. "Where is she?"

"You guys already picked her up," Witkowski replied.

"What? *Who* picked her up?"

"Two agents in a Ford Expedition. Agent Ross and—" He paused. "Actually, I didn't catch his partner's name."

"They had badges?"

"Yep. I wouldn't have let her go otherwise."

"There is no Agent Ross in my detail, Officer Witkowski."

"What? Then who—"

Maurer threw his notepad to the ground in disgust. "What the *Hell* is going on here?!"

"Sir?"

"Did you get a license plate on the Expedition?"

"No."

"Would you please advise your dispatcher to put out an APB?"

Witkowski nodded slowly as the realization of what happened finally dawned on him.

†   †   †

"ALL UNITS ARE ADVISED TO BE on the lookout for a late-model, black Ford Expedition heading east, containing two male suspects wanted in connection with a federal felony investigation. One suspect is white, approximately six feet tall, wearing a black suit, short blond hair, using the name Special Agent Ross, age approximately thirty-five. Second suspect is African-American, approximately six-feet five inches tall, wearing a black suit, bald, with a muscular build, age approximately thirty-five. If seen, approach with caution. Suspects are armed and—"

Rostov signaled for the driver to turn the volume down on the scanner. "We need to switch vehicles."

"I'll call ahead."

Rostov leaned back in his seat, smiled reassuringly at Elen, and said, "Just relax. Everything's under control."

While the Expedition blazed a path through the residential neighborhood, Elen braced herself between Griffin and Rostov. Two minutes after picking her up, the Expedition pulled into an unattended parking structure and came to a screeching halt. Rostov unbuckled himself, then Elen, and helped her out of the vehicle. Inside the parking structure, a large Mercedes sedan was waiting. Rostov helped Elen inside and sat beside her in the back seat. The Mercedes exited the parking structure heading for the freeway.

They made it to Interstate 70 quickly. As they drove toward the airport, Rostov saw an Indiana State trooper blow past them on the left, then flash its lights at a black Ford Expedition several cars ahead.

The Expedition quickly changed lanes toward the side of the road, followed closely by the cruiser. Rostov smiled to himself as the Mercedes passed by.

"Who are you?" Elen asked softly.

"Agent Ross, ma'am."

"How come you're evading the police?"

"Simplicity," he replied. "You're a special lady, and we don't want too many people around to muck up our investigation." He smiled reassuringly, and added, "Believe it or not, this kind of thing happens all the time."

She looked away, and muttered, "Sure. Just not to me." Though his explanation pushed the boundaries of believability, Elen saw no point in antagonizing him with more questions.

Ten minutes later, they arrived at the airport. The driver passed through security, eased his way onto the tarmac and stopped in front of the waiting Gulfstream. Rostov ushered Elen inside and showed her to a seat. Through a small window, Elen saw the Mercedes drive away. Griffin closed the hatch and sat down in a rear-facing seat. Rostov sat down behind her, pressed the intercom to the flight deck, and said, "Let's move out."

With their U.N. clearance, the Gulfstream was third in line for takeoff. The pilot taxied along the tarmac and reached takeoff position a minute later. After receiving final clearance from the tower, the pilot eased the throttles forward and the jet accelerated smoothly down the runway. As the wheels lifted from the ground, Elen stared numbly out the window, wondering if not running away from the police officer was the worst mistake she had ever made.

Unit Ten Headquarters

BIRAN STEPPED INTO THE HALLWAY with Ambrose and said, "We can't let him out of our hands yet."

"I agree. He knows faces and he knows the layout."

"How far are you willing to go with this, Mike?"

"All the way."

"Good. I need to call Elen. Do you have a secure phone?"

Ambrose led him down several corridors to the communications room. Biran lifted the handset on a secure phone, fished out the card with Elen's mobile phone number, and dialed. It rang once and then he was greeted by a recorded message that said her voicemail had not been setup and could not receive messages. He waited a minute, re-dialed, and got the same response. "That's odd. She's supposed to have the phone on in case I need to reach her."

"Problem?" Ambrose asked.

"I don't know. Her phone seems to be turned off." Biran looked at the card, then dialed the second number.

Terre Haute, Indiana

KEVIN MANAGED TO ELUDE THE FBI and police vehicles searching for him. He lucked by a taxi just around the corner, got in immediately, and told the driver he wanted to see the city. The driver was happy to point out what might have been, in other circumstances, interesting landmarks. Kevin was oblivious. Slumped in the seat, he stared va-cantly out the window. He noticed a sign for a military surplus store ahead. "Slow down," he said.

"What?"

"That surplus store. Stop there. I need to go inside for a minute." The driver pulled to the curb, Kevin got out and said, "Wait here. I'll be back in ten minutes."

"I've seen this before, son. You give me cash, and I'll wait."

Kevin handed the driver a twenty. "Ten minutes. No, better make it fifteen." He handed the driver another twenty.

"That's plenty."

Kevin stepped inside the store and his cell phone rang. He opened it quickly and said, "Yes?"

"Kevin?"

"Who is this?"

Silence. Then, "Is everything okay?"

It was Kevin's turn to be silent. They had Elen's phone. Was it the FBI calling? The police?

"Kevin? It's Avi. Is Elen there?"

"Thank God it's you," Kevin said. "Things have turned bad so fast my head is swimming." He found a quiet corner of the store. "They've taken Elen. We got separated and she told me to get away and contact you."

"Damn. Where are you?"

"Terre Haute, Indiana."

"Did the FBI take her?"

"No, it was the police. Maybe the FBI was nearby, I don't know. By now, probably, yes."

"What?"

Kevin noticed two customers looking at him. "Look," he said. "I'm not in the clear yet. Can I call you back in fifteen minutes?"

There was no response for a few seconds. Then Biran said, "Kevin? I'll call you back. Fifteen minutes?"

"Okay." Kevin disconnected the call.

A store clerk approached and said, "Can I help you?"

"Yeah. I'd like to get some woodland BDUs."

"Over here."

Kevin followed the clerk to the clothing section and selected trousers, a jacket, an undershirt, a web belt, hat, socks, underwear, and side-zippered boots. He added a set of electric hair clippers to an olive-drab duffel bag, and said, "Thanks. Do I check out over there?"

"Sure. Whenever you're ready."

Kevin walked to the register. On the wall behind the counter he saw a cabinet filled with unit patches and insignia pins. "Could you give me that unit patch, corporal's pins and that name patch?"

The clerk retrieved the items and set them on the counter.

"And a sewing kit," Kevin added. He paid cash, put everything inside the bag, and left the store. Outside, the cab was still there. "Where to?" the cabbie asked.

"Just take me to a cheap motel."

BRYCE MAURER WAS BRISTLING as he stormed into the Terre Haute police station. Forewarned, Lieutenant Mitchell Harris met him at the entrance, expecting a numbing verbal tirade. As pissed as he was,

Maurer was professional enough not to focus his indignation on the wrong party. "Lieutenant," he said quietly.

"Agent Maurer," Harris replied. "I'm sorry about the mix-up."

"Not your fault," Maurer said between clenched teeth. "This investigation has reeked from the beginning."

"Excuse me?"

"Nothing," he muttered. "Any sign of the Expedition?"

"No."

"Any sign of Edwards?"

"Nothing."

"Okay. Thanks, lieutenant. Let me know if anything develops."

"Of course."

Maurer turned and exited the building. Outside, he withdrew his phone and dialed.

"Assistant Director Smith's office," the secretary answered.

"This is Agent Maurer. Is the assistant director in?"

"One moment please—"

Maurer waited.

"Agent Maurer," Smith finally said. "I was just going to call you."

"Oh?"

"I just got off the phone with the director. Your investigation has been closed."

"What? Just like that? Do you know what just happened here? Twice within the last twenty-four hours I was minutes away from catching Biran and Edwards. At the Holiday Inn yesterday we were just unlucky. But—"

"Agent Maurer?" Smith interrupted. "I don't have time right now. Pack up your gear and get your men together. You can give me your report when you get back."

Maurer was speechless. "But—"

"The subject is closed, Agent Maurer. I appreciate your efforts."

Reluctantly, Maurer swallowed his frustration and said, "Yes sir."

KEVIN APPROACHED THE MOTEL counter cautiously. A disheveled woman stood up from her post in front of an old television and said, "Can I help you?"

Kevin placed five twenty-dollar bills on the counter. "I need a room."

"Sure," the woman replied, eyeing the cash. "Just you?"

Kevin nodded.

She took the cash and pointed to the guest book. "Sign in here."

Kevin hoped with cash on the line she wouldn't ask for ID. He signed the first name that popped into his mind.

The woman gave him a key, and said, "Room ten. In the back."

Kevin hefted his bag and left the office. The room was completely hidden from the street. He unlocked the door and stepped inside. Just then, his phone rang. He set the bag on the bed, flipped open the phone, and said, "Hello?"

"Are you clear?"

"Yeah. I just got a cheap motel room."

"Good," Biran replied. "Now, what's going on?"

"Elen was picked up by the police. It was just bad luck." He closed his eyes and explained what had happened.

"Damn," Biran muttered.

"What are we going to do?"

"What do you have with you?"

"Four grand, a Walther three-eighty, and some camouflage BDUs I just bought."

"Oh? You have an entire uniform?"

"I'm gonna buzz my hair in just a minute."

"Good thinking, Kevin. Can you lay low for a while?"

"Sure."

"Good. Listen, we're going to fly out there and pick you up. I'll call you as soon as we arrive."

"When are you coming?"

"Sometime in the next five hours."

"That fast? Great."

"Keep your head down."

"Yeah." Kevin disconnected the call and fell back on the bed, suddenly spent.

Chapter 15

U.S. Consulate, Munich

MIKE RUSSELL WAS STARING AT A large computer monitor, engrossed in research. Just as Neumann had predicted, everything regarding the assassination list had been appropriated by the CIA station chief. He was directed to stay away from any further contact. Even the Israeli told him to drop it, for his own good. But he couldn't.

He typed *Charles Richardson* into the Internet search engine and scrolled through the hits. He read article after article. Nothing shed any light. He clicked one more article, scanned the text, and stopped. The article was written by a watchdog organization. It contained a list of attendees to the annual, secret meeting of the Bilderberg group that had occurred the previous year in Zurich. Russell scanned the long list of prominent attendees, and saw the name *Gordon Henning*. He highlighted all the names, copied the contents, and pasted the list into a new document. While he waited for the printer, he took his cell phone and dialed.

"*Ici Bernard*," the voice answered.

"*Bonjour, Bernard*. Mike Russell."

"*Oui*, Monsieur Russell. What can I do for you?"

"Would you please have Alan call me? It's urgent."

"*Mais bien sûr*."

"*Merci*."

Russell retrieved the printout and placed it on the desk beside the monitor. He continued to search online for information. Nothing interesting. Two minutes later, his phone chirped. He opened it and said, "Russell."

"You asked me to call?"

"Alan, I have some interesting news."

"Oh?"

"Are you familiar with the Bilderberg group?"

"I've heard of them," Biran replied.

"Richardson and Henning were members. Does that make any sense to you?"

"How do you know they were members?"

"Someone infiltrated their meeting last year and published the list of attendees on the Internet. Alan, why would two members of this group be assassinated?"

"Mike, have you heard of the Sonneschwerten?"

"The what?"

"Look, Mike. You don't want to know. You'll be in danger."

"How so?"

"Trust me. It's in your best interest to drop this. Erase everything that connects you to this. Everything."

"I can't just—"

"Mike?" Biran interrupted. "It isn't worth dying for."

That stopped Russell cold.

"You don't want to know," Biran repeated.

"Okay. I'll drop it. Some day, though, let me know what this was all about?"

"Maybe," Biran replied. "One more thing."

"Yes?"

"Where did you get the original list?"

Russell hesitated, then said, "Lieutenant Erich Neumann. Bundeskriminalamt. Don't let it come back to me."

Russell disconnected the call, sat down at the computer and deleted everything he could think of. Satisfied his tracks were covered, he stared at the printout beside the monitor. After a moment of indecision, he stuffed the printout in his jacket, shut off the monitor, and left the room.

† † †

Unit Ten Headquarters

"HENNING AND RICHARDSON WERE Bilderbergs," Biran said.

"What's that?" Kenton asked.

McGrath said, "The Bilderbergs are a group of the most influential men and women in the world. About two to three hundred members, they meet once a year in secret to discuss international relations and global politics. Membership is by invitation only, and the content of their discussions is guarded more closely than our nuclear arsenal."

"Why would the Sonneschwerten assassinate two Bilderbergs?"

"It doesn't make sense," McGrath replied. "If the rumors are true, they are staunchly in support of unifying Europe and the U.S. under a world government. I would have guessed they were allied with the Council of Ten, not enemies."

"Two separate groups that want the same thing?" Kenton suggested. "Maybe some conspiracy-minded folks are expressing their disapproval."

"We know who is behind the assassinations," McGrath said. "Rostov. The real question is: Why did Rostov eliminate them? Could it be an internal power struggle?"

"Possibly," Ambrose allowed distantly.

Biran cleared his throat and said, "We're missing something here. The commonality between the Bilderbergs and the Council of Ten is the United Nations, right? The Bilderbergs support the U.N. and shape international policy. For all we know, the Council could be secretly running the U.N."

"Perhaps a small group is hiding within the larger one," Ambrose said.

"You mean a secret group within the Bilderbergs?" Kenton asked.

"The large group would be an excellent source of expertise and information."

"Not to mention cover and deniability," Biran added.

After a brief silence, Kenton cleared his throat. "Well, to me, it sounds like they're cleaning house."

"That's as good a guess as any," Ambrose said. "Unfortunately, we have no way to verify it."

"In any case," McGrath said. "The answers lie with the Sonne-schwerten, and with GlobalComm. If we can crack those two, we can get answers to the rest."

All nodded concurrence.

Terre Haute, Indiana

KEVIN WAS WALKING ALONG THE BANK *of a huge river with Elen at his side. She smiled at him as they strolled along the river-bank. The smile faded, though, as a gray mist seeped closer and quickly enveloped them. Before Kevin realized what was happening, Elen disappeared. He reached out for her, but his hands closed on cold, damp fog. He tried to call her name but no sound would come out.*

Just as quickly as the fog came, it left. Elen was nowhere to be seen. Deeply disturbed, Kevin searched for her desperately. Finally, he caught a glimpse. On the opposite bank, Elen stood looking in his direction. He tried to wave, but his arms wouldn't cooperate. He tried to yell, but no sound emerged. He looked around, hoping to spot a raft or something else he could use to cross the river. As he searched, he noticed for the first time that the water was rushing feverishly past him. Without a raft, he knew the river was uncrossable. And, much to his dismay, there was no raft in sight. Feeling helpless, he looked back at Elen.

There was a man beside her now, a giant—perhaps as much as eight feet tall. He was wearing the uniform of an ancient Roman centurion. A golden helmet protected his head, a large silver breastplate covered his massive chest, and a long skirt of leather and bronze girded his waist. The fearsome centurion began to guide Elen away. She obeyed his commands as if she was in the twilight of a deep, narcotic sleep. Kevin tried to yell again, but nothing came out. Without thinking, he dove head-first into the rain-swollen river.

The current was too strong. He tried to swim, but nothing worked. He slipped beneath the surface. As the realization of his own impending death dawned on him, he struggled desperately to breathe—

Kevin awoke, choking and gasping for air. The dream was so vivid, so palpable. Shivering from a draft, he turned his head and saw the door standing open. The wind must have blown it open. He looked around the room with concern. Had he been discovered during his slumber? Nothing had changed. Outside, massive storm clouds had moved in, creating a prematurely dark sky. He closed the door and turned the deadbolt.

Finally catching his breath, he opened the duffel and dumped the contents on the bed. He took the hair clippers into the bathroom and buzzed the hair off the sides and back of his head. He used a longer blade attachment for the top. When he finished, he rubbed his scalp and wondered what Elen's response would be when she saw him. If she saw him. He studied his appearance in the mirror. He'd never served in the military but he was reasonably confident he could pass as a Marine. He was in good shape. He'd learned some military discipline as a kid, so it wasn't much of a stretch. All he had to do was add the uniform to the haircut, and the disguise would be perfect.

He cleaned the bathroom, deposited the trimmed hair into a small trash bag, and washed the remaining residue down the drain. He showered and shaved, sewed the patches on the uniform jacket, then got dressed. As he studied his completed disguise in the mirror, he slipped into a new identity, confident he was unrecognizable as his former self.

Warrensburg, New York

THE GULFSTREAM LANDED SMOOTHLY on GlobalComm's private tarmac. After taxiing to a stop, Rostov ushered Elen out of the plane and into a waiting Expedition. Griffin got in and the threesome were whisked to GlobalComm headquarters.

The driver parked at the rear of the parking structure. Rostov helped Elen out of the vehicle, guided her toward the elevator, and pressed the call button. As they waited, Rostov removed her handcuffs. Elen looked surprised. "Out of respect, ma'am," Rostov said. "Please don't make me regret my decision."

Elen nodded, rubbed her wrists, and muttered something akin to appreciation as the elevator doors opened. Griffin entered first. Rostov motioned for Elen to follow. Once inside, Rostov pressed the tenth-floor button and waited for the short trip to the top. The doors opened and Griffin stepped out. Rostov led the way to the security door and pressed his hand against the scanner. The door hissed open and Rostov ushered Elen inside.

"Colonel Ross! You amaze me! Congratulations!"

Elen turned to see Ian Ferguson approaching.

"Thank you, sir," Rostov replied.

"Mister Wellesley will be very pleased when he arrives," Ferguson continued.

"He's not here?"

"He's in London. But he should be back sometime tomorrow evening." He turned to face Elen. "My name is Ian Ferguson, ma'am. I'm very pleased to meet you."

Elen's eyes narrowed as she studied him.

Ferguson smiled at her and said, "Jacob, would you please escort her to the Green Room?"

"Of course. This way, ma'am."

THE ROOM WAS WELL-APPOINTED, though nothing in it was green. A large television sat in one corner, a broad, full-length vanity mirror filled the wall to the left, a sturdy oak dresser was straight ahead, and a bathroom was to the right. Rostov steered Elen into the room and said, "If you get hungry, just pick up the phone. You won't be able to dial out, of course. The room is monitored by video. Out of respect for your privacy, the bathroom is not. Please do not abuse this privilege."

Elen sighed in resignation. Whatever else was happening, she realized it could be a lot worse. Taking her situation with as much grace as she could, she said, "Thank you."

Rostov was curious what Ferguson and Wellesley had in mind for her, but there was no way he was going to ask. He nodded once to her, then left the room. Elen examined the door after it closed. There was no handle. She pushed on it but it didn't budge. It was a nice room, but it was a cell.

Exhausted, she lay down on the bed and closed her eyes.

GRIFFIN DROVE ROSTOV BACK to the airstrip. The Gulfstream was waiting on the tarmac. Rostov got out, grabbed his bag, and walked towards the plane. Griffin walked with him.

"I'll be back in a couple days!" Rostov yelled against the roar of the jet's engines.

"Yes, sir!" Griffin yelled back. "Have a good trip!"

Rostov boarded the Gulfstream and closed the hatch behind him. Griffin stepped away from the plane and watched while the pilot taxied to the runway. The jet screamed down the tarmac and rocketed effortlessly into the late afternoon sky. With the roar of the engines fading in the distance, Griffin withdrew a cell phone and stepped away from the Expedition.

"Yes?" a voice answered moments later.

"Yo, dog," Griffin said.

"News?"

"She's in PC. Stable but guarded. The doc is away until tomorrow night."

"She's okay?"

"Yeah. She'll be fine. They want to keep her overnight for observation, though. I'll keep an eye on her."

"That's great news."

"Yeah."

"We should be getting into town in about four hours. You wanna meet for drinks?"

"Sure."

"Okay. See you at Mike's."

"All right."

† † †

Over Eastern Colorado

ABOARD THEIR OWN PRIVATE JET, the members of Unit Ten were already en route to Terre Haute to pick up Kevin. Onboard were McGrath, Biran, Ambrose, Kenton, Staff Sergeant Rodriguez, and Anna Cohen. Her medical experience and military training were considered important enough to include her on the trip. Joe was sitting next to her and they were chatting quietly.

Two rows behind them, at the rear of the plane, Dan Rodriguez was doing a final check on their weapons. He withdrew six Glock-17 pistols and six suppressors from a large, padded carrying case. Each man would have three fifteen-round magazines. He'd brought a sub-compact Glock-26 for Anna to use—due to its diminutive size it only came with three ten-round magazines. The next cases contained collapsed MP5 submachine guns. They were SD3 versions, configured with integrated suppressors and retractable stocks—very efficient in close quarters, yet also effective to a range of 100 meters. Rodriguez, Kenton, Ambrose and Biran would be carrying the submachine guns along with two spare thirty-round magazines—ninety rounds of ammo per weapon. Between the Glocks and the H&Ks, each man would have over a hundred and thirty rounds.

Another case contained eight flash-bang concussion grenades. Like the name implies, flash-bangs are designed to disorient opponents with a dazzling flash and a deafening explosion. They are very effective when used correctly. Rodriguez opened the fourth case and carefully inspected the six, one-pound rectangular chunks of plastic explosive he'd appropriated from the Unit Ten armory. Semtex, created in 1966 by a modest Czech inventor, is rubbery and exceptionally malleable, and is still one the best plastic explosives in the world. Digital detonators were kept in a separate bag. Rodriguez eased the case shut, locked it, then opened the final case. Inside were five sets of infrared night vision goggles. The battery housings were empty but he had plenty of batteries. They would insert fresh batteries prior to the actual assault.

At the front of the cabin, McGrath, Ambrose, and Biran were discussing options. "I don't want to burn Griffin," McGrath said. "If we can release Elen without his involvement, so much the better."

"But it's a fortress," Biran countered. "We need someone inside to pull this off."

"It just may come down to that," McGrath said. "But let's consider our options. First of all, we know security is extremely tight."

"Yes, but it's mostly technological security. If we can get past the first two security chambers, we're inside with the tactical advantage."

"Don't forget about the elevator," Ambrose cautioned. "Clearance is monitored via closed circuit video."

"At the bottom floor," Biran said. "That's why we need Griffin. He would be the only person in view of the camera."

McGrath was unconvinced. "What about the cameras in the primary security chamber?"

"I can disable the camera with an MP5," Biran said.

"There are two cameras in the secondary chamber," Ambrose said.

Biran nodded. "Keep in mind that whoever is monitoring those cameras doesn't always pay close attention to the board. All we need is five seconds to get from the primary chamber through the secondary. With Griffin on point, we have tactical superiority. If we move fast, we can do it."

Silence.

McGrath said, "You know, Avi. If you were part of a *sayeret* commando team, I'm sure you could pull it off. We can't expect to have that kind of unit integrity. If one thing goes wrong, we could fail."

"What other options do we have?" Ambrose asked.

"Well," McGrath said. "A direct assault is out of the question. That leaves an indirect assault. Subterfuge."

Biran and Ambrose nodded their heads in agreement.

"Why don't we just snatch Wellesley when he gets off the plane tomorrow?" All heads turned to see that Joe had joined the conversation.

"Not a bad idea," McGrath replied.

"Safer for us," Ambrose said.

"So, we exchange him for Elen?" Biran asked.

"Or we just kill him," Kenton suggested.

Eyebrows raised.

"Or not," Joe added softly.

"Uncle Sam's Misguided Children," McGrath said.

Anna slipped out of her seat and said, "You boys behaving yourselves?"

"Yes, ma'am," was the chorused reply.

Joe looked at her and winked.

She smiled back. "Boys and their lethal toys."

"Oo-rah," Joe replied.

Terre Haute, Indiana

KEVIN WAS SITTING ON THE BED in his motel room, numbly watching a sports program on the television. His cell phone rang. He opened it and said, "Hello?"

"It's Avi. We're going to be landing in about twenty minutes. Can you get to the airport?"

"Sure. How will I find you?"

"Just wait inside the terminal. I'll call after the plane lands."

"Okay."

Over Florida

ROSTOV WAS SURPRISED AT HOW EASILY he had apprehended Elen Biran. Ferguson was clearly pleased. Wellesley would be, too. A couple days off was just what he needed. He picked up a phone and dialed. The phone rang until it was finally picked up by the answering machine. He waited for the greeting to finish, then said, "Heather? It's Jacob. If you're there, please pick up."

Cayman Brac

HEATHER WAS LISTENING FROM the other end of the room.

"*Anyway,*" Rostov's voice continued, "*I'm on my way back, and I should be there in an hour or so. I've missed you. Hope you're doing okay.*"

She resisted the urge to answer the phone. Her bag was packed, the Rover keys were in her hand, and she was headed out the door. The last twenty-four hours had been a whirlwind. With Jacob gone, the magical aura had dissipated, the reality of her situation had dawned on her, and she didn't like what she saw. A sense of dread accompanied his return. She began to regret ever meeting him, let alone jumping into bed so quickly.

Heather looked at the floor and wondered what to do. Finally, she set her bag down and walked over to the phone. There was a memo button on the answering machine. She pushed it. The machine beeped and started recording. "Jacob," she began quietly. "I'm so confused. My heart is telling me to stay but my mind is telling me to go. I hope you understand." She felt tears welling in her eyes. "Good-bye," she said quickly, and pressed STOP. She wiped the tears from her eyes, picked up her bag, and left.

Terre Haute

KEVIN CALLED FOR A CAB and told the driver to take him to the airport. The driver pulled away from the curb and rejoined traffic. It was nighttime and there wasn't much to see. A light rain was falling and Kevin was lulled into a trance as he gazed blankly out the window. After several minutes of following the hypnotic array of city lights, his eyes glazed over.

He pictured Elen in his mind, and smiled as he recalled the twinkle in her eye and the tiny dimple in her cheek when she laughed at his jokes. He imagined the warmth and the comfortable weight of her body against his, and inwardly ached to hold her again. He opened his eyes—and sighed bitterly as his brief fantasy evaporated. He gazed numbly at the skyline. Still not much to see. Just a pervasive darkness occasionally pierced by a solitary streetlight woefully inadequate to overcome it.

When they finally arrived at the airport, Kevin paid the driver, got out and headed for the terminal.

Cayman Brac

HEATHER WAS SITTING INSIDE the Range Rover. The engine was off.

Fighting through a torrent of conflicting emotions, she finally realized she couldn't leave. Not now. Not like this. She sighed deeply and slowly got out of the vehicle. Back inside the house, she set her bag down beside the door and erased her memo from the answering machine.

She studied the interior of the house, wondering what to do, then looked outside through the dining room window. It was getting dark, but the temperature was still in the seventies. A walk along the beach would be nice. She went to the bedroom, put on a sweater, then left once again.

Terre Haute

INSIDE THE TERMINAL, KEVIN found a seat next to a large window, facing the tarmac. The place was so small, there was no chance of missing Avi when he arrived. He sat there for several minutes before his phone finally rang.

"Hello," he said quietly.

"Where are you?" Biran asked.

"Inside, by the front desk"

"Okay. Go to the desk. I'll be there in two minutes."

When Biran walked inside the terminal, Kevin knew it was him immediately.

Biran approached and said, "Kevin?"

"Avi?"

Both grinned as they shook hands. They walked out to the tarmac and were onboard the jet minutes later. The pilot raised the hatch behind them and secured it for flight.

"Nice to see you, again," Kevin said to Ambrose. After the colonel made introductions, Anna came over and hugged Kevin. "I'm sorry," he said.

"Don't be," Anna said. "You did your best."

"Well," McGrath said. "Let's buckle up and get back in the air."

Kevin sat next to Anna, unaware of Joe's intention to sit with her. Standing beside Kevin, Kenton hesitated for a second, but recovered quickly and found a seat across the aisle. As the Gulfstream taxied into position, Kevin took Anna's hand. She squeezed back and held on as the plane accelerated. Seconds later, they lifted off the ground.

Cayman Brac

THE REPETITIVE SOUND OF WAVES lightly crashing on the beach was soothing. Though noticeably cooler than the day, the nighttime air was still quite comfortable. Heather carried her sandals in her hand as she ambled along the feather-soft sand, remembering her first day here with Jacob. McGrath had come out of nowhere, and one conversation was all he had needed to plant the seed of doubt in her mind.

Jacob was an assassin.

She stopped to gaze out at the dark Caribbean waters.

He's also the most remarkable man I've ever met. The most enigmatic. In my heart I trust him—or at least want to trust him. But how can I be involved with a man who is a killer?

You don't have the courage to leave.

What convinced you to stay?

Jacob did. By being so charismatic, so full of intensity and life. By being vulnerable. And honest.

You flirted with him. Slept with him. Flew out here with him and you hadn't even known him a day. That's not just foolish, it's downright stupid. Haven't you got any brains?! You've acted like a spoiled, infatuated child from the beginning—no wonder you can't make an intelligent decision!

Numbed by her impromptu deliberation, she suddenly felt tired. She sat down in the sand, pulled her knees to her chest, and gazed out at the darkness covering the ocean. As she sat there, staring into the void that was the sky as well as her mind, she lost track of time and her thoughts wandered. To younger years. Innocent years. She smiled wistfully as she recalled her first kiss and how her heart had fluttered nervously. How she'd fallen in love. How she thought she'd fallen in love. *You haven't done much better now—so much for being an adult.*

It was a difficult reality to swallow. Weary of her tortured reflections, she sighed deeply and tried to blank her mind. Mysticism aside, she found it hard to do. Her mind continued to wander, but she paid little attention to the reflections or the conclusions.

AN HOUR LATER, SHE WAS SURPRISED by an odd tickle on her cheek. She turned to see Jacob kneeling behind her, brushing her cheek with the petals of a fresh rose.

"I'm so sorry," he said softly. He sat down and wrapped his arms around her. "I owe you a tremendous apology, Heather. I'm sorry for putting you through this. Are you okay, babe?"

In a numbed silence, Heather considered her response.

"How can I make it up to you?" he asked.

"I don't know," she muttered. She took the rose from his hand, raised it to her nose and inhaled the sweet fragrance. "What am I doing here, Jacob?"

"What do you mean?"

"What am I *doing* here?"

Rostov struggled for a reply. Finally, he said, "I care about you, Heather. More than you know."

"Do you?"

"Yes, I do. I guess only time will tell what's going to happen. But this I *do* know: You're a special person, and your happiness means a lot to me."

Heather rested her cheek against his and said, "Who are you, Jacob?"

"An enigma," he replied.

"So I've gathered. Do we have a future together?"

Rostov gazed into her eyes and said, "I don't know, Heather. I certainly hope we do."

She faced the ocean and said, "I almost left tonight. I know I'm in way over my head. But, I just can't seem to get away. I think I made a big mistake coming here. I hardly know you. Yet, I've slept with you. Come here to the islands with you. Found out you're a secret agent or something. I feel like I'm about to fall over a cliff."

"You're safe with me, Heather. I won't ever let anything bad happen to you."

"I believe you. But I have to know who you are, Jacob. You said you were one of the good guys. Can you prove it?"

He sighed, caressed her cheek, and finally said, "You're right. I need to tell you. But, I put my life in your hands by doing so."

"Are you willing to do that?"

He was silent for a moment. Then he said, "How good are you at keeping a secret? Once you know, you can never tell anyone. Not your mother. Not your father. Not your girlfriend. Not your priest. No one. *Ever*." He paused to gauge her reaction. "Do you still want to know?"

She closed her eyes, steeling herself for the truth. Finally, she nodded.

Rostov wrapped his arms around her and said, "Much of what I've told you is true, but it's a cover. I'm currently employed by a secret, very powerful intelligence organization. It's basically the secret police of a global shadow government. I've been working for them for six months. You've already guessed what I do." He sighed, and said, "That's true, but it's a means to an end. I'm not doing this for myself. I'm not a rogue mercenary."

"What do you mean?"

"For a number of years, the Israeli Government has been investigating this secretive organization. They seem to have their hands everywhere. Global politics. Finance. Manufacturing. Military armaments. Organized crime. You name it, they're in it. The world is being pushed towards political unification, and this group is leading that push. It's simply a matter of time. What concerns us is *who* will have ultimate control of this global government when it's finally implemented. What are their views on human rights, on liberty, on religion? Will it be an empire? A democracy? A republic? Will it be communist? Totalitarian? Will the people have freedom?

"We needed better intelligence about this group, and that's where I came in. I was personally authorized by the prime minister to use whatever means necessary to penetrate this organization."

"You *are* James Bond," she whispered.

He smiled reticently. "I've never told anyone about this. Can you handle it?"

Heather nodded. "What do I say you do, if anyone asks?"

"I'm a freelance security consultant. I travel a lot. I have a military background. Special forces. Israeli military. That's all you should say, because that's all you know. You don't know details, but it's a good job and it lets us live a good life."

"It *is* a good life," she said.

Rostov smiled, wrapped his arms around her, and kissed the back of her neck. Comforted by his presence, Heather smiled as she gazed up from the dark ocean to the bright pinpoints of brilliant light high up in the blackened sky. *Amazing*, she thought. *So clear, so cold, and so far away*.

Chapter 16

Glens Falls, New York

FIFTEEN MILES SOUTHEAST OF WARRENSBURG, the small town of Glens Falls was an ideal location for Unit Ten's prearranged rendezvous with Tom Griffin. McGrath and the rest of the team landed just after 8:00 p.m. and took refuge in a nondescript hotel. They quickly convened with Griffin at a local tavern, and Griffin left within the hour. It was a risk to be seen together, so he would have no further contact except in an emergency.

The next morning, the team assembled in McGrath's room. Weapons cases were stacked next to a large dresser. Each person was wearing a navy blue warm-up suit with USA BIATHLON TEAM emblazoned on the back. If anyone asked, they were part of a U.S. Olympic training program. It was a calculated deception, but clever. Anyone seeing them might be inclined to remember, but they would most likely only recall seeing a team of uniforms rather than individuals. The jogging suits were decidedly less suspicious-looking than woodland camouflage. In essence, they were hiding in plain sight.

After a quick survey of his team, McGrath walked to the center of the room. "Good morning, lads," he said. "And lady. As you know, today we will be doing team-building exercises in preparation for the upcoming Olympic trials. Our first exercise will be a hike in the Hackensack Mountains north of Warrensburg, where, by sheer coincidence, we will be in close proximity to GlobalComm's North American headquarters." He smiled. "At a private airfield nearby we will encourage our lad from England to join us."

He opened a small case and handed each person a device that looked like a tiny hearing aid. "These fit over and inside your ear. We will have an open comm net, so more than one can speak at a time. The mic picks up vibrations in your jawbone. Tap the earpiece to toggle the mic. You'll hear one short beep when you're live, two when you're not. We've already discussed tactical assignments, so, unless there are any last minute questions?" He paused briefly, assessing each person. "Okay, let's get our gear and move out."

Earlier, Ambrose used false identification to rent a nine-passenger van. Now, in front of the hotel, everyone boarded quickly and buckled in. Sergeant Rodriguez drove. Fifteen minutes later, they stopped for breakfast in Lake George, just south of Warrensburg. Inside an unremarkable diner, discussion was kept to common banter and nothing about the mission was mentioned. They finished breakfast quickly. Twenty minutes later, Rodriguez turned the van east into the Hackensack Mountains north of Warrensburg. After another five minutes he drove past the private airstrip and stopped a quarter of a mile down the road, between the airfield and the GlobalComm building. Kevin got out of the van and took a soccer ball with him across the street. As he juggled the ball with his feet, Anna stood next to the van watching.

While McGrath went to the front of the van and lifted the hood, Ambrose strapped on a backpack. He and Biran each grabbed a gym bag, crossed the street, and entered a thinly wooded forest between the road and the airstrip. They stopped a kilometer from the tarmac and settled in.

"One and Two, in position," Ambrose reported using the earpiece.

"Copy," McGrath replied. He was the communications net controller.

Ambrose opened his gym bag and withdrew a set of binoculars. The bag also contained extra clothing, an MP5, a Glock-17, and spare magazines for both weapons. Biran's bag was identical. Their immediate task was simply to identify Wellesley exiting the plane. After a positive ID, they would hurry back to the side of the road and establish a good firing position. Ambrose would use the vehicle spike-strip in his backpack to blow the tires of the vehicle ferrying Wellesley to the GlobalComm facility. Biran would cover him and shoot out the tires if necessary. If both failed, Kenton would disable the vehicle with the Barrett sniper rifle he had brought from Barstow. A favorite of long distance shooters, the Barrett fired a fifty-caliber round that could disable an engine block from over a mile away.

Kenton took the massive rifle, still in its case, farther down the road toward the GlobalComm building. He found a good location parallel to the road that would place Wellesley's vehicle directly in his line of fire. "Three, in position," he reported.

"Copy," McGrath said. He leaned over the engine as if trying to figure out why the vehicle wouldn't work. A holstered Glock was secured inside his zippered jacket.

Rodriguez was sitting in the driver's seat with an MP5 on his lap. If Wellesley's driver decided to stop on the way to the airstrip, Dan could shoot him immediately. That had its advantages. Hijacking the vehicle before pickup could make it easier to snatch Wellesley. However, he knew it was unlikely the driver would stop for anything except his boss.

BACK NEAR THE TARMAC, under cover, Biran and Ambrose hunkered down and waited. After a while, Biran caught a faint sound. "Two, possible contact," he reported. He brought the binoculars to his eyes and scanned the sky. The roar grew louder, and the plane gradually came into view. "Bird inbound," he said. "ETA, forty seconds."

"*Here comes the welcoming party,*" Rodriguez reported over the net. "*Three-hundred meters. Two-hundred. One-hundred. He's not stopping.*"

Biran watched the Expedition drive past the van, continue towards the airstrip, and finally pull onto the tarmac. "You watch the vehicle," he said to Ambrose. "I'll watch the plane."

As the Gulfstream landed, Biran saw a baby-blue United Nations insignia on the tail. He reported the information to McGrath. The plane taxied to a spot just short of the waiting Expedition. The hatch opened, the stairs came down and a tall man stepped into the sunlight. Biran identified him immediately as Wellesley. "Contact confirmed," he said. He was about to set the binoculars down when another man stepped into view. Biran froze and tried to get a better focus. As the second man descended the stairs and surveyed the area, Biran cursed quietly.

"What is it?" Ambrose asked.

"I know him," Biran replied. He tapped his earpiece and said, "This is One. Abort. Abort."

Half-a-mile away, Kenton picked up the Barrett and hustled deeper into the woods. The wave off was surprising—Avi wanted this mission to succeed more than anyone, so Kenton knew that whatever had happened was probably bad. He carefully weaved his way through the trees, returning in the direction of the van. Back at the van, McGrath waved for Kevin and Anna to get back inside.

Kevin said, "What's up?"

"The mission's been waved off."

"Why?"

"I don't know. Just get inside and stay out of sight."

Kevin helped Anna inside. McGrath realized there was no way for him to get to cover inside the van. He prepared to play out the charade, hoping Rodriguez had the presence of mind to hide the MP5. As the Expedition neared, McGrath leaned in closer over the engine block. The vehicle passed by and he resisted the urge to look. He knew Wellesley was gone, heading toward the impenetrable safety of the GlobalComm building.

McGrath tapped his earpiece and said, "Area clear. Report."

"Three, clear," Kenton said.

"One and Two, clear," Biran reported.

McGrath waited for the team to return. He trusted Biran knew what he was doing. He also knew they needed to get away as soon as possible. Waiting around much longer might look suspicious. When Kenton came out of the woods, McGrath motioned him to the rear of the van. Seconds later, Ambrose and Biran hustled over.

"What happened?" McGrath asked.

"I recognized the other man with Wellesley."

"Who was it?"

"Yossi Aharon. He's an assistant deputy foreign minister and a close advisor to Ben-Yakov."

"What's up with that?" Kenton asked.

"I have no idea."

"Well, what do you suggest we do now?"

"Regroup," Biran said. "He's not a member of the Sonneschwerten."

"What makes you say that?" Kenton asked.

"I just know. Maybe Wellesley brought him here to show him something."

"Elen?"

"Could be. If that's the case, he'll only be inside briefly. Maybe we can capture him when he returns to the airstrip."

"Okay," McGrath said. "How do you want to do it?"

ELEN HEARD A KNOCK ON THE DOOR as she sat on the bed watching the news. Griffin opened the door, stepped inside, and said, "Please come with me, ma'am."

He led her down the corridor, turned the corner, then stopped suddenly. The corridor was empty. Quietly, he said, "Before we continue, there's something you should know. Your brother is here in Warrensburg."

"What?" she whispered.

"I'm here to help you. If things start going crazy, trust me to protect you. Okay?"

Elen nodded.

"Good. Just play along, and don't treat me any differently."

"Okay."

SEATED AT THE MASSIVE OAK TABLE inside the boardroom were Yossi Aharon, Ian Ferguson, and Wellesley. Aharon, in his late-thirties with tanned skin and a receding hairline, was admiring the artwork adorning the walls. "They're beautiful," he said. "Where did you get them?"

"Here and there," Wellesley replied.

"They must have cost a small fortune."

"Or a large one," Wellesley countered. "Ah, here we are." Griffin entered the room with Elen. "Please have a seat, Miss Biran."

Griffin retreated to the wall behind her and stood at ease.

"Mr. Aharon," Wellesley said. "This is Elen Biran, the daughter of Gideon Biran. I believe you know him. He's a general in your air force."

"Miss Biran, what are you doing here?"

Wellesley said, "She's in our protective custody."

"Why? Has she done something?"

"Natan will know why."

"What is this?"

"You tell him," Wellesley continued, "that it's time for him to cooperate with us, with the U.N. We have no more patience for his posturing. He must give us what we want, what the world wants. For peace. For stability. For the future."

Aharon rose from his seat, indignant. "She's an Israeli citizen!"

Ferguson stood. Wellesley shook his head, and said, "Ask him, how many lives is he willing to sacrifice for his antiquated national-istic idealism?"

Aharon surveyed the room, and said, "What you are proposing is so ludicrous, I can hardly believe I'm hearing it. Is this blackmail? You think you can force him into doing this? Everyone in Israel has lost sons and daughters. The loss of one more life, though tragic, is noth-ing in relation to the safety of the Israeli People. You cannot possibly succeed in this endeavor, Mister Wellesley. This is an act of war, and you are a fool."

"Do not for a moment think, Mister Aharon, that I don't know what this means. Your ignorance of the larger issues makes you noth-ing more than a simple peasant messenger. A pawn. A puppet. Ben-Yakov will know what is at stake here, for it is more than you can see."

Aharon shook his head. "There is no room for compromise. You will not succeed. And if anything happens to this beautiful woman, do

not think for a moment you will escape retribution, Mister Wellesley. You are a terrorist. You know our track record on that score."

"You still have no idea with whom you are dealing, Mister
Aharon. Be a good lad and just deliver the message."

Aharon's eyes narrowed. He stewed in silent indignation, exud-
ing barely restrained hostility. Finally, growling through clenched
teeth, he said, "Will that be all?"

"You may go," Wellesley said.

Griffin noticed Aharon clench and unclench his fist. Clearing his
throat softly, Griffin said, "Sir, shall I drive him back to the airstrip?"

Ferguson raised an eyebrow, but Wellesley smiled and said, "Yes.
Thank you, lieutenant. Mister Aharon, good day." Aharon glared at
Wellesley one last time and stormed out of the boardroom.

Griffin gestured towards Elen and said, "Shall I escort her to her
room first?"

Wellesley brushed him off with a wave. "Colonel Ferguson can
do that. Make sure Mister Aharon boards the plane safely."

"Yes, sir," Griffin replied with a slight bow of the head. Resisting
the impulse to look at Elen, he turned immediately and left the room.

Ferguson went to the door and gestured for Elen to precede him.
"Please," he said. "I presume you remember the way back."

"Yes, as a matter of fact, I do. I can even find my own way, if you
prefer."

"Not at all," he countered, grinning at Wellesley. "It's my pleasure."

"I'm sure it is," she muttered as she left the room.

"I DON'T KNOW IF THIS IS SUCH a good idea," McGrath said.

"We'll be fine," Ambrose replied. "Avi and Joe are the best."

"I'm not worried about *them*."

Ambrose glanced at McGrath, then returned his attention to the
road. Biran and Kenton were hidden behind trees on either side of
the road, in excellent positions to approach the Expedition whenever
it happened to return. Once again, it was a waiting game.

"What if they don't stop?" McGrath wondered.

"That's why we're in the middle of the road. The driver will have to go out of his way to avoid us."

"If he's well-trained, you know he won't stop."

"Then he'll hit the spike strip," Ambrose said.

McGrath nodded.

"*Four, contact inbound,*" Rodriguez reported.

"Copy." McGrath turned to the rear of the van and said, "Anna. Showtime." She came around to the front and waved at the approaching Expedition.

"He's slowing," McGrath said.

Ten seconds later, the Expedition came to a smooth halt five feet from Anna. Rodriguez was still in the driver's seat of the van with the MP5 in his lap. Kevin had disappeared. McGrath cautiously approached the driver's side of the Expedition. The tinted window rolled down to reveal the toothy grin of Tom Griffin. "You guys better get in," he said. "You can talk on the way to the airstrip, but we don't have much time."

"Avi," McGrath said. "Let's get in. Everyone else, hang back."

With McGrath and Biran inside, Griffin continued towards the airstrip and said, "Mister Aharon, these are the good guys."

"Good work, Tom," McGrath replied.

"Mister Aharon, my name is Avi Biran. You may not recall, but we met several years ago, in the prime minister's office. My sister is Elen Biran. She's being held inside that building."

Aharon studied Biran briefly, then looked at McGrath. "Who are you?"

"British Intelligence."

"Sir," Biran replied. "I'm a Mossad case officer, but I'm operating in the dark. These men are helping me to get her out."

"You're Mossad?"

"Ken, adoni." *Yes, sir.*

In Hebrew, Aharon asked, "How many men do you have?"

"Shiv'a," Biran replied. *Seven.*

Aharon seemed to like that answer. Finally, he said, in English, "That idiot Wellesley is trying to blackmail Ben-Yakov. He brought me here on a pretext, with the intention that I confirm she is being held here and he might have more or can get more and he is more than willing to kill all of them until the prime minister cooperates."

"Cooperates with what?" Biran asked.

"I'm sorry, Mister Biran, but that's classified."

"Look," Biran said. "One way or another, I'm going to get her out of there. But knowing why she's in there could be critical."

Aharon was silent as he considered the situation.

"We're almost there," Griffin announced quietly.

"Tell me something, Mister Biran," Aharon finally said. "What was the first Gulf War fought over?"

"In Kuwait?" Biran reflected for a moment, then said, "Containment. Control. Power."

"No," Aharon said. "Ultimately. Why did the United States and the United Nations fight?"

"To free Kuwait and suppress Hussein."

"No," Aharon said, shaking his head. "Think. What is so special about the area?"

Biran shrugged and shook his head. "*Shemen?*" he finally guessed.

Aharon smiled.

"This is about oil?!" Biran asked.

Aharon nodded and said, "Last year, in the Negev we discovered two pools deep in the Paleozoic basin. They have the potential to provide oil for the entire region for at least the next hundred years. Three months ago, we struck the mother lode. It's deeper and broader than any reserve in the Middle East. Deeper than Iraq, Kuwait, Saudi Arabia. It appears their fields actually drain into ours. So, in effect, we'll be pumping their oil right out from under them. The preliminary production estimates are astounding. Within three years, Israel, per capita, will be the wealthiest nation in the world."

Both McGrath and Biran looked at each other in stunned silence. "But why is Elen involved?" Biran asked.

"That I do not know," Aharon replied softly. "It's stupid for them to think by kidnapping her they can force Ben-Yakov to capitulate. I told Wellesley he was a fool for even considering it, but apparently

Natan knows something the rest of us do not."

"What can they possibly gain from this?"

"For years now, this group of Wellesley's has facilitated the darker side of the United Nations' existence."

"Through the Sonneschwerten?" Biran asked.

"You know the name?"

Biran and McGrath nodded.

"That's interesting," Aharon mused. "In any case, the Sonneschwerten are responsible for collecting, among other things, secret, exorbitant taxes on global oil production."

"What the Hell?" Biran muttered. "What business is it of theirs?"

Aharon nodded his head enthusiastically and replied, "That's exactly what we've been saying. They refer to the collection as a sort of members' dues for status within the U.N., among other things."

"I've never heard that before."

"And why would you? It's not something they publicize."

"So, what's the fuss?" McGrath wondered aloud.

"The prime minister refuses to pay."

"Why?" Biran asked.

"Because it's none of their damned business!"

"But why would they threaten to kill Israeli citizens unless they get paid?"

"Because they're out-of-control," Aharon replied. "It's nothing short of extortion on the sort of grand scale that would make a Sicilian blush. They know about our newly tapped wells and they're drooling all over themselves."

"What are you going to do about it?" Biran asked.

"I don't know. Ben-Yakov will make that decision."

"But what happens to my sister in the time being?"

"They won't kill her," Aharon said quickly. "At least, not for a while. She's leverage."

"We've seen this before, Mister Aharon," Biran said. "We don't negotiate with terrorists. We hunt them down."

"I know, Mister Biran. But this is not that simple."

"It is for me."

Aharon regarded Biran intently, and said, "When I was younger, I was an operator just like you. I would just as soon cut Wellesley's heart out and piss on it. The difficulty we face, however, is any action taken against them will have serious repercussions. These people don't bluff. They have the resources and the will to do exactly what they're threatening. That's what makes their threat so intimidating, and that is why we have to carefully consider our options."

They reached the airstrip. Griffin braked to a halt on the tarmac next to the waiting Gulfstream. Aharon said, "I have to go now."

"Why do they give a damn about this money anyway?" Biran asked. "They're already the wealthiest people in the world. Why do they have to rape us?"

"And set a terrible precedent? No. Every nation lapses on U.N. membership dues, but no one refuses to pay the secret oil tax. That is, no one except Israel. With a five-billion-dollar budget, they need to get the money from somewhere."

"We can destroy them, you know," Biran replied. "This unit and I have the weapons and the experience to get her out, and enough explosives to put a serious dent in that building."

"You're serious, aren't you?"

Biran clenched his jaw intently, but said nothing.

"Give me a number where I can reach you. Maybe something can be arranged."

Biran scribbled on a slip of paper and said, "Decide quickly, Mister Aharon. I don't want her inside any longer than absolutely necessary."

Aharon took the paper, smiled, and exited the vehicle.

"Do you trust him?" McGrath asked.

"Yes, I do. I could see in his eyes he wants to make these thugs pay every bit as much as I do. If he can get approval from the prime minister, he might be able to help us get the job done."

McGrath nodded. They watched the Gulfstream taxi to the far end of the field. Once in position, the jet accelerated, its engines a throaty roar. Seconds later, the beast was airborne.

Chapter 17

Jerusalem, Israel

To most people who knew him, Prime Minister Natan Ben-Yakov was very charismatic, almost larger-than-life. During the hard fought election campaign two years earlier, the international media coverage managed to convey that aura to a certain extent, but were unable to fully communicate to global audiences the sheer strength of his character. As impressive as he appeared on television, he was much more so in person.

In ancient rabbinical writings, there is reference to an energy force, an aura, that surrounds the Eternal, YHWH. In Hebrew, that aura is called *shekinah,* a covering of glory and power that mortal man cannot look upon and live, much in the way a man cannot stare directly at the sun without destroying his eyes. Some believe that the first created Man may have initially shared his Creator's *shekinah.* Following an act of rebellion, however, he was banished from Yahweh's presence, the shekinah was severed, and, with only a residue of glory remaining, he became acutely aware of his inherent nakedness. From that day onward, his descendants have endeavored to cover their innate imperfection with expensive clothing, lavish jewelry, luxurious vehicles, extravagant living, titles of authority, and more—perhaps subliminal efforts to restore the lost glory.

Ben-Yakov occasionally wondered if his natural charisma was a remnant of that ancient connection. Though he did pay appropriate attention to his appearance, he was not so enraptured with his status as the premier government official in Israel that he fell prey to the trappings commonly associated with high office. His roots were from the common people, not from wealth, and he retained a firm memory of who he really was: a simple, idealistic man with a very intelligent mind and a deep commitment to the health and preservation of his nation. Unlike so many other politicians, he was not adept at creating a pleasing façade when he was disturbed, nor was he willing to pay lip service to idiots. He was a man of conviction, integrity, and honor.

But he was also a man of great sorrow and grave introspection. Today he was reflecting on a particularly cynical concept—specifically, that there is no stronger realization of the futility of striving to be a popular governor than when one has finally achieved office. Enemies both near and far come out of the forest like wolves to a stricken deer. In the process of trying to serve everyone, it often seemed he was pleasing no one.

He sighed deeply as he glared at the television. The footage was gruesome—yet another terrorist bombing on the Israeli-occupied West Bank. He clenched his teeth as he watched a young Israeli schoolgirl—her face and clothing battered by the explosion—stare in deafened shock at the twisted body of her dead mother lying askew on the sidewalk. How she had survived while her mother had not was nothing short of a miracle.

The young girl fell to her knees and took her mother's hand. The picture zoomed in on the girl just as a single tear trickled down her sooty cheek. A steady stream of tears soon followed unchecked as she realized her mother would never again hold her in her arms, would never kiss her goodnight, would never pick her up from school. Ben-Yakov suppressed a flood of his own tears as his heart reached out to comfort this little innocent child, this precious daughter of Israel. At that point, he felt something snap deep inside. He shook his head and closed his eyes. Seconds later, several tears finally managed to escape down his cheek. He heard a knock at the door, and turned his head.

An aide poked her head into his office. "*Adoni?*"

Wiping his eyes subtly, he replied, "*Ken*, Katryn?"

The aide glanced at the television, returned her attention to the prime minister, saw the evident pain in his eyes, and was profoundly moved. She knew Natan Ben-Yakov was a very serious man, a good man, but she had never before seen him in such a moment of deep vulnerability.

"Yes?" he repeated quietly.

"I'm sorry to disturb you, sir," she said. "Mister Aharon is on a secure line from our consulate in New York."

"Thank you," he replied. As she turned to leave, he added, "Katryn?"

She stepped back inside his office. "Sir?"

He inclined his head toward the television. "Would you please find out who that little girl is? I want to speak to her and her family. Quietly."

Katryn blinked, glanced again at the television, and said, "Of course, sir."

"Thank you."

Katryn averted her eyes and closed the door gently as she left.

The prime minister sighed once more, cleared his throat and finally lifted the phone receiver. "Hello, Yossi," he said as he watched the television. "How are you?"

"Good and bad, sir," Aharon replied.

"Yes?"

"The Council are flexing their muscle, sir, through GlobalComm and the Sonneschwerten."

"How?"

"They've kidnapped an Israeli citizen living in the United States and are holding her for ransom."

Ben-Yakov's eyes narrowed and his jaw clenched tightly. "Explain," he said.

Aharon quickly retold the heated conversation in Wellesley's boardroom. "The young woman's name is Elen Biran, the general's daughter. I told him he was a fool for even considering it, but he seemed to think you would have a different reaction."

The prime minister closed his eyes and sighed deeply.

"He gave me no specific terms," Aharon added. "So I have to assume you know what he is talking about."

Ben-Yakov nodded slowly and said, "Yes, I do."

Both men were silent—Ben-Yakov lost in thought, Aharon waiting for the prime minister to elaborate. When Aharon realized no such explanation was forthcoming, he said, "I had an interesting encounter after I left, though."

"Oh?"

"On my way from the headquarters building to the airstrip, the driver stopped and two men got inside the vehicle. One of them is Mossad. His name is Avi Biran, the kidnapped girl's brother. He wants to kick ass and take names, sir, and he wants to do it *now*."

"Of course," Ben-Yakov replied.

Both men were silent for a while. Finally, Aharon said, "Can we assist them to get her out?"

"No."

"This is *mishegoss*, *adoni*. Insanity! I don't care who these people are, they can't treat us like this!"

"Unfortunately, they can and they do."

Silence.

"Is this about the oil?" Aharon asked.

Ben-Yakov nodded as he muted the television. "Mostly," he replied distractedly. "There was a bombing on the West Bank twenty minutes ago. Five were killed, thirty injured."

"Yes, sir. I just saw the report. When is this going to stop?"

"I wish I knew."

"*Adoni*," Aharon said firmly, respectfully. "With all due respect, we've cooperated with these thugs for far too long and it's time to let them know they can't screw with Israel anymore." He paused. "Biran has a small team that can get her out and they have enough explosives to destroy a good portion of the building."

"Really? I didn't know we had that kind of team in New York."

"We don't, sir. Biran is doing this on his own."

Ben-Yakov pursed his lips and sighed. Though he couldn't afford to show it publicly, his sentiments mirrored Aharon's. "This can't come back to my office, Yossi."

"It won't, sir."

"Very well." He pursed his lips reflectively, and said, "I'm going to have someone call you. Wait until you hear from him."

"Yes, sir."

"*Shalom*," Ben-Yakov said.

"*Shalom, adoni.*"

The prime minister disconnected the call and pressed the intercom. "Katryn? Would you please contact General Biran and arrange for him to see me first thing tomorrow morning?"

"Certainly, sir."

Ben-Yakov disconnected the intercom, withdrew a personal phone directory and dialed a number he had—for safety reasons—never used before.

Cayman Brac

THE SKY WAS GORGEOUS AND THE ocean calm—another typically balmy Caribbean morning. Rostov was sitting beside Heather on the hardwood deck outside his house, chatting about everything and nothing. The earlier tension between them had evaporated. Things began making sense to her and her conscience was no longer at odds with her heart.

"So where do we go from here?" she said.

"One day at a time, I imagine."

"What a strange world," she mused.

"That it is."

"I mean, nothing is as it seems."

"To a large degree. But not entirely."

She sipped her iced tea, took a deep breath, and said, "Nearly everything I've been brought up to believe is only the *official* story. Some of it's true, but"—she hesitated, searching for the right words.

"It's a little mind boggling," Rostov sympathized.

"Only a little?"

"Or maybe a lot."

"So, only a small percentage of people actually know what's really happening?"

Rostov nodded. "That's just the way it is. The way it always has been." He suddenly looked down at a black satchel beside his chair.

"What is it?" Heather asked. She looked at the bag and heard a faint buzzing sound coming from within.

Rostov reached down and withdrew a small phone from the satchel. As he studied the phone, he glanced at Heather and said, "Only two people know this number."

Heather raised her eyebrows questioningly.

Rostov cleared his throat, brought the phone to his face and said, "Yes?"

"*Do you recognize my voice?*" Ben-Yakov asked in Hebrew.

"Of course, sir," he replied in kind.

"How are you?"

"Fine, sir. What can I do for you?"

"I want you to contact Yossi Aharon. Something's happening in New York you should know about. Here is the number—"

Rostov grabbed a pen and a slip of paper from the satchel and wrote down the phone number.

"Use your own discretion as to how involved you want to be," Ben-Yakov continued. "I don't want you to burn yourself."

"Understood," Rostov replied.

Ben-Yakov was silent for a moment, then added, "This may give you an opportunity to go deep."

"*Ken, adoni.* You can count on me."

"Excellent. *Shalom.*"

"*Shalom.*" Rostov disconnected the phone.

"Who was that?" Heather asked.

"My boss."

Near Warrensburg, New York

"HOW SOON CAN YOU GET HERE?" Biran asked over his cell phone. He and the rest of the team were in a hotel twenty minutes away from GlobalComm headquarters.

"A few hours, I think," David Anan replied.

"Okay. Call me when you arrive. But before you go, do you remember that fire protocol program we used last year in Marseille?"

"Of course."

"Do you have a copy with you?"

"I've got my whole bag of tricks."

"Great. Bring them all."

"Will do. See you later."

Biran disconnected the call and said, "He should be here in a few hours."

"Great," McGrath replied. "Every little bit helps."

"And I've got a new plan," Biran added.

"Oh?"

"We're going in tonight, sometime between nine and ten."

"What about Aharon?"

"We don't need him," Biran replied. "Better to leave him out of this anyway."

"You think so?"

Biran nodded. "If my plan works, this will be easier than we thought. We just need to act quickly and decisively. And we need to contact Tom."

"It's risky."

"Yes. But he's the crucial component for this to work."

ELEN, CONFINED TO HER ROOM, was horrified as she watched the news. The coverage of the West Bank bombing took top billing for the news day and the story was being recapped for the fourth time since she began watching forty minutes ago. At last count the death toll had risen to eight, as three of the thirty wounded bystanders had succumbed to their injuries. Five of the eight were children.

Elen wiped a tear from her eye as she watched the replay of a young girl kneeling beside her stricken mother. "When is it going to stop?" she whispered hoarsely. It was largely due to incidents like this that she had felt the need to seek sanctuary in America. There was no pattern to the madness, no way to completely protect oneself. Though definite hotspots existed, mainly in contested areas like the West Bank and Gaza, the violence could not be contained from spilling over into supposedly safer areas.

"*No group has yet claimed responsibility*," the on-scene reporter intoned, "*though Palestinian extremists are being blamed for this latest atrocity. Already angered over the proposed partitioning of Jerusalem, Israeli hardliners today are threatening to nullify all agreements made with the Palestinians. PLO spokesmen have condemned the attack and expressed their grave sorrow to the Israeli government. While it appears a minority faction may be responsible for today's bombing, heightened tensions may derail the peace process indefinitely. This is especially regrettable in light of the historic progress of recent negotiations.*

"*Reporting live from the West Bank, this is——*"

Elen turned the television off and closed her eyes.

IN HIS PRIVATE OFFICE, WELLESLEY frowned and shook his head as he watched the news. He heard a soft knock on the door. "Come."

The door between his office and the boardroom opened. Ferguson stepped inside. "Sir?"

"Yes, Ian?"

"Signals have intercepted and deciphered an encrypted transmission that originated not far from our location. It's an advanced encryption and the language is rather unusual."

Wellesley muted the television and turned around. "Indeed?"

Ferguson approached with a mini disc in his hand. He placed the disc into the drive tray of Wellesley's desktop computer. A graphic display appeared on the screen as the first distorted voice spoke:

Yes?

Yo, dog.

News?

She's in PC. Stable but guarded. The doc is away until tomorrow night.

She's okay?

Yeah. She'll be fine. They want to keep her overnight for observation, though. I'll keep an eye on her.

That's great news.

Yeah.

We should be getting into town in about four hours. You wanna meet for drinks?

Sure.

Okay. See you at Mike's.

All right.

The transmission ended and Wellesley nodded his head reflectively. "Can you ID the voices?" he asked.

Ferguson frowned and reluctantly shook his head. "Unfortunately, our computers can't reconstruct that aspect of the transmission."

Wellesley sighed and said, "Play it again."

Ferguson replayed the transmission.

Once finished, Wellesley's eyes narrowed as he looked at Ferguson. "What do you make of it?"

"It could be nothing. But the conversation seems directed. Purposeful. It just feels wrong. The signal source originated within two miles of here, and it happened the same day Miss Biran arrived. This close to home, I don't believe in coincidences."

"That's exactly what I was thinking."

Both men were silent for several seconds. Finally, Ferguson said, "I could send it down to NSA. They may have something that can resurrect a voiceprint."

Wellesley slowly digested the suggestion and said, "Send it. And if they can get a voiceprint, get their software."

Ferguson smiled and said, "Very good, sir." As he turned to leave, his attention was drawn to the muted television.

Wellesley noticed his glance and said, "Regrettable incident, wouldn't you say?"

"Aye, sir. Very regrettable." He paused and added, "But necessary."

"Yes. Regrettably necessary. Oh, Ian?"

"Yes?"

"About Mister Aharon. I didn't like his tone."

Ferguson nodded and said, "I was just about to call Colonel Ross."

"Thank you, Ian."

"Of course, sir." Ferguson turned and left the room.

† † †

Cayman Brac

"DO YOU HAVE TO LEAVE AGAIN so soon?" Heather asked.

"I'm sorry," Rostov replied quietly.

"You never get a chance to breathe."

Rostov chuckled and said, "Something big is happening, Heather. I need to be there."

Heather smiled and nodded her head.

Just then, another buzzing sound came from Rostov's satchel. He reached inside and withdrew a second phone, read the text message and shook his head.

"Who is it?" Heather asked.

"My other boss."

"You're a popular guy."

Rostov smiled.

Heather stood. "Well, big guy, I'll leave you to your work." She leaned down, kissed him on the lips and walked inside.

Rostov used the second phone to return the call.

"*Ferguson.*"

"Ross here."

"Colonel, I have an urgent assignment for you here in New York. I want you airborne within the hour. We can videoconference on the way."

"Understood."

"Excellent. I'll talk to you then—" The call was disconnected and Rostov set the phone down. He collected his satchel, stretched briefly and slowly walked inside.

"Do you have to leave soon?" Heather asked from the kitchen.

"Within the hour."

"Where are you going?"

"New York."

Heather was silent for a moment, and finally said, "Can I go with you?"

"I don't know if that's such a good idea."

Heather accepted the answer with an understanding nod.

"Then again," he added. "It *is* my plane."

She suddenly grinned with pleasure.

"It's probably not a good idea, but—what the Hell?"

Heather walked up to Rostov and gave him a big hug. "I promise I'll stay out of your way."

Rostov returned her embrace, then Heather kissed him and went to the bedroom to pack. They were at the airport thirty minutes later. The engines were warming up just as he and Heather reached the Gulfstream. Rostov helped her board, then stowed their bags in the rear of the cabin. The pilot stepped out from the flight deck just as Rostov sat down. "We're ready to go when you are, sir."

"Then kick the tires and light the fires."

The pilot grinned. "Roger that, sir. We should be airborne in sixty seconds."

"Excellent. As you were."

The pilot reentered the flight deck and closed the cabin door. The Gulfstream started moving forward and taxied into position for takeoff. The heavily insulated cabin reduced most of the engine noise. Rostov spoke in a low voice to Heather: "You have to become an actress, you know. Are you up for it?"

"You bet I am."

He took her hand and said, "Good. Once we're airborne, I have to initiate a videoconference. I won't make you go to the restroom or anything, but make sure you stay out of view of the camera and make sure you don't say anything. Okay?"

She nodded. Rostov leaned over and kissed her forehead. She smiled at him and buckled herself in as the plane turned onto the runway.

"*Please make sure your seat belts are fastened*," the pilot said over the intercom. "*We'll be airborne shortly.*"

Heather squeezed Rostov's hand and laid her head against the headrest as the plane began to accelerate. They were suddenly pressed into their seats as the plane rocketed down the runway. The cabin vibrated gently as the wheels raced across the tarmac, but the rumbling was short-lived. It ceased altogether the moment the plane lifted effortlessly into the sky.

"Wow," Heather said immediately. "I've never been on a jet this small. You take off so much faster than on commercial planes."

"Yeah. A lot of thrust and very little weight."

"I like it."

Rostov smiled at her, winked, and said, "Get used to it."

"Oh, you smoothie." Squeezing his hand, she peered out the window as the ocean and land faded away beneath them. "What a beautiful day," she said. And it was. Sunlight sparkled playfully off the calm Caribbean waters, and the sky was a deep, rich blue with patches of fluffy white cumulous clouds overhead. "It's as close to paradise as I can imagine."

Rostov nodded. They were silent as the plane continued its climb to cruising altitude. Finally, the plane leveled off and the pilot's voice came back over the intercom: "*We're cruising now at twenty-three thousand feet. Skies are clear and I anticipate a smooth ride. Flight time should be just under four hours.*"

The intercom clicked off and Rostov moved across the cabin to a seat with a computer monitor in front of it. He turned the computer on and patched in to GlobalComm headquarters. Moments later, Ferguson's face appeared on the monitor.

"Hello, Colonel," Rostov said. "What news do you have for me?"

"Hello, Jacob. We have a small problem that needs to be taken care of ASAP. I've sent the file to your e-mail so all you have to do is print it out for the details. The man's name is Aharon. Yossi Aharon. Perhaps you've met?"

Rostov recognized the name immediately but allowed no reaction to show. "I know who he is, but we've never met."

"He is, of course, a powerful Israeli official. I realize this may be a little close to home. Should I assign this to someone else?"

"Of course not. What do I care who he is?"

"Excellent. This is a favor to W. When you're finished, he wishes to express his appreciation personally."

"Tell him it's already done."

"I will. Good luck."

The picture disappeared and Rostov shut the camera off. He

pulled up the target file from his encrypted e-mail. Next to the computer, a color laser printer warmed up. When the file finished printing, Rostov studied it.

"Can I see?" Heather asked.

Rostov glanced at her and nodded his head.

She approached and studied the photo of Aharon. "Is this how you get your assignments?"

"No," he replied. "I'm usually briefed personally. This is only the second time I've used the videoconferencing."

"It seems so high-tech."

Rostov shrugged and replied, "It is, and it isn't. It's just a tool."

"Are you going to——?"

"To kill him?" he asked.

She swallowed and nodded her head slowly.

He didn't answer.

Warrensburg, New York

BIRAN WAS AWAKENED FROM A COMBAT NAP by the sound of his ringing phone. He opened his eyes, sat up quickly and answered with a groggy, "Hello."

"I'm here," David Anan said.

"Already? Where are you?"

"I'm at a Shell station on Highway Nine, just north of the city."

"Sit tight. I'll be there in ten minutes."

Twelve minutes later, Biran pulled the van into the service station and waved to his Mossad colleague. Biran parked the van and got out. Both men embraced warmly. "It's good to see you," Biran said.

"*Shalom*, Avi," Anan replied. "It's good to see you, too."

When they arrived back at the hotel, Biran found a secluded parking space in the rear and helped Anan with his bag. Biran led the way to McGrath's room and knocked.

Ambrose opened the door. "Hello, Avi. I see your friend made it."

"Hi, Mike," Biran said as they entered the room. While he made introductions, Anna handed David a sandwich and a drink. Then it was time for business. "I mentioned to Colin that I have a new plan," Biran continued. "This is how we're going to play it—"

IT WAS SEVEN O'CLOCK AND THE SUN had already set behind the mountains. Having traveled three time zones yesterday, it still felt to each man as if it was earlier in the day than it actually was. Not that it mattered. It would be another three hours before the night's activities would kick into high gear.

Anan and Biran were at a nondescript video store in downtown Warrensburg, slowly browsing through the available titles on the wall. The door opened and Griffin entered. No one else was inside. Griffin walked over. Biran handed him a DVD case and said, "There's a CD inside. You need to find the network mainframe and insert the disc. The program installs automatically so you don't have to worry about commands. All you have to do is remove the disc when the installation is complete. Get rid of it somewhere safe. It's a copy, so I don't need it back."

Griffin nodded.

"The program is going to give a cold to the building's main fire control computer," Biran continued. "The first false alarms should hit around nine and it should really hit the fan sometime around ten. We'll arrive as software technicians around nine-thirty. You have a crucial role. You absolutely have to be there to make sure we can get inside."

"I can do that," Griffin said.

Biran studied the imposing ex-SEAL for several seconds. Finally, he said, "Thank you. We'll see you then."

Griffin nodded and smiled briefly at the two men as he left the store.

National Security Agency
Fort Meade, Maryland

JASON FOLTZ WAS A MID-LEVEL ANALYST with the NSA, a position he had held for the last fifteen years. In his early forties, he had prematurely gray hair, but prided himself on having all of it. He was good at his job, but lacked the managerial skills to contend for promotion. To compound his lack of promotability, he also had two vices: fast cars and fast women. They were secret and unlikely obsessions he had managed to hide from everyone who mattered, but the effect on his pocketbook left him hunting for alternate avenues to satisfy those cravings. Freelance work was one of those ways. He discovered he could fudge a little on security regulations in order to help someone in a non-classified endeavor. Some months he was able to pull in an extra three to four thousand. Other months were completely dry. It was a cycle he'd become accustomed to over the last five years. And since this happened to be one of those drier months, he leapt at the opportunity to earn another consulting fee from Ian Ferguson.

Ferguson sent him an e-mail earlier in the day with an attachment containing the intercepted transmission. Just for looking at it Ferguson would pay him five-hundred dollars. If he could actually decipher a viable voiceprint, he would get an additional thousand. Fifteen hundred bucks for maybe a couple hours of work. It was a sweet deal, all the more so because he had the software at his disposal to get the job done.

He had been working on the transmission for a little over an hour when he finally hit paydirt. He played the deciphered transmission and clearly heard the voices of Griffin and McGrath, although he had no idea who he was listening to. He saved the file and e-mailed it to Ian Ferguson. Then he looked at his watch. It was just past seven. He shut down the computer, stood up to leave, and smiled as he imagined how he was going to spend the money.

GlobalComm Headquarters

ELEN WAS RESTING ON THE BED. Her eyes were closed but she was awake. The lights were dimmed. *Click.* She heard the unmistakable sound of the door slowly opening. She held her breath.

The door closed.

She heard footsteps approach the bed.

She was facing away from the door, but she didn't want to open her eyes. She sighed deeply, regularly, as if asleep.

Nothing happened.

As the seconds passed, it was all she could do to keep her eyes shut.

Still, nothing happened.

A minute passed. Then two minutes. Finally, the footsteps retreated.

She heard the door open softly. It stayed open for a few seconds. Then she heard it close.

She continued breathing regularly, but her heart was racing.

It was something she had feared might happen.

God, please.

Another minute passed. She opened her eyes and slowly looked over her shoulder at the door. She was alone. On the bed, though, was a pink negligee. She snatched it up, threw it into the corner, and glared at the camera embedded in the ceiling. "You"—the words stuck in her throat. She clenched her fists and started shaking, a furious rage burning inside. With no other recourse, she reached down, picked up one of her shoes from the floor, and threw it at the camera. "You *sick,* evil, bast—" She tried to stop, but she couldn't. The tears came out and she couldn't control them. She fell to the bed and curled into a fetal position, weeping. She screamed at the top of her lungs and called them every foul name she could think of, but it didn't make her feel any better.

GRIFFIN TOOK THE ELEVATOR TO THE top floor, cleared security and headed for the main computer room. As he neared his objective, he blanched inwardly when he noticed Ian Ferguson approaching.

"Evening, lieutenant," Ferguson said as he neared. He had an odd smile on his face. "What brings you here at this time of day?"

"Tired of chasing you know what, sir," Griffin replied. "What's so funny?"

Ferguson shook his head. "Nothing." He stopped and looked at the DVD in Griffin's hand. "You going to watch a movie?"

"I was thinking about it."

"Maybe I'll join you later. Where are you going to watch it?"

"In the lounge."

"Okay," Ferguson replied as he continued on his way. "Catch you later."

Once he was out of earshot, Griffin sighed and muttered, "That's the last thing I need tonight."

He continued down the corridor to the network mainframe room. He was surprised no one else was inside, but wasted no time inserting the disc into the main computer. A setup wizard appeared on the monitor. It started automatically. Griffin looked around the room. So far, so good.

Thirty seconds later, the setup wizard came up on the screen again. Installation complete. The CD tray slid out automatically. He took the disc, closed the tray, and left the room.

JFK International Airport, New York

ROSTOV USED A PUBLIC PAY PHONE to call Yossi Aharon, dialing the private phone number given to him by the prime minister. Heather was several feet away with her back to the wall, watching people go by. Their bags were still on the plane.

"Aharon."

"Ben-Yakov asked me to call you," Rostov said.

"Yes. I've been expecting your call."

"Good. We need to meet immediately."

"Where are you?"

"JFK."

Aharon paused for a moment, then said, "Lincoln Center, thirty minutes. In front of the opera house."

"Okay."

Twenty-five minutes later, Rostov paid the cab driver and stepped onto the sidewalk with Heather at his side. Rostov took her hand, led her across Broadway and up the steps into Lincoln Center. As they walked past Avery Fisher Hall, Rostov pointed to the right and said, "That's Juilliard. I have a cousin who studied there."

"Really?" Heather studied the large stone and glass building that looked unlike any school she had seen before. "It looks more like a hotel."

Rostov chuckled. "Over there is where the New York Philharmonic plays. The Metropolitan Opera plays over there."

"Have you heard them?"

"Of course," Rostov replied. He saw Aharon near the opera box office. "It was part of our training."

"Really?"

"Sometimes we have to be sophisticated, you know."

Heather grinned.

Rostov scanned the area. No threats he could see. He looked back at Aharon and saw four men in dark trenchcoats surrounding him in a spread-out, diamond-shaped pattern. "Those men are Mossad," he said quietly. "Security."

Heather's eyes grew large as she saw Aharon and his security detail.

Rostov squeezed her hand and changed direction towards Aharon, continuing to scan the area for threats. "He's going to think you're a player," he added. "Just be calm and don't say anything."

"Okay."

They walked the sixty or so yards to where Aharon was standing. As they neared, Rostov made eye contact with him and nodded once.

"It's okay," Aharon said to his security team.

"Stay here," Rostov said to Heather as he entered the protected diamond.

She stopped next to the lead Mossad man and watched as they continued to scan outwardly.

"*Shalom*, my friend," Rostov said quietly, extending his hand.

"*Shalom, haver*," Aharon replied as they shook hands.

"Natan said something big was happening."

"Yes."

"It must be GlobalComm."

Aharon nodded.

"You're in danger," Rostov said. "They've put a contract on you. From Wellesley, personally."

"Do you know who will do it?"

"It was supposed to be me," Rostov replied. Aharon's eyebrows narrowed, and Rostov added, "Ironic, isn't it? Not to mention fortunate."

"Yes," Aharon said solemnly. "I would have to agree."

Rostov sighed as he studied the assistant deputy foreign minister. "You should fly home immediately," he said.

Aharon nodded, turned away and said, "Follow me."

Chapter 18

Warrensburg, New York

BIRAN AND ANAN WERE INSIDE the parking structure of the GlobalComm building, dressed in gray coveralls. The first fire alarm had gone off thirty minutes ago and stopped seconds later of its own accord. The second alarm went off a few minutes later, lasting for just a few seconds. A security check found nothing wrong in the building. When the third alarm went off minutes later, only to cancel itself after a few seconds, Ferguson concluded something was wrong with the fire control system. A short-circuit, maybe. The fire department called and asked if they had a problem. Ferguson told them he thought it was a software glitch. No, the fire department didn't need to roll out. He called a crew familiar with the fire control software to come in from the city. Since that call, three more alarms had gone off in the last fifteen minutes, each lasting for only a few seconds. Ferguson was convinced his assessment was correct.

The crew that came from the city never made it. The two Mossad men made sure of that. Biran hefted a large coil of super-lightweight, half-inch cable over his shoulder. Anan had an identical coil over his shoulder. Both men carried large rucksacks in one hand and large tool belts around their waists. Biran approached the elevator, stopped at the doors, and looked up at the security camera.

Seconds later, the elevator button turned green. Biran pushed it and the doors opened. Both men stepped inside and rode the elevator to the top floor. They stepped out just as another fire alarm went off. The security guard eyed them suspiciously.

Biran glanced up at the ceiling and said, "Yeah, I guess you do have a problem."

"Show me your IDs."

Biran looked down at his chest and patted himself in confusion. "Where the Hell is it? I thought I had it just a moment ago." The guard raised his MP5. "Whoa, there, soldier. I think I must have dropped it or something. Damn."

"I can't let you guys in."

"Look," Biran said. "Why don't you just let us in to fix the problem."

Keeping his MP5 leveled on the two technicians, the guard shook his head and picked up a security phone.

Just then, the security door opened and Griffin stepped through. "What's the holdup?" he inquired brusquely.

The guard put the phone down. "No ID, sir."

"Damn! When are you guys gonna learn to bring your IDs?!" Griffin boomed at the two Mossad men. "This is a secure facility. You *have* to bring your ID!"

Both men cringed.

Griffin shook his head in disgust. Then he said to the guard, "Let them through."

"I can't do that, sir," the guard objected. "Regulations. They have to have ID."

Griffin stepped closer to the guard and growled, "I know about the damned regulations. They're here to find out what the Hell is wrong with the alarm system. I suggest you lower your weapon and let them through."

The guard swallowed nervously. Finally, he nodded and safed his weapon. Without another word, Griffin turned on his heel and escorted Biran and Anan through the security door. Anan sighed in relief as the door slid shut behind them. The final blast door opened in front of Griffin and he ushered them inside.

Ferguson was the first person to meet them. "Lose interest in the movie?"

"Yeah," Griffin replied. "These false alarms don't help"

"These the techs?"

"Yeah."

"What's with the cables?"

"Hopefully we won't need 'em, sir," Biran replied. "I don't wanna go back downstairs if we need to replace some wiring."

"That seems like a lot, though," Ferguson said.

"Tell me about it. This stuff ain't light."

Ferguson hesitated. Finally, he simply shook his head, continued on his way and muttered, "Civilians."

IN THE BOARDROOM, WELLESLEY was standing with a glass of cognac in his hand. He stepped closer to a painting on the wall, sipped his drink, and studied the detail. It was a 1909 Alma-Tedema depiction of an ancient Roman communal bath. Gorgeous women, pristine marble, clear water, fine clothes, beautiful flowers. He was captivated.

The door opened and Ferguson walked in.

"Any word on the fire alarms?" Wellesley asked without averting his attention.

"Two technicians have arrived to fix the problem."

Wellesley nodded distractedly and said, "Good." He studied the painting a little longer and added, "Fix yourself a drink, Ian. I'd like to speak with you on a personal level."

Ferguson walked to the table. A bottle of cognac and a folded sheet of parchment lay next to an empty glass. He poured himself a drink.

"I love this painting, Ian. It reminds me of another time, another generation. A different world."

"It is nice," Ian agreed.

Wellesley continued to gaze at the painting as he said, "A council member has passed away."

"Sir?"

"I just received a letter from the council." Wellesley sipped his cognac. "A chair has opened at the table."

Ferguson nodded slowly, waiting for him to continue.

"How long have you been with me, Ian?"

"A long time, sir."

Wellesley nodded as he turned away from the painting. "In that time, we have seen many things, have we not? The world has evolved tremendously. At no other time in history have we been so close to achieving peace. Yet at the same time, we have never been so far. Economic prosperity was at an all time high until recently. And still we struggle for the ideals of a utopian society. Have you ever imagined what it would have been like to be Alexander, or Caesar, or Nebuchadnezzar? To be the ruler of the entire world?"

Ferguson reflected on the question before replying cautiously, "Not really."

"You've never once had that thought?"

Ferguson shook his head.

"Of course not," Wellesley suddenly agreed, as if struck with the realization for the first time. "You are a great warrior. You would have served them honorably as a prized champion." He nodded pensively, then said, "I've imagined it my whole life. I've been selected to join the council."

"The council, sir? Congratulations!"

"Thank you, Ian."

"You must be overwhelmed."

"Yes, I suppose I am. And you know, I think Jacob is at least partly responsible for the appointment."

"How so?"

"His handling of the Richardson affair. I never told you why he was eliminated, did I?"

"No, sir."

Wellesley sipped his cognac, inhaled through his nose and said, "Charles Richardson had a seat on the policy committee. Not a council member, but close."

Ferguson raised an eyebrow and said, "Is that so?"

"Yes. He was one of us."

"Why was he eliminated?"

"He went out of school, Ian. He and Gordon Henning spoke about sensitive council matters. They knew the rules, they broke them, and the council decided they were too much of a liability. A statement needed to be made. Sometimes, Ian, I swear some of our members have no idea what is really going on."

"So, Rostov dealt with them."

"Precisely."

"And he has no idea how important his role was, does he?"

"No, he doesn't. And the irony is we killed two birds with one stone. All of the people on the list were either liabilities or misguided fools. Yet their eliminations have strengthened our position with Ben-Yakov. Allowing the list to be leaked was a stroke of genius. Ben-Yakov simply *has* to take the threat seriously. Yet, if Rostov had failed anywhere along the line, we could have severed the connection easily. Blamed the Israelis, even. Exposed him as a rogue. The international fallout against Israel would have been priceless." He smiled reflectively, and said, "He was always expendable in my mind. But now, I think he is extremely valuable to us. He's simply too talented for us to lose, Ian."

"I agree," Ferguson replied softly. Both men fell silent as they reflected. Finally, Ferguson said, "When do you join the council?"

"I fly to Zurich tomorrow."

"That soon?"

Wellesley turned to his chief of security and said, "Ian, you've earned the right. You're my champion. I want you to come with me."

Ferguson was pleased. It was what he had hoped might happen. So much power. So much wealth. So much influence. "Thank you, sir. I'm honored."

GRIFFIN STEPPED OUTSIDE THE MAINFRAME room and watched the corridor. There was no activity. He leaned back inside and said, "Clear."

Inside, Anan was seated at the mainframe computer. "Diagnostic's almost complete."

Griffin stepped back into the corridor.

"Almost done," Anan said as he watched the progress.

Biran opened his rucksack and withdrew a one-pound block of Semtex. He unscrewed a panel on the mainframe, placed the explosive inside, then inserted a detonator. He screwed the panel back on, withdrew another block from the rucksack and followed the same procedure at a computer terminal on the other side of the room. A third explosive was placed inside the air conditioning unit on the opposite wall, leaving the mainframe between them. The explosives, however plain looking, were actually quite unique. Each block contained a special Israeli-designed chemical compound that tripled the destructive power of the Semtex alone. Set to detonate simultaneously, only one was really necessary to destroy the room. However, with double redundancy and ten times more explosive power than standard, Biran knew the three charges would easily obliterate the mainframe, the rest of the room, and cause severe damage to everything in the vicinity.

Griffin stepped inside and closed the door. "How are we doing?"

"The charges are set," Biran said. "When they go off, power to the building will completely shut down. The elevators will be offline. We'll need to find Elen, get to an exterior room, blow out a window and rappel down the side of the building."

Griffin smiled. "That sounds like fun."

"Where's a good location?"

"Elen's room is two floors down. There's a lounge with an exterior window just down the corridor."

"Okay," Biran said. He withdrew a pair of infrared night vision goggles. "You'll be blind as a bat when the power goes, so be ready to put these on."

Griffin took the goggles.

At the mainframe terminal, Anan removed a high-capacity USB memory drive, and said, "Let's go." He slipped the drive into a pocket, then grabbed his rucksack and coil.

"What was that?" Griffin asked.

"The crown jewels," Anan replied.

"Let's get this gear down to the lounge," Biran said. "Then we can get Elen."

FERGUSON LEFT THE BOARDROOM dizzied by the sudden change in his life. For years, the Sonneschwerten had been the pinnacle of professional achievement. He was already a millionaire because of his time with Wellesley, and now he was going to be propelled light-years beyond. The ultra-secret Council of Regents was the pinnacle of power in the entire world. Though the identities of the council's ten members were closely guarded, Ferguson knew those members controlled, directly or indirectly, over half of the world's wealth. They were the chosen ones, the ultimate elite. Ferguson's tenure with the Sonneschwerten had only scratched the surface in relation to the power he would now wield through Wellesley. A brave new world was indeed coming. He had known it for years.

On the way to his office, he walked past the computer room and stopped. The door was closed. He opened it and stepped inside. The technicians were gone. He stepped further inside and his eyes narrowed as he sensed something out of place. He deliberated on the sensation for a few seconds, then went to the mainframe and looked at the monitor. System normal. No more alarms had gone off, so the techs must have found the problem and fixed it. After one last look around, he left the room and closed the door.

It took him thirty seconds to reach his office. Once inside, he sat down at his computer.

BIRAN SCANNED THE HALLWAY one last time and checked his watch. 9:59. The MP5 was resting on his back, slung over his left shoulder, pointing at the ground behind him. The Glock was holstered on his hip. He secured the night vision goggles to his head, looked at Griffin beside the door, and nodded his head. Griffin was wearing goggles, too. He inserted his keycard into the door lock and the door clicked open. Biran drew his pistol, pushed the door open further and slowly eased his way inside, surveying the room quickly. He had expected to see Elen immediately. Except for a bed, a television and a dresser, the room was empty. He looked at Griffin.

Griffin mouthed the word *bathroom*.

Biran nodded and walked toward the door he had missed. "Elen," he said softly.

Nothing.

"Elen. It's me."

Nothing.

He tried the doorknob. It turned. He pushed the door open.

FERGUSON OPENED HIS E-MAIL ACCOUNT and noticed his contact at NSA had responded. He clicked on the file attachment. After it downloaded, the fully deciphered transmission played. He screwed his face in concentration, and muttered, "That voice sounds familiar."

He looked at the clock. 10:00.

Just then, he heard a mind-numbing explosion and the entire building shook violently. Before his brain could process what had happened, his office went completely dark.

SUDDENLY BLIND, BIRAN TURNED on his night vision goggles. As an infrared beam of light illuminated his field of vision, the bathroom took on a bright greenish hue. He swept both directions, but the bathroom was empty. "Where is she?!" he whispered.

"She's not here?!" Griffin said from behind.

"Where could she have gone?"

AS SOON AS THE LIGHTS WENT OUT, Elen froze. Everything was pitch black and darker than anything she had ever seen before. She had stumbled into a large room just before the explosion, and had closed the door behind her. Sightless, she quickly lost her sense of direction. She slowly backed into a wall, then slid along it until she bumped into a doorknob. Relieved, she opened the door, and——

Nothing happened.

With the loss of sight, her other senses gradually began to compensate. She could hear the blood rushing past her ears. Her breathing intensified. Quicker. Deeper. She was starting to panic. Disoriented by the discomforting sounds and her complete lack of visual references, she finally began to lose her balance. She leaned against the doorframe for support, hoping to stabilize the sudden, overwhelming sense of vertigo.

✝   ✝   ✝

"NO," BIRAN WHISPERED HARSHLY. "The last thing we need to do is split up. Let's check all the rooms along the corridor."

"Okay," Griffin said.

Biran, Griffin, and Anan made their way along the hallway using their night vision goggles, checking rooms as they went. Biran stepped inside one room, scanned quickly and moved to the next one. Anan leapfrogged him. By the time they reached the end of the corridor, they still hadn't found her.

FERGUSON SWORE AS HE BASHED HIS SHIN against an unseen object. He found his way to a cabinet, wrenched it open and fumbled blindly for several seconds. Finally, he found a flashlight. He turned it on and breathed a sigh of relief as his office was illuminated. He unholstered his H&K pistol and said to himself, "Griffin, if you're behind this, I'm going to kill you."

But first, he had to check on Wellesley.

He exited the office. His flashlight beam revealed a corridor haphazardly strewn with football-sized chunks of concrete and plaster. A long light fixture was hanging precariously from the ceiling to his right. Ferguson shook his head in dismay as he put the pieces of the puzzle together. "Those damned false alarms," he growled through clenched teeth. "How was I so blind?" He kicked a chunk of drywall in frustration, sending it skittering into what was left of the corridor wall.

He picked his way through the rubble. When he reached the mainframe, he couldn't believe what he saw. What had been a room was now only a big hole in the side of the building. Somehow the corridor had reflected the energy away from the center of the building and blown it outward. A four-foot wide section of floor was completely gone, obliterated by the explosion. Ferguson leaped over the hole in the floor, slipped on something wet and lost his balance. Twisting in the air, he used his forearm to brace the fall and his head barely missed a large chunk of concrete. Close call. He breathed a sigh of relief as he got back on his feet. Next to him was the mangled corpse of a security guard.

"Sir!"

Ferguson turned to see an approaching guard.

"The whole floor is demolished, sir! What should we do?"

The chief of security swore through clenched teeth as he deliberated on damage control. "First, find someone and go secure our female guest downstairs. If you see Griffin, arrest him at once and bring him to me. If he resists, shoot him. But please, try to keep him alive."

"Yes, sir."

As the guard turned away, Ferguson resumed his immediate task. He labored his way through mound after mound of rubble. Finally, he found his way to Wellesley's boardroom. He shined the light inside and entered the room with his pistol up. The interior had only been slightly damaged by the blast. After a cursory examination of the room, he found the secret door to Wellesley's private office. He pushed it open. Wellesley was standing in the middle of the office with a small flashlight in one hand and a Beretta in the other.

"Are you okay, sir?" Ferguson asked.

"I'm fine, Ian. What the Hell happened?!"

"Saboteurs," Ferguson replied. "I'll deal with them."

"Thank you."

Ferguson left the room.

"THERE!" ANAN WHISPERED. "An open door!"

All three ran toward the door. Biran reached it first and looked inside. Nothing. He shut the door and ran to the end of the corridor. Before he reached the corner, he saw a flickering flashlight beam illuminate the intersection. He pressed himself against the wall and eased closer to the intersection. He heard footsteps approaching.

"*Halt! Don't move!*" a voice yelled from behind him.

Biran turned his head to see another guard approaching with a flashlight. His goggles compensated for the brighter illumination and prevented him from being blinded, but the surreal-looking device was a dead giveaway he was an intruder. Biran brought his suppressed pistol around to engage the new threat, but before he had a chance to fire, two deafening gunshots boomed, and the guard went down. Biran saw the tip of Griffin's pistol protruding from a darkened doorway.

Biran turned back just as the guard who had been approaching from the other corridor rounded the corner. The guard slammed into him at full speed. Biran's face was sprayed with something hot and wet and he was knocked back against the wall. His goggles fell to the floor and the guard's flashlight skittered away against the far wall. Stunned by the impact, Biran was slow getting his pistol back on target. When his hands came up empty, he suddenly realized he was no longer holding it. He looked around quickly. The light from the flashlight cast shadows everywhere, but he finally noticed the Glock on the floor. It had fallen next to the guard, who was still on the ground. Biran knew he wouldn't be able to reach it in time. On instinct, he lunged at the fallen man and pummeled him with a flurry of blows. Soon, his hands were slick with blood.

He backed away in surprise and studied the guard closer. Even in the darkly shadowed illumination of the guard's flashlight, the man was obviously dead—a bullet had entered under his chin and blown the top of his head off. Biran realized what must have happened. As the guard turned the corner, he had run right into Biran's pistol. The impact had caused it to elevate and discharge simultaneously. Only luck had prevented it from blowing his own brains out in the process.

Biran breathed a sigh of relief, leaned down to pick up his pistol, then slipped in the guard's blood. He fell hard on his hip and cursed through clenched teeth. He grabbed the Glock, rolled away, and got back on his feet.

Anan came around the corner, took one look at his friend's bloodstained face, and said, "Jeez, Avi! Are you okay?"

"I'm just earning my paycheck." He wiped his face with his shirt, then retrieved his goggles. He put them back on, turned off the flashlight, and said, "Where's Tom?"

"Coming," Griffin replied as he turned the other flashlight off.

Everything went dark again.

Biran looked at Griffin through his night vision goggles and said, "We're running out of time. We've got to find her."

"I hear you, man," Griffin said. "One thing at a time."

Biran continued down the corridor. Still no sign of her. He slowed his pace as he approached another intersection. Clear. He walked down the hallway with his gun up, ready for any threats. At the next corner, he stopped and peeked around it. She was standing with her back to the wall. In the greenish glow of the goggles, she looked really scared. "Elen," he whispered, running to her side.

"Avi?" she asked incredulously.

Biran embraced his sister with all of his might. "How did you get out of the room?"

"The fire alarm must have unlocked the door."

"Of course."

"You made it," she said, hugging him tighter.

Biran kissed her cheek and said, "Take these."

Elen put on the extra set of goggles. "Thanks," she said. "Now I can actually see."

"Good. Now, let's get the Hell out of here. Tom, how do we get back to the lounge?"

"Follow me."

The foursome hurried back the way they had come. When they got near the lounge, Griffin raised his hand and slowed down. Just before the intersection he stopped. The hulking ex-SEAL got down on his knees and peered around the corner from about eight inches off the ground, allowing only the smallest silhouette to be visible for anyone who might be waiting for them. He eased his head back, turned to face Biran, and said, "There are three guards on the other side of the lounge entrance. They have some small emergency lights illuminating the hallway in front."

"Damn," Biran whispered.

"Here," Anan said. He pulled two flash-bangs out of a small bag and handed them to Griffin.

"Those are gonna draw a helluva lot of attention, my friend."

"You have a better idea?"

"Whatever we do," Biran muttered, "let's do it quickly. We're running out of time."

"Okay," Griffin agreed. "I guess we don't have any choice."

"Tom?" Biran whispered. "Which way does the lounge window face?"

"North."

Biran walked back down the corridor, tapped his earpiece and said, "Six? This is One, do you copy?"

"*Six, five-by,*" McGrath replied over the comm net.

"Five is secure," Biran said. "We're still inside."

"*Copy.*"

"Can you get Three over to the north side of the building?"

"*Three copies. Moving now.*"

"Three, keep an eye on the eighth floor," Biran said. "We may need your help."

"*Copy, One. Good luck.*"

Biran returned to the group, looked at Griffin, and said, "Let's do it."

Griffin nodded. "All right. The door to the lounge is about twenty meters away. The guards are another five beyond." He paused, then muttered, "Damn."

"What?"

"I'm gonna have to send another one into the lounge. We have no way of knowing who's inside."

"What's wrong with that?" Elen asked.

"We'll have lost the element of surprise. Timing can get screwed. They could come out of the door at the wrong time. I could trip on my—well, it could go bad before we know it, that's all."

"We have to go, Tom," Biran insisted quietly.

"Right. When I chuck this, count to three, then haul ass right behind it. Close your eyes, cover your ears, and keep your heads down until you hear that little firecracker go off, or you're gonna be hearing the fat lady singing so loud you won't know which way is up. Avi and David, you two make sure to wax those guards. If they're prepared for a flash-bang, you might only have a couple seconds before they figure out what's going on. Elen, you stay back. I'm going to secure the lounge first, then you get in there as fast as you can, okay?"

Elen nodded her head. Beside her, the two Mossad men checked their MP5s, then nodded at Griffin. Biran finally said, "Let's go."

Chapter 19

GRIFFIN PULLED THE PIN ON THE first grenade, released the spoon, and lobbed the flash-bang around the corner. "Fire in the hole," he quietly warned his partners.

Eyes closed and ears covered, the quartet waited for a count of three, then the floor shuddered with the force of the explosion. Griffin immediately turned the corner and ran for the lounge while Biran and Anan rushed the stricken guards with their MP5s leveled from the shoulder. Two guards were writhing on the ground, palms pressed to their ears, eyes clamped shut. Their retinas had been seared by an explosion brighter than the sun. The third guard saw the grenade coming and reacted instinctively. But even with his eyes closed and ears covered, the blast from the grenade still knocked him flat. Simultaneous bursts to his head and chest leveled him as he tried to get up. The first two guards, though momentarily incapacitated, were still a danger. Biran knew they couldn't afford to take chances. He shot one and Anan shot the other. Not pretty, but they had no choice.

Griffin reached the lounge door and pulled the pin on his last grenade. He tested the door handle. It was unlocked. He released the spoon on the grenade, opened the door, and tossed it inside. He shut the door, stepped away quickly and hunkered against the concrete wall. The explosion rocked the room and rattled the door. Flinging the door open, Griffin rushed inside with his weapon drawn. Biran was right behind him.

No one was inside. The blast had blown out all the windows, scorched the carpet, and left a darkened blast mark on the wall.

"Clear," Griffin yelled. "Let's get the Hell out of here!"

"Right," Biran replied. He stepped over to the window to examine the newly created exit. He flipped up his NVGs and looked down. It was a long drop. Fortunately, they had come prepared. Eight stories is about eighty feet. Each coil of lightweight rappelling cable was one hundred feet long. They would have more than enough length to spare.

Anan grabbed the rucksacks and coils they had stashed earlier in the corner of the room. Griffin grabbed a coil from him, clamped a titanium grapple to one end and secured it against the steel window frame. Once Biran finished securing his cable, both men flung them out into the darkness. On his knees beside the shattered windows, Anan fished through the rucksacks for the rappelling harnesses. He had brought four, just in case. He handed them out along with thick rappelling gloves. Biran helped Elen secure her harness, then he did one last check of the room. The wind was bitterly cold and loose papers were blowing around.

"Elen and I will go down first," Biran yelled against the wind. He turned to her and said, "You remember how to do this, right?"

She nodded.

"Okay. Let's go."

Elen slipped the cable through her harness and stepped toward the window. Biran hooked himself up beside her. They turned around at the same time and placed their feet on the edge of the window. Biran eased himself out the window and kicked away. Squeezing with his gloves, he controlled his descent until the harness and cable pulled taut. He dropped ten feet and stopped one floor down with his feet against the side of the building. Elen joined him a second later.

"Good," he said. "Just take your time and relax."

Both kicked away at the same time and both halted one floor lower.

"Good," he said. "Almost there."

Again they kicked away and again they stopped one floor lower. Kick. Stop.

Kick. Stop.

Kick. Stop.

Finally, they were only ten feet off the ground.

"Careful on the last one," Biran warned.

"Right."

Elen dropped the final ten feet, stopping two feet off the ground to ease herself down the rest of the way.

"Great job," Biran said as he unhooked his cable. "You're a pro."

Elen laughed softly.

Biran looked up to see two shadows emerge from the window. "Great. We should be out of here soon." He took Elen's hand and headed for the protection of the nearby woods.

FERGUSON, FLASHLIGHT IN HAND, stormed furiously down the corridor. When he came upon the dead guards outside the lounge, he threw open the door and looked inside. The cold breeze coming through the window caught his attention, but the rappelling hooks on the window frame drew him in. He cleared the room quickly, then approached the window and peered down the side of the building.

GRIFFIN HEARD A RESOUNDING *boom* from above and felt the .45-caliber bullet streak past, missing by only inches. He glanced up, saw Ferguson's pistol hanging out the window, then shouted "Move!" to Anan, one floor below.

ALARMED BY THE GUNSHOT, Biran looked up at the building, aimed his MP5 at the opening eight stories up and squeezed off four controlled bursts of automatic fire.

THE WINDOW FRAME BESIDE FERGUSON was quickly peppered with 9mm bullets, but he barely flinched. The flash from the submachine gave him a new target and he immediately redirected his fire to the ground. He squeezed off five rounds, then remembered his quarry escaping down the side of the building.

† † †

GRIFFIN KICKED AWAY FROM THE BUILDING and launched himself to the side. Holding on to the cable with one hand, he drew his handgun and returned fire, but his aim was off. He just hoped to gain a few precious seconds while he descended, controlling the rate of fall with his left hand. As he dropped, the bullets from above started coming rapid fire. He landed against the building and quickly pushed off again, dropping even farther. A bullet nicked the tip of his boot. Another hit him in the thigh. Swearing through clenched teeth, he felt helplessly exposed as he continued to descend. He kicked off the building and braced himself for the next volley when he heard an even louder *BOOM* from somewhere behind.

FERGUSON'S EYES WIDENED IN SHOCK as he looked down at his bloodied chest. "Wha—" His mouth began gurgling blood, choking off his protest. Suddenly dizzy, he looked behind him and saw a bloody spray pattern on the ceiling. Still in disbelief, he stumbled backwards toward the open window.

ELEN FLINCHED WHEN SHE HEARD the last gunshot. Everything became eerily silent. A shadow distinguished itself against the night sky. As the body hurtled downward, Biran hugged Elen close so she wouldn't see it land. Seconds later, the body hit with a heavy, bone-crushing *thud*. Biran ran to the body and stopped short.

"Hey guys," Anan said from the building's shadow as he disconnected his harness.

"David?" Biran said. "Damn, that was close."

All three looked up and watched Griffin rappel the rest of the way to the ground. He disconnected his harness and surveyed Ferguson's body. There was a very large, unnatural hole in the center of his chest.

"Well done, Tom," Biran said.

Griffin nodded. He looked one last time at Ferguson's body, then said, "Let's get outta here."

The foursome turned away from the building and jogged into the woods. They were joined by Rodriguez with his unused MP5, and Kenton with his once-used Barrett. They slowed to a walk.

"Just keeping an eye out," Kenton said with a satisfied smile. "Looks like you needed it, too."

"I had it all under control, Jarhead," Griffin replied. "One SEAL is all it takes."

"Not this time, seal pup. Normally I'd kick your ass for saying that. I'll make an exception this one time and buy you a beer instead."

"Maybe Marine pukes aren't so bad after all." He put his hand on Kenton's shoulder. In a more serious tone, he said, "Hell of a shot, man. I owe you one."

"Well, you can buy *me* a beer, then."

Griffin laughed, but it suddenly turned into a grunt. He started hobbling, favoring his left leg. Then he collapsed.

"Oh, my God," Elen said. "You're injured!"

"Yeah," Griffin grunted.

"Let's get him to the van," Joe said. He helped Griffin to his feet, then got under his shoulder. Rodriguez took the other side. Together, they helped Griffin walk on his one good leg, like an injured football player being taken off the field.

Joe added, "You gonna be okay, buddy?"

"I've survived worse. I'll be fine."

McGRATH AND KEVIN WERE WAITING in the shadows beside the van when Kevin, using night vision binoculars, saw movement from the building. Two shadowy forms exited like ghosts, followed by another two, then another three.

"Oh, no," Kevin said, still watching the building.

"What is it?"

"I think some guards just came out."

"How many?"

"Seven."

"Take this," McGrath said as he handed over his MP5. Into his lapel mic he said, "This is Six. You've got company. Seven bandits at your six o'clock."

"It's loaded?" Kevin asked, suddenly nervous.

"Safety's off. You good?"

"Yep," Kevin replied with more strength than he felt as he turned and started running up the road. His heart was racing. In the distance, he heard crackling branches and leaves, probably from the rescue team as they trekked back to the van.

"Kevin!" McGrath shouted. "Come back."

Up ahead, automatic gunfire suddenly exploded in the night.

"WE DON'T HAVE TIME for this," Biran grunted as he took cover and returned fire. "Elen, you take Dan's spot and get Tom back to the van! David, cover me. D-Rod, cover the flank! Looks like you get to fire that thing after all!"

Rodgriguez, grinning ear to ear, took off to the west.

Meanwhile, Joe, Elen, and Griffin double-timed it deeper into the woods.

KEVIN IGNORED MCGRATH'S ORDER as he continued toward the battle. "Not very often you get to shoot a submachine gun at bad guys," he muttered to himself, trying to pump himself up. "How hard can it be?"

Still following the road, he slowed to a jog, then suddenly dropped to the ground. A dark shape moved ahead, materializing into a security guard seconds later as he came out of the treeline heading south. Kevin held his breath and froze, hoping he hadn't been seen. More shots rang out to the west and the guard started running along the other side of the road, coming within thirty feet of Kevin's position. But the guard's attention was directed toward the woods and he missed Kevin entirely.

Once the guard passed, Kevin got up as quietly as he could and shadowed the guard from the opposite side of the road. He stayed on the pavement, hoping that by doing so he would avoid stepping on a branch or something else that would give him away. He then realized, belatedly, there was no cover if the guard decided to turn around.

He suddenly felt naked.

The guard slowed to a walk and raised his head to listen.

Kevin raised the MP5 to his shoulder and pointed it at the guard. He crouched and walked heel to toe, in a smooth, quiet rolling motion he'd learned during his days in the marching band. The familiar thought calmed him, but the closer he got to the guard, the more terrified he became. Soon he was sixty feet away, gaining ground and doing his best impression of a SEAL sneaking up on a terrorist.

The guard never turned to check behind him.

Tunnel vision, Kevin realized, as he remembered how, with adrenaline coursing through the bloodstream, soldiers in battle tend to lose peripheral awareness and fixate on a target.

But the same thought applied to Kevin, as well. With a sinking feeling, he slowly turned his head to check his own six—

And breathed a sigh of relief.

No one was there.

Meanwhile, the sound of gunfire intensified deeper in the woods.

The guard headed toward the sound of battle.

Kevin followed.

RODRIGUEZ FLANKED THREE OF THE GUARDS, emerged through the trees from behind and took them down with well-placed, three round bursts. With his sniper training and marksmanship skill, they didn't stand a chance.

A short distance away, Biran and Anan dispatched three other guards in similar fashion.

Biran keyed his mic and said, "This is One. We took three bandits down."

"Four here," Rodriguez reported over the radio. "I got three of 'em."

"There may be more," Biran continued. "Keep your eyes open, but let's get the Hell out of here."

Chapter 20

THE GUARD SLOWED TO A WALK as he heard voices in the distance. He eased his way through the trees and raised his M16 as he caught sight of the van and the rescue team huddled around it.

KEVIN WISHED HE HAD A RADIO. The rescue team were like sitting ducks at the van. What were they thinking?

He checked his six one more time, then continued stalking. Suddenly a branch snapped at his feet.

The soldier turned around.

Kevin's heart sank. Without thinking, he yanked on the trigger and did his best to keep the barrel on target as he emptied the entire magazine.

To his amazement, the guard went down.

"Oh my God," he whispered, feeling lightheaded.

"Kevin!" Elen shouted as she ran toward the guard, pointing a Glock at the body. She kicked his rifle away, then dropped to a knee to check his throat.

The guard's eyes blinked several times. Bloody foam bubbled up out of his mouth and down his chin. Elen knew he'd been shot in the lung. The guard slowly reached for her hand but she stepped back, unwilling to be drawn closer. He could have a grenade or a knife or a handgun. His hand dropped back tiredly to the ground and his chest was suddenly racked by a coughing fit.

Still pointing the Glock at the soldier, Elen said to Kevin, "Are you okay?"

"I'm fine."

The guard closed his eyes.

Elen waved for Kevin to approach.

He hugged her tightly. "I'm so glad to see you safe."

"I'm glad you're safe, too."

Elen let go and took a step back. "Nice shooting, by the way."

"I was so nervous. I'm lucky I hit anything."

Elen rubbed her hand through his newly buzzed stubble, and said, "What did you do *that* for?"

"I was depressed." He grinned sheepishly. "Seemed like the thing to do at the time."

"Come on, guys!" Ambrose yelled. "The police could get here any minute."

"Let's go," Elen said, taking Kevin's hand.

BACK AT THE VAN, ANNA grabbed a medical kit and looked at Griffin's leg while he stretched out on the backseat. Once everyone was onboard, Rodriguez eased the van through the trees and onto the street. As the van passed the road to the airstrip, no one noticed the Gulfstream approaching off in the distance.

"Slow down," Ambrose said.

Red and blue flashing lights were approaching rapidly. Rodriguez glanced at the speedometer. Under normal conditions, driving five over the speed limit would hardly raise an eyebrow, but now was not the time to take chances. He eased off the accelerator and the van slowed to forty-five. A convoy of three police cruisers rushed by in the opposite direction. The van shuddered from the high-speed passes. When the police vehicles continued on their way, there was a collective sigh of relief.

"Where do we go from here?" Elen wondered.

"Glens Falls," McGrath replied. "We have a jet waiting for us."

"Where's that?"

"South. Less than an hour away."

"And from there?" Biran asked.

"Where do you want to go?"

"Quebec."

McGrath grunted. "Actually, I don't know about Canada. We're carrying cargo that might raise some eyebrows."

"Can you bluff diplomatic clearance?"

"It's risky. If it doesn't work, we'd be in the wrong country to bluff our way out of."

"So, we stay in the U.S.," Biran concluded. "How about D.C.?"

"Washington?" McGrath asked. "Right into the lion's den, eh? Don't forget, there's still an FBI hunt for these two."

Biran said, "Everyone knows lions spend most of their time sleeping. I should be able to get us covered by the Israeli Embassy. We'll be flying *El Al* out of the country by the time the sun comes up."

McGrath smiled. "D.C. it is, then."

THE GULFSTREAM LANDED AND ROSTOV quickly disembarked, puzzled why they'd lost contact with the communications room. No Expedition was waiting to pick him up. He hiked the half-mile it took to reach the building. The power was back on and Rostov was unaware of the brief skirmish. He took the elevator to the top floor and entered the security corridor. A serious-looking guard greeted him with an MP5 and asked for identification.

"As you were," Rostov said coldly. He showed the guard his tattoo and the guard backed off with a quick apology. Rostov nodded his head and passed through the remaining security barriers. Once inside the main corridor, he was taken aback by the rubble strewn over the floor. He grabbed a shaken security officer walking by, and said, "What the Hell happened?"

The officer looked at him oddly and replied, "Someone blew up the mainframe, man. The whole room. It's gone. Where the Hell have you been?"

Rostov released the man and made his way to the boardroom. He figured he would find Ferguson and Wellesley in deep discussion. Instead, he found only Wellesley facing a delicate painting on the wall. "Sir?" he said gently.

Wellesley turned to face Rostov and nodded his head. "Hello, Jacob. What are you doing here?"

"Excuse me sir, but what the Hell happened?"

"Ian is taking care of that."

"Where is he?"

"I don't know."

"I'll be back in a moment." Rostov turned sharply on his heel and left the room. After picking his way through the rubble, he strode briskly toward the elevator. He was outside of Elen's room a minute later. As he entered, he wasn't surprised to see she was gone. He left the room and continued down the corridor. He came across three security guards on the floor. He checked their pulses, shook his head, then went into the lounge. He saw the shattered window and cautiously approached the windswept opening. At the edge, he knelt down, fingered the two cables, and carefully poked his head out the window. The exterior of the building was lighted now. He was able to make out the body lying eighty feet below.

He went back to the elevator. Three minutes later he was on the ground, staring at Ferguson's body. A pistol was on the ground near his right hand and there was a large hole in his chest, unmistakably the work of a large-caliber rifle. "Yossi was right," he said to himself. "I wish I could've seen it." He looked up and scanned the area. Nothing. He'd seen enough. He nodded his head absently and made his way back inside. When he entered the boardroom, Wellesley was sipping a glass of cognac and studying a different painting.

"I'm sorry, sir," Rostov said. "Ferguson is dead."

Wellesley turned to face him and raised an eyebrow questioningly. "Ian? Dead?"

The tepid response was clearly due to shock, Rostov figured. Apparently, even someone of Wellesley's prominent stature could be hampered by common human weaknesses. "There appears to have been a skirmish in the lounge," he explained. "He was shot in the chest and fell out the window."

"You're positive?"

Rostov nodded and said, "I'm afraid so, sir. He's gone."

As the harsh reality of the information sank in, Wellesley finally appeared genuinely horrified by his champion's untimely demise.

"And the girl?"

Rostov hesitated.

"Well?"

"She's gone, too."

"Good. Serves her right."

"Not dead, sir. She's gone—as in disappeared. Rescued."

"Damn! How could this happen? And Mister Aharon?"

This time, Rostov simply shook his head and looked at the floor as he resisted the sudden urge to smile. "I'm sorry, sir. He fled the country before I could get to him."

Wellesley nodded slowly, then numbly muttered, "I'll be damned, but a lot of things have happened today."

Rostov was silent. Outwardly he portrayed sympathy, but inside he was wondering just how *deep* he would be able to go now that Ferguson was out of the way. The beauty of it all was he hadn't done a thing. Having taken no part in the debacle, he was completely free of blame, and there was no way he could be linked to it. "We can start rebuilding first thing tomorrow, sir," he said. "I'll find out who was behind this."

Wellesley finally seemed to come out of his reverie. He turned to study Rostov. After a moment's reflection, he said, "Fix yourself a drink, Jacob. There's something we need to discuss."

Near Washington, D.C.

UNIT TEN ARRIVED AT DULLES INTERNATIONAL at one in the morning. After a smooth touchdown, the Gulfstream taxied to a private terminal. A dark limousine with Israeli diplomatic plates waited for them, flanked on either side by two smaller vehicles.

The lights came on inside the cabin. Kevin touched Biran's shoulder and said, "So, what happens now?"

"The chief legal attaché from the embassy is meeting us. You and Elen are still in a gray area in terms of the FBI's investigation. We can probably prove the two of you were legally justified taking the actions you did. Self-defense. Corrupt cops. For now, though, I think the best thing is for you to disappear from the radar for a while. Let this whole thing blow away."

"I can't go home?" Kevin asked.

"No one's stopping you, of course, but I don't recommend it. Maybe later, when everything gets cleared up. This can never go to court, you know. They'll never let it. The best thing is to simply get out of the way. Besides," he added, "there are a few people who want to meet you."

"Really? Who?"

"You'll just have to wait and see."

Kevin nodded as he followed Biran out of the plane. Elen was right behind him, holding Anna's hand as they reached the cold tarmac.

"What about Anna," Elen said quietly. "What's best for her?"

Anna leaned close and whispered in her ear. Elen turned around and looked at her in surprise.

"What?" Kevin asked, feeling left in the dark.

"Joe's promised to look after me while I finish my degree," Anna said. "Colonel Ambrose has offered me a job when I'm done."

"Don't worry," Kenton said. "She's in good hands, and her field medical experience will be a valuable addition to our team."

Elen smiled.

McGrath touched Biran's arm. "A word?"

"Of course."

McGrath led him away from the group, and said, "Now, Avi. This was, without a doubt, a successful operation. We freed your sister, of course. We're all proud of that. But, as you must certainly be aware, we've taken a tremendous loss by doing so."

Biran nodded. Griffin couldn't possibly return to GlobalComm. He'd be dead two minutes after showing up. That loss of an inside asset was a huge blow to Unit Ten's position. "I understand. With your permission, the prime minister will learn of your support. I'm sure he will wish to show his appreciation."

McGrath nodded, and said, "Good luck, Avi."

"You too, Colin. *Shalom*."

"*Shalom*." They shook hands one last time.

Epilogue

Jerusalem

"THIS FEELS SO SURREAL," Kevin said as Elen pulled her father's five-year old Volkswagen into the crowded visitor parking lot on Kaplan Street. They were in the Kiryat HaMemshala, the main government district three kilometers west of the Armenian, Christian, Jewish, and Islamic Quarters of the Old City—and also not far from the controversial Dome of the Rock, the Temple Mount, and myriad ancient artifacts at dozens of active archaeological sites. "So much history," he added.

"It does seem like a dream," Elen agreed as she found a parking spot. She turned to Kevin and said, "Are you ready?"

"To meet him? Absolutely!"

Elen smiled as she gazed into his eyes, where she saw the same, magnetically warm and innocent exuberance she'd come to enjoy seeing so much. As she got out and locked the door, Kevin stood beside the Volkswagen and looked around, soaking in the environment. Across Kaplan to the north was the Bank of Israel, a five-story, squarish concrete edifice that he thought looked rather inelegant—not at all like the shiny glass-and-steel highrises of Manhattan. Nevertheless, it was a remarkably powerful financial institution in its own right, and the stolid design seemed in keeping with the Israeli predisposition towards pragmatism over flashiness. To the east, across Yoel Zusman Street, the T-shaped Supreme Court building was just visible through a façade of olive and pine trees.

Immediately to the south was the government building housing the office of the prime minister.

As they walked toward the entrance, Kevin turned to her and said, "Can I ask you a question?"

"Sure."

"Do you think God helped us get here?"

She smiled wistfully and replied, "I'm not ready to make a judgment on that."

"Neither am I," he said, staring blankly into the sky. "But, if he's up there, Elen, do you think he brought us together?"

"That's a sweet idea, isn't it? I hope so."

Kevin chuckled. "So, what's going to happen now?"

"I don't know. What are you thinking?"

"Well, I—" He laughed at himself, and said, "It's just—I'm not sure what to . . . what will happen to us—"

"Elen!" General Gideon Biran interrupted as he approached from the building's entrance. In his fifties, with closely-cropped gray hair and wearing an impeccable uniform that was otherwise understated—without medals or other paraphernalia—he projected the serene confidence common to many seasoned combat veterans.

"Dad!" she said excitedly as they embraced warmly.

Once they separated, her father said, "Are you ready?"

She looked at Kevin, who simply smiled back at her. She turned to her father and said, "Let's go."

PRIME MINISTER NATAN BEN-YAKOV was speaking privately to Avi Biran in his office when his secretary buzzed the intercom. "Yes?" he said.

"General Biran is here, *adoni*, with his daughter."

"Thank you, Katryn. Give me another minute."

"Yes, sir."

"Here's the file," Ben-Yakov said to Biran as he withdrew a green folder from his desk. "You'll be working directly for me on this project now, with the most stringent regard for security."

"Yes, sir." Biran looked at the edge of the folder and read the embossed codename: *ZEL / SHADOW*.

"Only Benny Nakom and Yossi Aharon know about your new status," Ben-Yakov went on. "You may only discuss this with them or myself. Understood?" Nakom was head of the Mossad. Biran nodded. "Good. Jacob has gone deeper than I had even dared to dream possible, Avi. You are his case officer now, his only lifeline to the real world. Put a list together of people you want to help, then take the list to Benny for final approval. Good luck."

"Thank you, sir," Biran replied. "Uh—about the assassination list."

Ben-Yakov waived his hand, brushing the subject aside. "They wouldn't dare. Just trying to intimidate me, that's all. Nothing to be concerned about."

It sounded like false bravado. "If I may, sir," Biran ventured carefully, "then why did they put your name on the list?"

"And why did they kidnap your sister?"

Biran nodded with evident curiosity.

Ben-Yakov smiled, but it was without humor. "This is classified, but two months ago, your father was appointed head of security for the new oil fields. Wellesley is a devious little devil, I'll give him that, and he obviously has good sources. But he didn't count on your involvement, and he still doesn't understand Israel. Perhaps he never will."

"Was Wellesley trying to blackmail my father? Or, was he just trying to blackmail you?"

"Both, I suppose. Two birds with one stone."

"But would he actually have gone through with it? Would he have killed Elen to get to you and my father?"

Ben-Yakov sighed, pursed his lips in concentration, and said, "I think he would have. Yes. He had the stones to eliminate his own cronies, Richardson and Henning, so she may very well have been in mortal danger. Killing me, on the other hand, from the beginning was never a viable alternative, in my opinion. The outcome is simply too unpredictable. If word leaked out, the backlash against the U.N. would be staggering. Aside from that, had an assassination taken place, especially so soon after Yitzhak's death, the peace process would have been completely derailed. The U.N. can't want that."

"What if they do, sir?" Biran asked.

Ben-Yakov raised a curious eyebrow.

"Think of the reaction," Biran said. "Two prime ministers assassinated in less than twenty years! What would that say for the security of our country? The government would be in shambles. Think of the international reaction. The U.N. might even step in and try to take over."

"That's a chilling idea," Ben-Yakov said. "At least one thing is clear: the Council want to control us—at any cost. This is a warning to be vigilant, Avi. Wellesley and his goons will be back, sooner or later, pushing for limits again."

Biran nodded soberly.

Ben-Yakov rose, came around the desk and shook hands with the intelligence officer. Biran slipped the folder into a padded leather briefcase. The prime minister pressed the intercom button and said, "Please send them in."

General Biran, Elen, and Kevin walked in, followed by a staff photographer. Ben-Yakov came around the desk and greeted General Biran with a warm handshake, then moved to Elen and kissed both of her cheeks. "I'm so glad you're safe, Miss Biran."

"Thank you, Mister Prime Minister. It's such a pleasure to finally meet you."

"The pleasure is mine, I assure you. And who is this?"

"Kevin Edwards, sir. It's truly an honor to meet you."

"Again, the honor is mine, Mister Edwards. You have helped prevent a major national disaster. We are grateful for your sacrifice."

"Thank you, sir."

Elen smiled at Kevin, then slipped her arm around his.

"Now," Ben-Yakov said. "The least I can do is give you a memento to remember this occasion."

Ben-Yakov turned Elen and Kevin to face the photographer. Elen motioned for Biran and her father to join them. Both begged off and stepped away. Elen held Kevin's hand as the photographer captured the trio on film.

"Thank you again, sir," Kevin said as the photographer left.

"It's my pleasure," Ben-Yakov replied. "So, what do you plan on doing here in Israel?"

"I'm just taking it one day at a time, sir."

"Maybe you should write a novel."

Kevin looked at Elen and grinned. "Why not? But I wonder if anyone would believe it."

"Oh, that doesn't matter," Elen replied. "It's more mysterious."

"Maybe you're right."

"Of course she is," Ben-Yakov said. "Good luck, in any event. I'm sure you'll do just fine."

"Thank you, sir. And good luck to you, too. *Shalom*."

The prime minister smiled approvingly. "*Shalom, haver*," he replied with genuine warmth. *Peace, my friend.*

Zurich, Switzerland

THE GULFSTREAM'S ENGINES WHINED at low idle as the plane waited on the tarmac. Two impeccably dressed pilots stood on the ground next to the extended boarding ramp, smoking American cigarettes and laughing. As three vehicles approached in the distance, one pilot nudged the other, stamped out his cigarette and boarded the plane. The second man took one last drag, blew a cloud of smoke into the air, then stamped his cigarette out. Two white-and-orange Zurich *Polizei* motorcycles approached the Gulfstream, followed by a large, black Mercedes S600 sedan. Beside each of the sedan's mirrors, a small white and blue United Nations flag fluttered in the wind. Both flags slowly drooped as the Mercedes rolled to a stop next to the jet. The motorcycles continued on.

The right rear door of the Mercedes opened and Rostov stepped out, dressed in an immaculate, black Armani suit. Wellesley emerged from the other side wearing a dark-blue, three-piece bespoke suit from Saville Row. The pilot quickly pulled two pieces of luggage from the Mercedes, bowed respectfully to the billionaire, then followed Wellesley and Rostov up the boarding ramp. As the Mercedes drove off, the pilot closed the hatch, stowed the luggage onboard, then asked Wellesley if he would like a drink before takeoff.

"Gin and tonic," Wellesley replied. "Jacob?"

Rostov removed his coat and sat down in the plush leather seat opposite Wellesley. "Rum and Coke," he said. "Thank you."

After a minute, the pilot returned with the drinks and said, "We should be airborne shortly, sir. Is there anything else I can get for you?"

Wellesley shook his head.

"Very good, sir." The pilot nodded respectfully, then left.

"So," Rostov said. "What happens next?"

Wellesley took a drink, then smiled at Rostov. "London, Jacob. There are a few people who want to meet you."

Rostov nodded soberly. "I'm honored, sir. I look forward to meeting them." He looked out the window and resisted the urge to smile.

Acknowledgments

Although I have made every effort to present factual details in this book, *The Rostov Ascension* is a work of fiction. It was inspired, however, by an actual person who, thankfully (and to the best of my knowledge), is nothing like Jacob Rostov. When I first read Victor Ostrovsky's non-fiction exposé, *By Way of Deception: The Making of a Mossad Officer*, I was fascinated by the stories of intrigue, survival, and cunning. While many others have written excellent books about recent Israeli history—most notably, Dan Raviv and Yossi Melman—Victor was the first (to my knowledge) to unveil the inner workings of the Mossad from an insider's perspective, including operational successes and failures. Twenty-some years after his New York Times Bestseller was first published, Victor is a talented artist and author who owns and operates a fine art gallery in Scottsdale. When we met in 2010, I found him to be kind, warm, approachable, and encouraging. So, thank you, Victor, for presenting your story to the world, for inspiring me to take an amazing literary journey, and for being willing to chat with and support an aspiring writer. It is refreshing to consider you a colleague and a friend.

I especially want to thank James and Barbara Allen for their untiring help in reviewing and preparing the manuscript from beginning to end. The following also deserve recognition: Michael Allen, Nancy Flor, Ilse Meier, and Jayna Newbold. To everyone else who helped, thank you for your support!

About the Author

In the three years MATTHEW ALLEN served as a deputy sheriff, he mastered many essential skills—such as report writing, handling evidence, and how to not sound like an idiot on the radio—before unceremoniously departing for browner pastures. As a SoCal native, he graduated from Long Beach Polytechnic High School, where he earned, among other things, an award for Outstanding Instrumental Music and the distinction of having an actual picture of not-yet-famous Calvin Broadus, aka Snoop Dogg, in his yearbook. He loves to travel and has lived in San Francisco, Scottsdale, Washington D.C., and Arkansas City, Kansas, where he currently resides with his lovely wife and four, slightly dinged-up remote control helicopters.

Author's Note

And so it begins! Thank you for reading *The Rostov Ascension*. I hope
You enjoyed it, and I welcome your comments! Please let
others know what you think by leaving a candid
review on Amazon.com.

If you would like to contact me, please send an e-
mail to mattallen.ma@gmail.com. I always personally respond,
and I would love to let you know when future projects are published.

Thanks again!
Regards,

Matthew Allen

17359557R00150

Made in the USA
Charleston, SC
07 February 2013